ON FIRE AND UNDER WATER

A CLIMATE CHANGE CRIME FICTION ANTHOLOGY

EDITED BY CURTIS IPPOLITO

PRAISE FOR
ON FIRE AND UNDER WATER

"Raw, brutal, tender, tragic—these are fifteen stories of people smashed flat by the Invisible Fist, people flailing and fighting against the huge and hidden violence at the center of our world. This is crime fiction that matters, crime fiction that is ready to face what comes next."

—Jordan Harper, author of *She Rides Shotgun* and *Everybody Knows*

DEDICATION

For anyone who has installed solar panels, switched to an electric or hybrid car, reduced their use of plastic, and to all those who consistently sort out plastics, paper, and other recyclables to keep them from taking up precious space at our overflowing landfills. You're doing your best to improve our planet—oil barons, billionaires, and crooked politicians be damned.

And, for our children. God forgive us.

Contents

Introduction

Curtis Ippolito

C limate change is an existential threat to the survival of our planet and every species living on it.

No well actually-s, nos, or maybes about it. This is scientifically proven fact. And we are seeing its devastating consequences playing out in real time. Floods, fires, and hurricanes occurring out-of-season and with greater intensity. Centuries-old glaciers melting. Increased hunger, malnutrition, wars, and displacement. Numerous plant and animal species staring down the barrel of extinction.

Also indisputable is that humans are the ones who put the Earth and all of us in this perilous position. More specifically, the oil barons, who, for decades, lied, sowed misinformation, and paid for erroneous studies saying oil production did not play the central role in causing climate change (they are still lying, greenwashing, and downplaying their role to this day). Other industries are at fault, as well, of course. Even newer ones. Staring right at you, AI.

So, what can writers and editors do about it?

We do what artists have done throughout history. We sharpen our art and employ it as a weapon. We shine a light on the injustices and wrongs being done to us and our neighbors. With that in mind, I'm proud to say *On Fire and Under Water* accomplishes exactly that.

I was thrilled and honored when the **Rock and a Hard Place** editors asked me to assist with this anthology. Climate change is an issue I'm very passionate about. I see its effects not only when observing the devastating events occurring globally, but also right around me. A hurricane hit in San Diego in 2023, causing major flooding that unhoused families and shuttered small businesses. Early this year, unseasonable fires destroyed neighborhoods in Los Angeles and Altadena, burned parts of San Diego, and in between. This summer, hundreds were killed in devastating flash floods in the Hill Country of Texas. And as an animal and nature lover, I'm also tuned into the species that are already threatened by development and human activity, and whose futures grow even dimmer when climate change is added to the equation.

While there are things we can do as individuals to improve our climate, it feels like making any positive impact gets tougher every day when compared to the industrial scale damage being wrought by the greedy, soul-sucking oil industry. That's why partnering with **RHP** on this anthology appealed to me so greatly. This is a moment and a project that has emboldened us to stand our ground, say our piece—to use crime fiction as a way to explore the humanity and atrocities of this crisis.

The stories between these pages reveal a glimpse of the peril in which climate change is placing everyday people. While these are works of fiction, you recognize the prescience, and you will feel the authenticity and urgency of the characters. As a reader of **RHP**, you know the editors stand in a class of their own in the crime fiction community when it comes to curating stories that speak to the times in which we are living. Every issue holds up a mirror to our cruel and sick society. A society where corporate greed runs unfettered, where the ultra-rich reign as the ruling class. Where police brutality and corruption run rampant. Where schools and places of worship are no longer safe from violence, yet our politicians do nothing to address any of it despite our pleas. No matter the issue, every story you find in **RHP** is focused on people, the stories of those put in the crosshairs of an unfair world. The desperate, the beaten-down, those who find themselves in impossible situations and try, right or wrong, to somehow improve their situations.

The stories in this anthology revel in this tradition. With the lens squarely aimed at climate change, the focus of each story remains on how this issue impacts real people at their most desperate.

Like in "Poison is the Wind that Blows," by C.W. Blackwell, where an incarcerated fire fighter finds himself caught between his crooked crew chief and a dangerous billionaire in the middle of an all-consuming wildfire. Or how in "The Devil Doesn't Live Hand-To-Mouth," Puja Guha paints a vivid picture of how climate change can completely upend someone's life dream and make them question their entire identity in order to survive. And prepare to be emotionally wrecked by our last story, "What You Lost," by Meagan Lucas—an epic story of three women with vastly different but equally human motives trying to escape a hurricane.

Although I've highlighted these three specific stories, I could have picked any three. Every story in this anthology is high quality. I am so proud of, and excited for, these writers. They poured their hearts into their stories, and I can't wait for you to read them.

Bringing this anthology to life was a true team effort, and I am honored to have assisted. The journey from the call for submissions to publication has been incredible. Behind the scenes there were multiple rounds of reading and scoring, then selection, editing, layout, design—so much hard work. I extend my sincere gratitude to the entire **RHP** team.

Roger Nokes, Jay Butkowski, Albert Tucher, Paul J. Garth, Morgan Sullivan, Rob D. Smith, Ashley-Ruth M. Bernier, Victor De Anda, and Susan Jessen.

Each of you is a gem and a talent in your own right. Thank you for letting me be on the team these past few months. And I can't go without mentioning how incredible the cover is, designed by Heather Garth. It's dope as hell. I also have to say how much I loved reading every story submitted to this call. I considered it a privilege. I felt like I was in the middle of a huge protest, all of us marching through the streets together, supporting a righteous cause. To every writer who submitted a story, thank you. You have my respect.

In closing and speaking for everyone at ***Rock and a Hard Place***, thank you for purchasing this anthology. We know money is a precious resource these days, so we are extremely grateful for your support.

Now, turn the page and read these 15 excellent stories. When you're finished, I believe you'll gain a little more empathy to the plight of everyday people and be filled with a little more rage for what's being done to our planet.

– Curtis Ippolito

"At only six bucks an hour, the smoke brings a sharper sting, the air tastes more metallic and bitter."

Poison Is the Wind That Blows

C.W. Blackwell

A t only six bucks an hour, the smoke brings a sharper sting, the air tastes more metallic and bitter. The supervisors are making *ten times* what I'm making just to tell me where to dig. Still, cutting a fireline in the redwoods beats sitting in gen pop while some suck-face wife killer threatens to chew my throat out with whatever teeth he's got left. The crew chief—a potbellied old man named Reed—likes to call us fire felons. The other guys in the program don't like it, but I don't mind. To me, it sounds metal.

"Get your asses into the cut or I'll send you straight back to Mule Creek," yells Reed. Of all goddamn things, he's smoking a cigarette. Our piss break is over, but his will stretch long into the afternoon. For guys like Reed, his whole life is one steaming piss break. "Scrape it down to bare soil, boys. I want to see you sweat."

There's a house nearby. A two-story clapboard moldering in the shadows. Dry needles piled in the gutters, heavy brush growing wild in the yard. It's a fire hazard even in the off-season. He shouts to keep digging while he inspects the house for refusers and disappears into the low gray smoke.

Eddie Milligan, a short, square-shouldered inmate with a blue spider tattoo sucking his carotid artery, sidles next to me with a

Pulaski axe and makes a few scrapes in the dirt. Eddie's a talker, and everyone already knows his rap: burglary and car theft with a conspiracy enhancement, which he insists is *utter bullshit*.

"We got a wager going that Reed's looting them houses," he says. He doesn't look up when he says it, as if anyone could have said it. Just a rumor carried in the hot, dry wind. "Twenty bucks—you want in?"

I glance over my shoulder.

"Don't look, he knows we're onto him."

"How the hell do you know that?" I say.

"Saw him coming out of the last house with a gym bag. You think he was using their rowing machine? We've all been around the block." He taps a scarred index finger to his temple. "Think about it. You know I'm right."

I don't want to know what Reed is up to. Reducing my sentence, CAL Fire training—that's what I'm focused on. I want to become a salaried firefighter and retire with whatever pension I can build before my knees turn to gelatin. I don't need a betting pool to know Reed's a crooked asshole. So I stay quiet, dig harder, and pull big shovel-loads of redwood needles out of the cut.

"Just think about this," says Milligan. He won't stop talking. "If one of those homeowners files a report, who's Reed gonna pin it on? I say either he cuts us in, or we start making some noise."

I pretend not to listen. But as the hours roll toward evening, and Reed enters more houses looking for refusers, I start to appreciate the setup. With wildfires up and down the coast, the state can't handle all the staffing, and for most of the day, it's just us and Reed. I'm sure the supervisory ratio violates official policy, but in an emergency, sometimes the rules melt away. For a guy like him, it's almost too good to be true. Now I'm worried that my sentence will go the wrong direction, all while some mid-level bureaucrat pads his pension with family heirlooms.

◆

We sleep at base camp with the career firefighters and a handful of civilians. We're not supposed to drink, but the other inmates in the program have a little hidden away. I get a whiff here and there. I can see it in Milligan's eyes—a wildness that wasn't there before, the elated look of a man whose only booze for the last few years was brewed in a prison toilet.

The food is good and there's enough for second helpings. I'm scouting for another pork chop when Reed catches me by the shoulder. He has one of those smiles that never feels friendly, like he's holding a knife behind his back while showing teeth.

"What's your crime, felon?" he asks me. "You've been working hard, keeping your head down. Like you're trying to stay invisible. A man who doesn't want to be noticed always sticks out."

"I'm sure you've read my file."

"Of course. But I want your side of the story."

"Caught a looter on my property," I say, making the words sting, letting him know I'm on to him. "During the Laurel Fire a few years back. I ran a mobile mechanic service, and I caught him stealing tools from my garage. Not much more to it than that."

"I read that you cratered his skull with a pneumatic lug wrench."

"If you say so."

"It's not your first bit, is it?"

"You making a point?"

"A few years ago, they wouldn't let you into the program with a beef like that. You know that, right? Violent felonies were a big no-no." He makes a *tisk-tisk* sound. "Desperate times, I guess."

I concede that the times are indeed desperate, but all I really want is a second pork chop, not idle chit-chat.

"Listen," he says, lowering his voice a notch. He still has his hand on my shoulder, and it's all I can do to keep from shirking away. "Tomorrow we're working the Los Gatos hills. Lots of big money up there. Tech money. You ever heard of Ger Hollander?"

I give a tentative nod, like the name sounds vaguely familiar, but I know Hollander better than anyone here. He'd been a client before my stint at Mule Creek. A collector of WWII vehicles—cargo trucks, armored cars, some exotics. Even had his own shop with two lifts and pneumatic lines. I wrenched on his private collection as long as I could stand him. Of all the tech billionaires on the scene, Ger Hollander was the most arrogant, pugnacious son of a bitch there was.

"Made himself a gazillion dollars in AI," he continues. "In a way, you owe him for the opportunity. All those hot servers burping loads of CO_2, driving all the tree-huggers crazy. It was his idea to gut the EPA, wasn't it? Now you're here, putting out the fires he made, earning a reduced sentence. If Hollander keeps destroying the planet, you'll be out in no time."

Someone comes around to collect the leftovers. Not a pork chop in sight. They leave out a platter of cold broccoli, and it wilts sadly at the edge of the table.

"You got something you want to ask me, Reed?"

"Word is, Hollander has his own crew of private firefighters up there. The rich fucks always do. If we have to evacuate them, the situation might get tense. Those guys get paid good money. They may not come willingly. Hell, they could be armed. I could use a guy like you to give our little squad some teeth."

Our little squad?

"That's the sheriff's job—I don't have a badge."

"It's a tricky situation, that's all I'm saying. We could have minutes to get everyone out. Deputies are already working around the clock. And if you happen to find a little something of value to slip into your pocket, well, I'd just look the other way. This job has perks, you know."

"Find someone else," I say. "I don't like playing stupid games. Why don't you ask Milligan? He's the one who likes to chit-chat."

His face sours.

He turns away, mutters: "That's what I'm afraid of."

❖

Reed is bad at this.

He's told me eighty percent of his plan, and what he hasn't told me is easy to figure out. I see him later that night, gabbing to Eddie Milligan, Ruben Ortega, and Tyler Benke, no doubt recruiting them for his big play. Maybe plying them with booze and weed to seal the deal. Even though they're suspicious of Reed, I know that if he keeps floating Hollander's name, my colleagues will grow curious about what's inside that big eight-figure mansion in the Los Gatos hills. In the end, they're just career thieves making 1980s wages.

But I want to be sure.

Sometime after midnight, I slip from my tent and thread the maze of trailers and porta-potties. The fire crew has long retired to their bedrolls. The camp is silent. Now there is only moonlight and the brown veil of woodsmoke. Even with the haze in the air, the moon is bright enough to light the way. I find Reed's trailer at the edge of camp, his CAL Fire truck parked toward the exit like he's planning to leave in a hurry. At the door of his trailer, I wait and listen. Soon, I hear the long, guttural snores of an overweight alcoholic. It's the sound I'm hoping for.

The toolbox in the back of his truck is made of cheap alloy with a simple barrel lock. I'd stolen a fork from dinner service, and with one of the tines bent back, it makes a decent lockpick—I've picked better locks with worse tools. It only takes me a few minutes to open the box lid, and what I find in there is enough to send Reed straight to county jail. I count four handguns—two revolvers and two Glocks—all placed in individual one-gallon Ziploc bags with loose ammunition inside. There's also an ounce of weed, four teeners of crystal meth, and a stack of vintage nudie magazines from the 1990s. But that's not all. In a black gym bag, I find old silver dollars, gold necklaces, loose cash. There's even a fully-charged burner phone tucked neatly among the spoils.

"Find anything interesting?"

I spin around—it's Milligan. It's too late to hide what I'm doing.

"Plenty," I say. I keep my voice to a whisper and hold up one of the stolen guns. "You were right about him, man. I just wanted to make sure before whatever happens tomorrow."

"He talked to you, didn't he? He's been making the rounds, blabbing about Ger Hollander, *the AI king of Silicon Valley*. You think this place is as juicy as he says?"

I don't want to mention that I turned down Reed's proposal.

"Something's going to happen," I say. "Be careful. I think your first instinct was right—if he makes a play, we'll all be convenient patsies."

He glances at the trailer. Reed's snoring sounds like an old hog choking on a truffle.

"Fighting fires is a dangerous job," he says, too loud for my comfort. There's a sinister edge to his voice that wasn't there before. "Tragedies happen all the time. Double-crosses turn into triple-crosses in a heartbeat. People get burned."

I can't tell if the threat is for me or for Reed.

I lie awake all night, thinking about it.

❖

When a neighborhood catches fire, the smell is unlike anything else. A demonic brew of woodsmoke, molten plastic, and burning cars. It makes its own caustic weather—a storm whose only purpose is to feed and choke and destroy. We line up on the windward side of a scrubby slope and dig among the bone-dry tanoaks and redwood trees. It's the hottest day of the week, and in minutes, we're all drenched in sweat. We go through liters of water without needing a piss.

Some houses are already lost, but not all. You can see the doomed structures burning on the opposite side of the ravine, a foul black smoke churning at the sky.

I nudge Milligan, point my chin toward a large Italian villa in the distance with terracotta tiles and adobe walls—more of a compound than a residence. Hollander has added to his trophy home since the last time I worked in his private shop. A guest house, a second pool. It looks like he's imported dozens of trees, none of them native. We spot a small crew digging along the slope in bright orange vests and full respirators. There's a backhoe stripping the topsoil bare, unearthing rocks and letting them tumble into the ravine below.

An unease grows as we near the mansion.

Reed can't take his eyes off the place.

"I'm gonna have a talk with them," he says, snubbing out his cigarette on the sole of his boot. "We'll see how many there are. Ortega, I want you to come with me so they don't think I'm alone."

Ortega takes off his helmet and wipes the sweat with the back of his arm.

"Sure, boss," he says, coughing. "Right behind you." His hand lingers on the cargo pocket of his right pant leg as he turns. He's given himself away. One of the guns I found last night has made its way into Ortega's pocket, and that means the other guns have found homes, too.

I clutch my Pulaski tight, take a few whacks at the dirt. I sense Milligan and Benke watching me in their peripheries.

"Whatever you're up to is cool with me." I say it calmly, almost like I'm bored with the situation. "I'm not a snitch."

They don't respond. The silence speaks for them.

It's not long before we hear gunfire.

A dozen shots ring out across the scorched hills. At least, it sounds like a dozen—it could be echoing through the ravine. Someone screams, and I can't tell if it's Reed, Ortega, or one of the private firefighters. Another sound tears out of the smoke—the *dut-dut-dut-dut-dut* of automatic rifle fire. It's anyone's guess what's happening. We wait uneasily until Reed's voice calls out from the direction of the villa. He yells something like *Let's go, boys* and now Milligan and Benke start reaching into their pockets. It's the signal they've been waiting for.

"Man, I'm sorry," Benke tells me.

I know what the apology is for, but I don't let it get that far.

I swing the pick-end of the Pulaski at Benke. It makes a *shlump* sound as it pierces his chest like an oversized meat hook. His jaw hangs open, eyes roll back. A silver revolver topples into the dirt and slides toward the edge of the ravine. He falls onto his ass like he's just taking a break, not yet realizing what a long fucking break it will be. Milligan has his gun out already, but I drive his arm up before he can shoot me. It goes off. One shot, two, three. It's a Glock, and I know he's got at least a dozen rounds left in the magazine.

"It's a set-up, Eddie," I tell him, but he doesn't listen, just squeezes another round into the air. I'm taller and stronger than him, and it isn't hard to keep the gun pointed away from me. "I called Hollander from the burner in Reed's toolbox. He knew we were coming. You listening? We both heard the machine gun. You guys never had a goddamn chance."

He glowers like I've betrayed him somehow, like he wasn't just about to shoot me.

"Toss the gun," I say. "There's a spare set of keys in the visor of Reed's truck. You saw what was in the toolbox. Take it all, I don't care."

"Reed gave the *all clear*, man. He called for me."

"They have him at gunpoint. He's cooked. All they're doing is flushing you out."

He gives up, and I let him throw the gun into the ravine.

"You're a snake, man," he says, but he's smiling when he says it. "I can dig a snake. They slither just like I do."

Milligan climbs to the road where the CAL Fire truck waits on the steaming asphalt. He pats the toolbox with the fat of his palm and slips behind the wheel. He gives me a depraved look of triumph, like he's just won the whole game. Then he beeps the horn twice and races down the mountain where all the pawn shops of the world await.

◆

When I hike to the villa, I see Ortega sprawled on his back in a pool of blood. It's so hot, I can almost smell him decomposing right under my nose. Maybe it's the shit leaking from his blown-out guts. At the top of the circular driveway, I see Reed. He's on his knees with his hands tied behind his back, a trio of serious men standing behind him in the same yellow wildland gear I'm wearing. But there's someone else, too. Not Hollander, and not quite a person, either. A figure made of shiny mirrored steel stands over Reed with a Tek 9 in its hand. It looks like something from a 1960s comic book, like a straight razor has come to life. Its face is a strange black lens that tracks me with deadly interest as I ascend the driveway.

"Please state the security code," it says—a female voice. Polite and flat, like a telephone directory.

"Arroyo 858," I say.

It turns from me and focuses on Reed, the Tek 9 is inches from the back of his head. I hear a loud click, and a godlike voice booms all around us.

"I appreciate the advance warning," says the voice. This time it's Hollander. I recognize the over-pronunciation of the consonants, as if he's trying to pack as much arrogance into each word as possible. "I like to reward loyalty, as you know. It's a rare virtue in this age of dishonesty."

"That's why I'm here," I say. "To talk about a reward."

Reed erupts in frothy anger. "They're gonna find your ass," he says. He sounds wounded, maybe shot somewhere I can't see. There's a small pool of blood gathering around his knees, blackening the hot pavement. "This time they'll jam you up for life."

"Maybe we'll be bunkies," I say, with a laugh. "You better plead out if you ever want to see the light of day. I'm sure they caught your stupid heist attempt on camera."

"Oh, we're no longer recording," says Hollander. His voice is so loud, it feeds back in shrieks and whistles like a cheap megaphone. "We'll say it had something to do with the fire. A power surge, maybe.

As much as I like to reward loyalty, I love punishing treachery, too. Please kill the prisoner for me, Samantha."

There's a brief silence as the machine shifts its weight.

A gust rises off the ravine. A bitter, poison wind.

"Hold on—we can talk this out, can't we?" Reed has the same look of utter loss that I had when my house burned to the foundation, or when I pled to involuntary manslaughter after beating that pock-faced looter to a bloody pulp. It's a look you make when every thread unravels and all you can do is bargain. "I can help save this place. Just give me a shovel and—"

The Tek 9 rattles. Reed's face is no longer a face. A chunky red spray fans out before him, a wet pile of failed schemes and gimmicks. The body falls forward into the mess, and the three private firemen shuffle uncomfortably, eyeing each other like nervous birds.

"Follow Samantha to the garage," says Hollander. He sounds remarkably calm for disintegrating a man by remote control. "She'll pay your reward from petty cash. And please, I know you're as much of a car guy as I am. Take what you want from the garage. Anything you like. Enjoy the ride, killer."

The voice shuts off for good, and I follow Hollander's killing machine as it lumbers toward the garage. I'd prefer not to follow that thing anywhere, but I'm unarmed, broke, and on foot. Without help, I won't get far.

"Which vehicle will you choose?" the machine asks me. It feels like there's a right and wrong answer, like it'll turn me into pink goo if I make the wrong choice.

"I don't know. Which one can I drive the farthest?"

"None of the vehicles in our inventory are considered fuel efficient. However, the 2026 Jaguar F-Pace is the most economical at twenty-two miles to the gallon in the city, twenty-seven on the highway."

I take the keys off the pegboard, and Samantha hands me a small duffle full of hundred-dollar bills. Then I put my foot into the Jaguar, fishtail past the bodies, and hit the smoke-shot highway. In the rearview, I can see Hollander's chrome assassin watching me as I go. Or maybe it's him, watching through its eyes, wondering if he should have let me live.

❖

I drive from town to town through the bone-dry West, staying off the grid, paying cash for everything. I sell the Jaguar at some greasy dealership in Elko, Nevada, for half its value. By spring, I settle in a former ski town in Wyoming. I say *former* because it hasn't snowed in three years, and most of the ski resorts have folded—or they're about to. The locals still think climate change is a hoax even as they watch the town crumble before their eyes. Some blame immigrants, but there aren't many of those around, either.

There's a dive bar in the center of town called The Witch's Tit, and it's one of the last places in America you can put real money into a jukebox and let your mind coast while nursing a cold bottle of beer. I'm listening to Iron Butterfly when a reporter from the *San Francisco Chronicle* pushes through the door and squints into the darkness. She stands with her hand resting on her bag, as if she's ready to pepper-spray the first cowboy hat that turns her way.

I wave her over and slide a chair out.

"Just so you know," she says, "if this isn't as good as you say it is, I'm calling the Marshal Service and sending you back to Mule Creek."

"I've heard that before," I say. "It never works out like you think."

The reporter's name is Sheryl Bronson. She works the domestic politics beat and has been following Ger Hollander's surprise presidential bid for the 2028 election. He's up in the polls, too. He says his technology can somehow stop the erratic weather, and many are stupid enough to believe it. Lately, Bronson has been running stories on the weaponization of AI and the industry's impact on the climate. I'm surprised he hasn't found a way to sink her yet.

It's a quality I admire.

I slide a thumb drive across the table, and she covers it with her hand.

"I'm not leaving until I see the video with my own eyes," she says.

"I knew you'd feel that way."

I hand her the burner phone, the same one I'd stolen from Reed's truck last year. The one I'd left recording from the pocket of my yellow brush shirt as Hollander's killing machine turned my crew chief's head into tomato soup. Bronson watches the video and winces, shuts her eyes tight. Then she watches it again—and again. She sets the phone down and orders a rum drink from the sleepy bartender. We both know that *weaponization* is too buzzy a word for the kind of violence Hollander is about to unleash.

"This video isn't AI?" she says, but she knows it's not. It's too imperfect—the smoke, the scratchy microphone, the physics of the execution. "If it is, I'll find out."

"The video's not, but Samantha is."

"Samantha?"

"If you listen, that's what he calls the machine."

"And you don't want money for this?"

"Just a plane ticket to Chile. I hear it still snows down there."

"I'm assuming you have a new passport."

"Yeah. It cost me, though."

She has another question—but hesitates.

"You tipped Hollander off. From what you've told me, I don't think you had much of a choice, but I need to know why you're turning on him now."

I scroll through the video one last time. I still have a painful cough from that day, the poison air buried in the deepest pockets of my lungs. Now the political winds are blowing poison, too. I know there is nothing that kills quicker than bad politics. It gets into the air and the water, it gets under the skin and into the blood—it hollows a country from the inside out. You can see the deep corrosion if you're halfway paying attention, but lately people seem content to float around in all that toxic wind like paper trash in a dollar store parking lot.

"Reed was a crooked asshole," I say. The organ solo from "In-A-Gadda-Da-Vida" has come and gone, and now some AI-generated country star named Colt Remington appears on the jukebox, singing nostalgically about an America that only really existed in country songs to begin with. "But Reed was small-time. If Hollander wins, we'll be a country full of crooked assholes."

"Maybe we already are," she says.

"Maybe." I reach down and yank the jukebox power cord out of the wall. A few cowboys turn around with sour faces as the bar goes silent. "Maybe I'm hoping you're that last one left. A cure for poison."

"I'm not anyone's cure," she says, finishing her drink with a quick tilt of the chin. "But I'll do you one better."

"What's that?"

"I'll send Hollander to Mule Creek over this."

I picture him in yellow bush clothes, cutting a fireline while some salty crew chief tells him to get his ass in gear, the bitter taste of ash in his mouth, the heat lashing his pampered, billionaire forehead. It's a much better outcome than squads of dead-eyed killing machines marching in the streets.

"I want a front-page story with mugshots," I tell her.

She takes the phone and thumb drive and settles them into a black Faraday bag. "I'll even put it in a nice frame for you."

"I knew when I opened the door that it was going to be a bad day. That heat hit me the same way that wind does downtown, like you feel it push in when you are trying to breathe out, and there is a second when you're scared you can't."

Hot Child in the City, 1995

Mary Thorson

It's hot. It's very hot **(1):** It was early, so it wasn't so warm yet—I didn't think so, anyway. We had our windows closed because nobody keeps them open at night with all of *that* out there. Not how it used to be, anyway. Drake had fallen asleep watching Bob Newhart on the La-Z-Boy in the living room. Now, some obnoxious kids' crap was blaring out in his face. I told him to turn it off—that it was too loud, and he didn't move. At first, I was annoyed. His hearing had been going for years, and you know how men are. Especially old men. So I yelled again. I remember the way his name sounded coming out of my mouth, and it was a sound I hated. I used to hate it. Now, sometimes when I'm by myself, I'll scream it just to hear his name, because nobody else is saying his name anymore.

Yesterday we broke records **(27):** Everything smelled so so bad. Like kids always do, right? But this was the worst it had ever been. I knew when I opened the door that it was going to be a bad day. That heat hit me the same way that wind does downtown, like you feel it push in when you are trying to breathe out, and there is a second when you're scared you can't. That's what it felt like. I opened Miss Mary's apartment door, and after the smell and the heat, it was the noise. Every kid was crying, slow and long. There was a window open, but it might as well have been a fireplace. And that baby was underneath a blanket. Why?

We all have our little problems, but let's not blow it out of proportion (95): Until then, my biggest fear had been drowning. Lake Michigan. And I lived really close. On certain days, when the winds were right, you could smell the lake, and it smelled like fish. But you couldn't smell the lake that week. I left my apartment, and I felt an actual moment of panic. I think I even said, out loud, to nobody, that it was too hot. I just had to walk a few blocks, but there was a thought I had that I might not make it. Then I thought I was overreacting. My mind does that, sometimes I spiral. So, I walked and looked for any water source on the way there. Like "oh, I know that library has a water fountain," or "if it gets really bad, I can always jump into the river." When I finally got to the lake, it was packed. And it looked like a lot of people were setting up camp, literally. Tents and everything. It was a land grab, and I had barely gotten there in time. And then I thought, "damn, there are 2.8 million people in this city."

It is a crisis. It's hot out there (124): We'd only been on shift for 90 minutes or whatever. Not long at all. But I swear the radio wouldn't stop going off. My partner and I have responded to something like five calls already. Person down in the street. Fights. Lots of DV popping, and that was strange before 10 a.m. Broken off fire hydrants. The paramedics started to get real sick of the sound of my voice *laughs*, but then I got my first DOA right at 9:41 a.m., I remember staring at the clock when the call came in. Taxi driver behind the wheel of his car. He probably fell asleep on an overnight. Parked it for a few hours before starting up again, and well—he just never got up again. The person who found him didn't even open the door. But I guess they didn't need to. He was middle-aged, had a bumper sticker stuck on the glove compartment above a picture of some kids. *It said I'm not deaf, I'm just ignoring you . . .*

Then we got a lot more calls like that.

We all walk out there. It's very, very, very hot (183): I watched the weather the night before. I remember his name and exactly what he said. Joe Sliker told us it was going to be a scorcher. Air conditioning on. Stay hydrated. The big graphic of the red, sweating thermometer on the side of the screen. So I wasn't expecting an easy day, but I couldn't fucking believe what I walked into. You couldn't sit down in the waiting room at Mt. Sinai. Lots of people vomiting. We couldn't get fluids into them fast enough. Their veins were collapsing before we could stick them. While me and the paramedic that was handing off continued CPR on an old man, the paramedic said something to me between breaths. I asked him to repeat himself. He told me they didn't open a single cooling center. That's when the kid came in. A woman shouting with him in her arms. She'd broken past check-in and triage. She locked eyes with me and just said, "Please."

It's like getting heavy snow. It's like getting real cold weather (216): There is a thing that happens in cities, it's called a heat island. You know when you're a kid and you're at school during recess. Your shoes, if they were made of rubber, would sometimes stick to the blacktop. That's because they were melting. When you don't have trees or grass and all there is is concrete and glass, you're basically a grasshopper underneath a magnifying glass. Temperatures in heat islands can be 20 degrees higher than those with some green, but when was the last time you saw grass in Chicago?

Yes, we go to extremes in Chicago (392): A woman by a garbage can. She melted into a puddle on the sidewalk. I mean, seriously. Her skin was sagging. It was almost like the bottom of the garbage bag inside the container had ripped and then leaked out through some crack, except that leak was wearing shorts and a 4th of July tank top. When we went to get her up on the stretcher, my gloves stuck to her skin, and when I let go, her skin peeled right off. She was all blister. Not twenty feet away from her was the shadow of the Sears Tower. That's when I noticed something that had been bugging me all day. A feeling I had that something else was going on besides the heat. It was the wind. There wasn't any. Not a single breeze all goddam day.

And that's why people love Chicago (500): Some people didn't even know it was happening. Like the people on Lake Drive or the South Loop. It was just summer to them. Nice. No school. Air-conditioned cars and houses, and apartments. They just stayed inside, watched whatever was on TV, and didn't know that people thirty blocks west were cooking. They didn't know that the hospitals were so backed up with bodies that they were storing them in a fleet, and that's not me exaggerating, a fleet, I tell you, of refrigerated trucks. Like a caravan. They just went on about their day, picking their kids up from daycare and turning on the stove to make them dinner. Maybe they took off their suit jackets when they got home. But maybe they didn't even have to.

***We go to extremes* (651):** First, I tried calling. After we had one hundred or so that first day. I called the mayor's office, and I didn't talk to him, but I tried. I told whoever to tell him he had a big problem. That this was bigger than a hot day. That something was happening, I'd never seen so many bodies in one day. And it was all the same thing. Over and over and over and over. Heat exhaustion. Fried up. Then, the next day, we got even more, so I called again because I heard the city wasn't opening up any cooling centers. Hand out portable air conditioners, send out firetrucks, and spray down the neighborhoods, something. Then the mayor got on TV, and I thought, good, you know? He's going to say something. He's taking this seriously. But he goes out and says it's nothing. He rambled about what? Nothing. Told everyone to relax. Then, the day after that, the trucks come. I didn't even have to call for them. They knew what was happening, and they just wanted us to load them up like produce. Then the kid came in. Really little, only three years old. Daycare worker found him in his bouncer. I stopped calling the mayor's office and called the Tribune. They knew me. I just told one of them to come down to the morgue. That I wouldn't say anything. The bodies told the story of exactly who was dying and why, but it was a story they already knew. They were bored with that story. Everyone was.

❖

* Between July 12th and July 16th, a heat wave descended upon much of the Midwest. Chicago, in particular, saw temperatures as high 110 degrees, which was 20 degrees above average. Conditions were exacerbated by high humidity and notable lack of wind. While there was no official death toll from the event, the Cook County Coroner at the time stated around 450 people died due to heat over that five-day stretch. Now, it is believed the actual number of excess deaths was closer to 800. The vast majority of the victims were elderly, hitting African-American males and people who lived in low-income neighborhoods particularly hard. Mayor Richard Daley gave a press conference during the heatwave. The transcript of that press conference is the bolded text within the story above. It is written exactly as Daley said it. Word for word.

Thomas, Mike. 2015. "How 739 People Died in a Chicago Heat Wave." *Chicago Magazine*. 2015. https://www.chicagomag.com/Chicago-Magazine/July-2015/1995-Chicago-heat-wave/

"That night, he powered down his laptop and put his cellphone inside the oven. Then he closed his bedroom door and read Shelly's research in bed with the blackout curtains drawn and a loaded AR-15 beside him."

Novel Entities

Zakariah Johnson

It started with the box turtle. Mathias Baumberger was standing on the shore of his organic fish pond, tossing in handfuls of cornmeal for his prize trout, when the tank-like little animal caught his eye. The hand-sized creature's face and limbs were covered in black tumors. Its carapace, evolved to blunt a fox or raccoon's teeth, was soft, and it bowed in where he handled it.

"What's wrong with you, old girl?" he asked, calling her "old girl" because the animal was clearly female as well as old, with a fully-healed crack in the shell to demonstrate her antiquity. The species could live to be a hundred, but he knew no way to calculate its exact age. Growths on its neck prevented it from drawing into its shell, and Mathias was amazed a predator hadn't made an easy meal of it. Intrigued, he placed the animal into the five-gallon bucket of feed that he'd already emptied so she wouldn't wander off. He noticed a sticky puss on his hands where he'd handled the reptile, and, always a man of caution where his animals were concerned, decided to clean up before finishing feeding his fish.

◈

"What do you think, doc?" Mathias asked the veterinarian examining the turtle.

"I'm shocked it's still alive," Shelly answered. "There're more tumors growing in its mouth. See?"

"She must have an insatiable will to live, like us." Mathias had been fighting melanoma for a decade, while Doctor Shelly White had had a double mastectomy she'd openly discussed and blogged about, a candor which had been approved of by most, but not all, in the community.

"Is she the only one you found like this?"

"There aren't many box turtles left. But I haven't really been looking. Why?"

"These types of tumors suggest exposure to a triggering toxin, an immune system collapse, or perhaps both, one leading to the other. You might want to inspect your property."

"What are you implying? My farm's been certified organic for twenty years. Not just by the state ag department but by the growers' association, too. The latter don't cut corners."

"Calm down, I'm spitballing here. Turtles travel, especially when they're looking for food. Mind if I keep it? I'd like to run some tests on these growths."

"Won't that hurt her?"

Shelly gave him a pitying look. "I'm sorry, Mathias. There's no way this one's going to make it. We'd best to put it down."

He sat down heavily on the chair next to the examination counter, eyes staring at nothing.

"Do you remember when we were kids?" he asked. "Everyone used to catch box turtles and keep them for a week or two before letting them go. I haven't even seen one in years and now we have to kill it?"

Shelly reached a hand toward his shoulder before retracting it and laying it on the counter, her other hand firmly holding it down. The charismatic but volatile bachelor farmer had been there for her through many struggles, but ultimately his emotions had proven more disruptive than soothing, and she'd told him their future could only be platonic.

"I'm sorry," she repeated.

❖

Mathias didn't believe for a second he had anything toxic on his property, but Shelly's warning had put the fear in him. He provided his dwindling and, ironically, grocery-deficient farm community with much-needed vegetables, fruits, and, most notably, fresh fish, since no one in their right mind would eat anything from the local river, awash as it was in pesticides from the farms now tilled to both banks for subsidized cash crops. While the big operations and other monocroppers might not care what lurked in their soil, his own livelihood depended on his products' reputation not to give his customers cancer, an immune-disorder, or just a bad taste in their mouth.

In the following weeks, he did a thorough reconnoitering of his property, checking for any source of contamination. The groundwater in his area was known to contain high levels of arsenic, so he always used rainwater to fill his pond and ran his drinking water through a reverse osmosis filtration system.

But the arsenic had always been there, and the turtles had done fine despite it for millennia. There were no old waste barrels, no unmarked gas wells venting into his air, no burn pits, and no visible signs of contamination anywhere on his farm. That meant looking for the invisible.

He remembered a scandal in the neighboring county a few years back, when the state department of agriculture had discovered PFAS contamination in the local soil. PFAS, perfluorinated alkylates, were the chemicals used in firefighting foam, high-tech rain gear, and nonstick cookware. Known as "forever chemicals," many PFAS had been banned but companies worldwide could get around the bans by slightly modifying the chemical compounds and rebranding them.

Before it had closed, the local newspaper ran a series of articles about in-state farmers who'd been duped into accepting sludge from a city waste treatment plant to spread as fertilizer on their fields.

The sludge was supposed to be PFAS free. It wasn't. He couldn't remember what the outcome had been, and further investigation showed the case seemed to have disappeared.

"Could it be PFAS?" He tried several searches, getting similar batches of AI-generated double-talk that didn't provide any guidance. Since the Environmental Protection Agency had been privatized, accessing the records on its website required a subscription, which he had as a member of the co-op. He tried there, quickly finding the same noncommittal soundbites the AI had been paraphrasing: research "suggested" that immune system failures "might" be induced by exposure to PFAS, but danger levels were unknown.

"Unknown, my ass," he said, and logged onto his VPN.

Spoofing his location to Sweden, he logged onto the website of an environmental NGO based in Holland. There, he found links to a 2010 study demonstrating rainwater throughout the world now contained levels of PFAS that exceeded the environmental standards of many national governments—including the USA—for "lifetime exposure" rates. Unsafe exposure levels were listed in measurements of billionths and trillionths of a gram.

"Nasty stuff," he muttered.

He printed the page, exited the location spoofer, and returned to the EPA website. It was tricky, but he finally found the page listing the levels of PFAS currently deemed safe for consumption. Those limits were much higher than the ones regulators in the USA had considered safe in 2010, according to the Dutch study of the same year.

"That can't be right." He checked several other articles published prior to January 2025 and found a plethora of exposure rates considered safe, depending on the polity, but the current EPA recommendations were far higher than any of them.

Excited at discovering evidence to share with Shelly, he instinctively hit "print screen" on the EPA website, triggering the warning dialog box: "STOP! This website contains classified information and may not be printed. Further attempts may result in legal action."

"Damn it, damn it, damn it . . ." He picked up his phone to take a picture before hearing an almost subliminal chuckle in its speaker that froze the blood in his veins. Recovering, he opened a music app on the phone, turned the volume to max, and then walked into the kitchen where he left the phone on the table. Closing the door to his study, he took the shot with his digital camera. Seconds later, his computer screen went blank.

❖

"I got another tumor turtle," Shelly said, climbing into his truck with her Wendy's order. "Dolores McIntosh's daughter brought it in, crying all to Betsy, poor girl. And Buck Jensen said he euthanized one with the same condition."

"Buck doesn't have a pond," Mathias said.

"No, he doesn't." She handed him her receipt from the burger joint. "To what do I owe the honor of this free meal?"

"Look at this." He held out a sheaf of papers. "See? It's a study from the Faroes. 'Estimated exposures to perfluorinated compounds in infancy predict attenuated vaccine antibody concentrations at age 5-years.' The PFAS don't just cause some diseases, they also set you up for others."

Shelly swatted the papers away like they were on fire. "The Faroes? Like the Faroe Islands? That's in Europe. Where'd you get this?"

"I used a spoofer to imitate a user in Sweden. There's tons of articles like this."

"A VPN? Jesus, Mathias. That's a felony now! What are you playing at?"

"I have a right to know."

"You idiot. Are you trying to get a visit from the Farm Labor Bureau? They don't mess around."

A recent bureaucratic shuffle had moved the federal Farm Labor Bureau from the Department of Agriculture into the Department of Homeland Security to facilitate the USDA's evolution into prison management. With foreign countries increasingly unwilling to accept deportees, the federal government had run out of room to incarcerate the hundreds of thousands of foreign farm laborers rounded up in immigration sweeps. Simultaneously, farmers were crying out for workers.

A solution had been found in renting out the detainees for only dollars a day back to the same farms, ranches, and slaughterhouses where they'd previously worked. Keeping workers near the farms that needed them had necessitated building a system of gulags across the country. The government maintained the pretense that the situation was temporary. The country needed food, after all, and the solution essentially meant that the system of dependence on and exploitation of immigrant farm labor developed over the previous century continued on as before, except now the workers wore ankle monitors and spent their evenings in trailers provided by FEMA instead of by their former employers. The gulags also doubled as holding jails for citizens awaiting bail hearings or trial, sometimes for months, often for years.

"The FLB?" Mathis laughed. "I'm not going to get arrested for doing research."

"What do you want from me?"

"They've walled off the reports on human subjects, but there must be veterinary studies on immune system decay in animals from PFAS. Can you get me some?"

"Why?"

"Because the public has a right to know—I have a right. I've thought about this. Do you know why we're seeing tumors in the turtles but nothing else, at least not yet? Because there's only two animals in North America that live long enough to absorb PFAS in excess of lifetime safety levels before dying of natural causes first. Turtles are one. You want to guess what the other one is? Rhymes with cumin. You think it's a coincidence all the NIH information about cancer clusters in this state has disappeared? That all those NSF grants have been cancelled? Just let me airdrop these screenshots to you."

"Please, no . . ."

"Done."

She took out her phone as it pinged and looked them over. "Damn it, Mathias."

"Come on. Just do a search for those studies. For old time's sake."

"Stop yourself right there, mister! This is the same pigheaded nonsense I left you over in the first place."

"Then think of the children. For God's sake, Shelly. I fear something terrible is happening here, and we've hardly scratched the surface."

Barely audible at first, Shelly's phone began to chuckle, rising to a level anyone would have noticed before abruptly cutting out.

"Oh my God," she rasped. "What have you done?"

◈

Unlike many of his neighbors, Mathias refused to rent prisoners from the local Farm Labor Bureau camp. He knew slavery well enough when he saw it. His fellow congregants at church mostly didn't see it that way, citing the clear exception for conscripted labor in the Thirteenth Amendment, not to mention the biblical precedent.

"Legal don't make it right," he'd said, and stopped going to services.

There were still enough landless, country Jakes around to help him with the harvest, and he managed the daily chores alone by working sixteen hours seven days a week. However, he still set up a stand at the farmers market in the parking lot between the United and Baptist Churches each Thursday. That Thursday, he had a pair of unusual visitors.

"How you doing?" asked the first man. Like his double, he was dressed in brand new work clothes and boots that had never trod the soil. His hair was cropped short, and his expensive sunglasses were clearly not the variety from the spinning rack at Wal-Mart. Both men were beefier than the typical tourist.

"I can't complain," Mathias said. "Yourself?"

"I could, but who'd listen, right?"

Mathias snorted in acknowledgement of the joke.

"No, really. If I had a complaint to make, who'd listen? Who is there to talk to around here?"

"What is your complaint?" Mathias asked.

The man picked up an apple, bit into it, and began chewing.

"Suppose this apple was sour. Or had a worm in it? Or maybe, a report came out that you'd been cheating a little, spraying a little something on your crops here or there. Not really organic." He paused to chew and swallow. "Now, I suppose I could complain about that, start talking to your neighbors, saying I suspected your food might contain novel entities. But then I might run afoul of the FFADA." The man said it like a word, emphasizing the "f" to draw it out. "You know what that is?"

"The Family Farm Anti-Defamation Act."

"That's right. It doesn't do to panic people about their food supply. Especially an upstanding member of the community like yourself. Head of the local Toastmasters Club, weren't you? Slandering food safety is also illegal." The man dug around the circumference of his inner lips with his index finger, flicked the loose apple pieces onto the ground, and spat. "That, though, that was a good apple. You know what a bad apple does, pard?"

"Spoils the barrel?"

"Indeed, it does." He tossed the remnants of the half-eaten apple back into the carton. "Pay the man, Charlie."

The mute member of the team stepped forward and peeled five one-hundred dollars bills off a roll onto the counter.

"Don't spoil the barrel, Mr. Baumberger," said the first man. Then they turned and disappeared into the crowd.

Mathias went back to work, trading friendly banter with his neighbors and customers as he rang up sales on his phone. He did good business for the next hour.

Shelly had promised to stop by the market to let him know what she'd found. She hadn't shown up yet, so when his phone dinged, he yanked it out of his overalls to check the message. Instead of one from her, there was a text from an unknown number displaying the side-by-side emojis of an apple and a worm along with a picture of the inside of his garage showing a gas can surrounded by rags. The can wasn't where he'd left it.

A few minutes later, Shelly came by his stand. She set a manilla folder on his table.

"I did what you asked. Never call me again." With that, she picked up a carton of his famous garlic, handed him five dollars, and walked away, leaving the folder behind.

❖

Arriving home, Mathias removed the gas can from his garage. The can was full. It hadn't been earlier.

That night, he powered down his laptop and put his cellphone inside the oven. Then he closed his bedroom door and read Shelly's research in bed with the blackout curtains drawn and a loaded AR-15 beside him.

She'd hit paydirt. Research on PFAS poisoning of farmland in the state had been all but scrubbed when it came to human subjects, but Shelly's veterinary resources showed an uptick in tumors in elderly horses whose owners had put them out to pasture. Increased mouth cancers in dogs were also suspected to have a PFAS link, as were increasingly common cases of body tumors in long-lived animals in Africa, such as giraffes.

More germane to his fears, Shelly's info showed that over the past twenty years, even as research had consistently lowered the amount of PFAS exposure considered to be safe, governments around the world had simultaneously raised the allowable rates, sometimes by several magnitudes. A law in the Netherlands to protect the public from PFAS soil poisoning had been repealed under pressure from developers after 70 percent of construction projects had to be cancelled. And still, the chemical companies proliferated the toxins.

Shelly's final printout confirmed what the old box turtle had told them from the start: their own county was saturated with PFAS, and the information had been suppressed.

"Sons of bitches."

The "classified" notice from the USDA website was still on the top of the final pages Shelly had printed from an archived version she'd found. The public had not been informed, and the clear plan was that they never would be. Just as the Family Farm Anti-Defamation Act (FFADA) and other "Ag-gag" laws had been passed to protect against public panic or de facto boycotts (organized boycotts had been declared illegal), federal agencies, public and privatized, had retooled their mission statements from public safety to public relations. What the public didn't know couldn't hurt them, or at least they couldn't lay the blame at the feet of Big Ag, Big Chem, or Big Brother.

Mathias slept fitfully that night. When he drove to Shelly's clinic the next day, her receptionist told him she hadn't come to work. When he called later to check, she still hadn't shown up. He stopped in once more the next day and found the receptionist feeding patient files through the shredder.

"Where is she, Marlys?"

The young woman looked up with a start from the whining machine. "Jesus, you scared me!"

"Where is she?"

The terrified receptionist looked around the empty office as if the men in sunglasses were standing there, then whispered low, "She's at The Farm."

❖

The Cass County Bureau of Farm Labor Detention Center, known colloquially as "The Farm," was the largest community in the county. The earliest residents had been housed in trailers formerly used by FEMA to house victims of floods, tornadoes, or other natural disasters. After those filled up, the late-arriving residents were packed into heated tents, sometimes one family per each, sometimes more. Surrounding the entire facility was a double circle of razor wire, its corridor patrolled by guards with German shepherds. Few escape attempts were made, and guard work paid better than most local options, so there was a waiting list of applicants wanting to sign on.

It was dusk when the rattle of metal sounded and the rumble of engines began to be felt. Inmate families looked up at one another as the noise became louder, eventually running outside to see what fresh hell was descending upon them. It turned out to be a row of thirty huge farm vehicles. Threshers. Tractors. Heavy trucks. Hay balers. And leading them all, a row of giant red combines riding five across, their horizontal cutting blades of spinning steel whirling chaff into the wind created by the oncoming convoy.

The line of vehicles was traveling in a wedge across the newly plowed corn field between the tent city and the highway. The noise of their radios could be heard playing the same song in unison: "Jailbreak" by Thin Lizzy. It wasn't Wagner's *Ride of the Valkyries*, but it got the message across: this convoy had come to liberate, not to kill. Anybody who wanted to come along only had to jump on board.

Shelly stepped from the communal tent she'd been assigned to see what the commotion was. Squinting through the swirling dust and fading light, she made out the "Cass County Growers Asso." lettering on the front of the central combine, making it clear where it came from and who was driving it.

"Jesus Christ, Mathias," she muttered and rubbed her newly blistered hands over her face. First he'd got her stuck in here, now he was coming to make her a fugitive. "You pigheaded son of a bitch." That stubborn streak had always been the worst and best thing about him, she reflected.

At a double blast of the convoy leader's horn, the other vehicles moved into a single file behind the five combines as they tore through the first, then the second coil of razor wire, and then toppled the guard tower standing beside the warden's HQ, the falling guard firing his automatic rifle all the way down.

"Shelly White! Shelly White! Where are you?" Mathias shouted into the mic of the lead combine, with old Buck Jensen literally riding shotgun beside him, his 12-gauge returning fire on any guards who hadn't run.

A Mack truck plowed through the warden's HQ just as he ran out the front door, barely avoiding being run down.

Dolores McIntosh was shouting in high-school-accented Spanish over her hay baler's PA, competing with Phil Lynott's soulful baritone for attention: "¡Corre, corre, toma a tus hijos y corre, tómalos mientras aún sean tuyos ¡corre ahora!

"Run!"

The crowd got the message. Men and women grabbed their children and quickly overpowered the outnumbered guards, at least those had hadn't obviously joined with the attackers.

Mathias stopped his machine and leapt down, bolt cutter in hand, to where Shelly was standing beside her tent. "Be still." He snipped off her ankle monitor, then handed the tool to a prisoner carrying a child on his back. "Cut off your tracking devices! They can't find you if you cut it off."

"What the hell are you doing?" Shelly demanded.

"You're getting out tonight."

"I have a bail hearing in just two months! I can't . . . I . . ." She looked around at the mass of vehicles demolishing the camp. Prisoners, and most of the guards, were climbing on board, into cabs, onto the beds, anywhere. Some ran in groups through the openings plowed through the wire. Others stood around stunned and confused. "What's the plan here?"

"There are three more camps between us and the state capital. We're going to hit them all. Then we're going to the capitol building."

"To reveal the truth?"

"To burn it down. Truth will follow."

"You'll never make it."

"Maybe not." The liberation song replayed through the stereo systems on the various farm vehicles, blaring about the jailbreak in progress. A helicopter had arrived, but so far wasn't firing. "I read your reports, Shelly. We don't have enough time left to worry about failure."

"We?" She was screaming over the music, motors, and sporadic gunfire. "What do you mean 'we'? You and me? These people here? Your co-op buddies you've tricked into this insanity? Is that your 'we'?"

"I mean the human race. And the turtles. And the horses. The fish. All of it."

"Yo, Mathias, let's roll, buddy!" Buck Jensen shouted down from the cab as he took the combine out of idle.

Mathias climbed two rungs up the ladder to the cab then turned back and held out his arm to her. "Coming?"

Shelly wrapped her arms around her torso. She thought about the missing parts of herself: of her life, her body, her chosen role as a healer in a dying world. Of her suffering patients and their sickened owners. Of her parents and brother, gone too young. Of the poisoned earth, her longshot chances with the parole board, and of Mathias's nearly certain to fail but likely final offer for redemption.

"I pick the next song," she said, and climbed aboard.

"Climate change. He'd heard about it as a vague concept back in school but had never expected it to affect him. Global warming, greenhouse gases, polar ice caps melting. It all sounded like someone else's problem."

The Devil Doesn't Live Hand-to-Mouth

Puja Guha

Mozambique had been destroyed—at least, each and every part of the country that mattered to him.

Would giving away intel on what's left of it even matter?

Antonio kicked at a piece of rubble in the sand. He'd begun the day determined to sort through the debris for anything salvageable. But half an hour into the task, he fought off the urge to curl into a ball under one of the few trees still standing anywhere in the vicinity as he looked over the edge of what had once been part of the pier at Bahia Mar Sanctuary. A boutique resort. His resort. Except it was all gone. All that was left was this rotting wooden platform. The rest was wreckage. Carnage.

He caught a glimpse of color and pushed through a layer of palm fronds to find a triangular piece of azure stone about the size of his palm. Several seconds went by before he recognized it as part of the mosaic wall hanging that he'd hung next to the reception desk. His sister had spent an entire month's salary on it as an opening gift for his resort. Antonio grimaced and tossed the haunting memory aside.

After three days of Cyclone Jasper, he was surprised anything had survived at all. There were moments during the storm when he thought that if he dozed off, even for just a few minutes, he'd awaken to find the entire country gone. And maybe he, too, would be lost in the wind and the waves. Swept away before the tides receded and the clouds parted. When the first rays of sunshine appeared, he was overjoyed. He and his sister had survived. Her children had survived. He'd run out into the grassland near her place and fallen to his knees. Prayed to Jesus, and every god in every other religion for good measure. If they could live through the end of the world, there was no hurdle they couldn't conquer.

Yet now, less than a week later, he could only admit the grim truth to himself. Surviving the end of the world was the worst curse imaginable.

I wish I had died.

The prospect of salvaging anything from the dump that was left of his business was too daunting to imagine. There was no way forward. No creative path to reopening. Despite his plan to begin with cleaning up the pier and the beach, he didn't even have access to a vehicle that could truck out the rubbish. And, even if he did, the nearest serviceable dump was over three hours away on mostly dirt road. The best he could do was pile it in a corner of the beach to deal with later, but the mound he'd created already reached his shoulders. With every second it threatened to ooze outward and merge into the pile of ubiquitous rubbish that was the rest of the property.

The foundation was reduced to a few cracked concrete slabs. Where the beach had been was now nothing but a roiling array of brown water. Tawny brown surf surrounded and abutted by every other shade of brown imaginable. Peanut-brown palm fronds were cracked and dry despite the thick layer of moisture that still permeated the air. The hickory and mocha-brown remnants of the pier. Previously white sand had turned the color of stale wheat toast. The entire resort would have to be reconstructed from the ground up.

I don't even know where to start . . .

The task of rebuilding weighed on him like a three-hundred-pound barbell. Pressing down on his shoulders at the bottom of a back squat. No matter how hard he tried to stand, his muscles refused to cooperate.

Much like he would probably never be able to lift three hundred—his current one rep max was two twenty-five—he would never be able to return the resort to what it once was. Or what it could have been. He didn't even have the money or supplies to repaint the pier, let alone reconstruct the boutique adventure resort.

And even if I did—what for?

During his childhood, he remembered his father saying the big storms were only once or twice in a lifetime. Yet, it was only by chance that the Inhambane region had escaped the devastation of Cyclones Idai, Kenneth, and Freddy, all of which had occurred within the last six years. Then there were the countless other cyclones whose names he couldn't even remember that had passed nearby and wrecked other parts of the coastline.

I need to find another dream . . .

Having his own coastal B&B for snorkeling, scuba diving, and other water sports no longer had a future. He had already called a few of his old clients to put food on the table. Thankfully, Mozambique's expat community and elites were still interested in swimming lessons. And while returning to Maputo felt like a step backward, he didn't have any other choice. He could teach every day and try to build his bank account back from the red. The loan payments on the resort were still due, and he had to send money home to his parents for the farm—if you could call the tiny plot of land where they slaved over cassava that. Their previously meager yields had dipped even further in the last few years, and he'd been telling them for months to invest in better seeds. Climate-smart agriculture or whatever the guy from the World Bank Agribusiness Support Program had called it.

It's my only option.

He blinked away tears and looked out across the bleak landscape once more.

I should be grateful. I'm alive.

So many others had lost everything. Yet he had an income-generating skill to fall back on. And even if he couldn't teach anymore, he could head to his sister's place an hour inland where he had weathered the storm. Or as an absolute worst-case scenario, he could always go home to the farm in Nampula. He'd grown up sleeping on the floor in their one-bedroom cottage, and it would be a roof over his head. One a lot of other Mozambicans would kill for after all of Jasper's devastation. But all Antonio wanted to do was kick and scream and rage at the world.

Climate change. He'd heard about it as a vague concept back in school but had never expected it to affect him. Global warming, greenhouse gases, polar ice caps melting. It all sounded like someone else's problem. But then he'd heard one of his clients mention climate change when Cyclone Idai was upgraded from a tropical storm to Category 1. Apparently, the increased severity—and frequency—of these storms had something to do with that phenomenon. Even then, the notion had remained abstract. Not something that could or would ever affect his life.

I should have known this was coming.

His insurance coverage for Bahia Mar was woefully inadequate. Something he'd planned to address, but hardly as pressing as meeting payroll for his staff. Another point to add to his list of regrets. If he ever wrote them down, the would've-should've-could haves would fill an entire novel the size of *Lord of the Rings*. The entire series, not even just one book.

You don't have time for that.

And he didn't. In fact, he ought to head back to Maputo that very night. His first swim lesson was scheduled for the next morning, and he couldn't afford to miss it. That cash would fund his dinner for three days, and, if he was careful, for the rest of the week. He'd done it once before. To buy and upgrade the resort property, Antonio had lived on a shoestring budget for almost five years. Eaten only one real meal a day. Taken his friends out on diving lessons as the occasional treat.

While the margins weren't as good as regular old swimming lessons at the pool, being out on the ocean fed his soul. Reminded him of what he was working toward.

It's all gone now.

The thought of a lifetime of daily pool sessions made him want to retch, but what else could he do? His dream was dead. Its last vestiges would disappear as the brown tides receded.

There's one other option.

Antonio had dismissed it immediately the first time the man had approached him at the market near the community center. Of the many Chinese people in Moz—both descendants of immigrant families and expats working in every growing industry—this man stood out in his memory. Something about the way he carried himself and slipped into conversation far too easily. Ernest Mao, if the business card was to be believed, although Antonio had his doubts. He preferred to think of him as 'the Chinese spy'. One moment he was picking vegetables, conversing with someone he'd run into briefly at the market several times over the past month, the next he was being asked to inform on one of his clients. A trade attaché at the American embassy who'd been posted in Moz for a two-year stint that had now been extended to six.

Antonio might be in need of cash, but a one-time payout of a few thousand dollars was hardly worth more than the relationship he had built with his clients. Especially when he considered Fred and his wife Gina to be more like friends. They had invited him over to dinner, come to the resort for diving lessons, and stayed up late playing board games with him. He didn't have many friends in the expat community—which was so privileged they lived a very different life—but Fred and Gina were special. They didn't brandish their wealth and flash it in your face. Instead, they'd made him part of their community. Several of his other clients had come from their intros. After they heard about the damage at Bahia Mar, they'd even invited him to stay while he sorted out his plans. Using that relationship to generate some extra cash felt like spitting in their faces.

So what?

Despite how welcoming Fred and Gina were, Antonio couldn't deny he felt some tendrils of resentment. Even though they worked hard—at whatever they did—they had everything handed to them. He'd had to suffer and save for every dollar. Every metical. And no matter how hard he worked or how much he saved, there never seemed to be enough. Even when things were good—like during the high tourist season over the last two years—he could never hope to have what they had. The gated five-bedroom mansion with a yard and swimming pool. The best he could strive for was a studio apartment in the loft of his seaside B&B. And when there was enough demand, he'd even given that up to a client just so he could put the extra cash away.

Placing a few bugs in their house the next time he visited wouldn't do any harm anyway. He could check on the devices once in a while and meet with the Chinese spy intermittently to hand over the recordings.

But what if Fred and Gina were spies too? If they were, perhaps they deserved their fate. All the government meetings they had and dealings with the lucrative mining industry. The road trips to Durban and other meetings in South Africa. Were they all just clandestine? Perhaps Fred and Gina had been stealing information from his government since they got here. Yet he struggled to think of them as bad people.

"*They specialize in lies and deceit. So, they've made you trust them . . .*"

That was what the Chinese spy had said. He'd pressed Antonio over again for two weeks, then simply left his contact information if Antonio had ever changed his mind.

Why didn't I throw away his card?

That question had haunted Antonio for the last three months. Every time he opened his wallet he saw the name *Ernest Mao, Huaxin Cement, Maputo.* Just another potential client for swim lessons if anyone spotted it, although no one ever had.

Antonio reached into his pocket and retrieved the card. Stared at the handwritten mobile-phone number etched in the top right corner.

His ticket to some easy cash. But the loss of every ounce of dignity he had left. He slid it back into one of the card slots and put his wallet away, then headed back to his car. The ten-year-old Toyota Corolla was parked at the end of the resort's old driveway. The asphalt had always been littered with potholes—something Antonio had planned to fix—but now he barely noticed them on his drive back to the city.

To Fred and Gina's opulent home.

He drove through the gate three hours later. The bitter taste of bile filled his mouth as he parked in their driveway. Their two Lexus SUVs were parked side by side, with the yard and swimming pool in the background. Straight out of a Lexus advertisement. His Corolla had never looked as drab or battered. Normally he was proud of owning a car, period—so many of his local friends couldn't afford one of their own—but alongside the luxurious vehicles, it was another reminder of what he would never have.

He grimaced and slammed the door. It crashed into the frame, and he immediately regretted it. The first thing the dealer had told him when he'd bought the car was to be gentle with it. Toyotas were built to last, but you still couldn't treat them like crap. Not when you couldn't afford a new car. Or even the most basic repairs.

Antonio grabbed his shoulder bag from the trunk and approached the main door to the house. As he waited for someone to answer, he noticed his hands were clenched into fists. Forcing them open, he tried to calm down. To believe everything would be okay. That he would find a way through the sludge to a better future on the other side. But the inner peace that had gotten him through the years of scrimping and saving to invest in the Bahia Mar property—which had been nothing short of a shithole until he'd poured another six months of work and money into it—was nowhere to be found.

Nancy, the housekeeper, appeared a moment later. She led him to the formal sitting room to wait—a room he'd only passed by in all the times he'd been over. "Fred and Gina will be back in an hour," she said in broken Portuguese.

Antonio nodded. Until his hosts returned, he was to stay here. Take in the pristine décor while he waited for them to lead him to his bedroom. The whole thing made him want to vomit.

You should be grateful, he reminded himself. They were being so kind to him. Always had been.

Or do they just want to rub their wealth all in your face? He shouldn't think that. Didn't want to.

The grating sound of the property gate yanked him from his train of thought. Five minutes later, Fred was pouring him a glass of scotch while Gina led him to his new bedroom. It was on the far side of the house. The window faced west, and the evening sun was shining through the blinds, lighting up the sky-blue bedding and chestnut wood décor.

"Thank you," he said to Gina with a small smile. "This is lovely."

"I'm so sorry about what happened to the resort," she gushed. "It's all so awful. I can't imagine how you are coping."

Antonio gave her a tight nod. He wasn't sure what to say. Her tone was dripping with sympathy, but he didn't want to engage anymore. If he could take the bottle of scotch into the room and drown in it on his own, that would be his preference.

But you have to be social. And thankful.

She led him back into the sitting room where Fred topped off his glass of scotch. "I know it feels bleak right now, but it'll be no time before you're hosting another one of those amazing gatherings at the resort. We met such interesting people there. I especially remember the official from the Ministry of Commerce you introduced us to. He helped Fred with a major mining deal."

"I didn't know that, but that's great," Antonio replied in a halting voice.

"You must have the best conversations with all your clients. They're such an interesting group."

After three drinks and all the associated revelry, Antonio finally managed to excuse himself.

Gina led him back to his bedroom and wrapped him in an unexpected hug. "Let me know if there's anything you need. And I really meant what I said earlier. You'll be back on your feet in no time. Besides, a few swim lessons with all those interesting clients can't be so bad."

"I hope you're right."

Why does she always ask so much about my other clients? Antonio stared at her, wondering if her slightly off behavior was merely a product of the extra alcohol consumption.

"Besides, you can always vent to us about the bad ones. Stay as long as you want and come by anytime."

"Thank you." After saying those two words so many times already that night, Antonio almost choked on them, his thoughts still lingering on her earlier question.

"Anyway, I'm so glad you're here. Whatever you need, we're here for you, no matter what. I promise." Gina lingered by the door with a small smile.

She's expecting another thank you.

Antonio forced himself to return her smile and sound out the words. "Thank you both so much. I don't know what I would do without you." He enunciated every syllable, but it didn't sound like his voice. Just a more subservient version of himself. The African in service of another colonial power.

As she shut the door, the Chinese spy's words came back to him once more.

"Why do you think they've been so nice to you? Sure, they're your friends. But it makes them feel better about themselves. Plus, your client base gives them access to all kinds of people they can get intel on..."

Antonio shook his head. Anything to rid himself of such a cynical outlook.

Ernest Mao—or whatever his real name is—is a spy too. You can't trust him.

Since their first encounter at the market, Antonio had clung to the belief that his friends couldn't be spies. But there had been signs from the very beginning. Little bits of curiosity the couple had displayed. Questions they'd asked about Antonio's clients, especially the government officials and businessmen whose kids he taught to swim. And now, facilitated by copious amounts of scotch, an indisputable desire to hear more about them.

They are *spies.*

At 3 a.m., Antonio awoke to a wave of nausea. He fumbled his way into the ensuite bathroom and buckled over the toilet. A fitting end to one of the worst days of his life.

By the time he stumbled back to bed, his mind was made up. Fighting through the drunken haze, he switched on the bedside lamp and reached for his wallet. The card for Ernest Mao was exactly where he'd left it. A little worn at the edges, but very much still legible.

Before he could talk himself out of it, Antonio sent a text to the number in the corner.

"Let's meet for a drink next week."

He set the phone back on his bedside table when the screen lit up with a notification. He sat up in surprise and checked it. *A reply at three in the morning?*

"Absolutely. Let's do Thursday. 6 pm at Botanica."

Antonio's torso went rigid as he stared at the words. He could still back out. Pretend it was all a mistake. But that wasn't what he wanted. Not deep down.

Phone still in hand, Antonio ventured over to the window. Because of the city's light pollution, the sky bore no comparison to what he'd seen every night he'd spent at Bahia Mar. A shiver ran up his spine as he once again recalled the empty misshapen pier, all that was left of his earlier vision of the future.

They're spies. This is what they signed up for. And what they deserve.

Regardless of how murky the stars were, they were clear enough for him to see the path forward. Antonio reopened the text thread and sent a thumbs-up emoji in reply.

It was time to make a deal with the devil. Because that was what it would take to sleep in a house like this every day.

And the devil doesn't live hand-to-mouth. It was time for him to stop living that way.

"JOIN OR DIE"

Refugees

Colin Brightwell

A merica inherited thousands of acres in brand-new beachfront property, and only the rich got new cabanas. The other poor saps—retirees turning their skin to leather in Florida, working-class stiffs hustling for a buck in Houston, and the artsy types from New Orleans—were forced into retreat to the Midwest. The Republican-controlled government gave them each a check worth eight grand, and guys like Floyd Henderson thought about ripping it to shreds. Eight grand, was that how much he and millions of others were worth? He hung around the new Mississippi Gulf for a few weeks, bumming cigarettes and drinks from the newly moved uber-rich with his check in his back pocket. New high-rises and McMansions overlooking the ocean went up with a furious speed this country hadn't seen since they beat the Nazis. The rich were excited. They always were when they got what they wanted.

After a while watching the construction, the new shorelines got too depressing—the rich moving in like vultures while the carrion was still breathing. Floyd hot-wired some douchebag's Porsche and hiked it up to Memphis, left it at a gas station off the interstate, wiped the insides clean. He knew folks who still drove Porsches had the money for scorched-earth retrieval. They took his home and his country, so he figured it was only fair he borrowed their ride.

Motel rooms were sparse. Floyd slung his backpack holding everything he could take with him over his shoulder and made his way downtown. There wasn't much in the bag. Clothes, mostly. The National Guard helping with evacuation made everything feel so apocalyptic that Floyd and the rest couldn't even get a U-Haul and hit the road Steinbeck style. Made him glad he was alone, at least. Less baggage to carry in the long run. Looking back at it, they did have the time. The rich just wanted them out faster.

By dark Floyd had no luck finding a room. Must have been the last antelope to the watering hole, something he was used by now. At least it was summer, and he wouldn't freeze to death in some alleyway. His watch said half-past seven, and the neon lights of downtown Memphis swayed him on. He wandered into some dive bar that was half-empty and found a stool with his name on it.

Two televisions hung over the bar. Both were on the national news, squares with talking heads yelling over each other. The world-weary bartender sweating through a grimy tank-top came over and asked Floyd what he wanted to drink. There wasn't much cash in Floyd's wallet—a few fives stashed with the government check.

"Whatever can's the cheapest," Floyd said. "And a water."

The bartender obliged and left Floyd to brood over his drinks like a thousand others before him. The volume of the televisions were turned up enough that Floyd could hear nothing but the shouting of the pundits and politicians, the vultures, the opportunists, the apologists, the deniers. The anchor showed footage of some northbound interstate leaving the Gulf congested with traffic, like the blocked artery of a ready-to-burst heart. Floyd thought it was fitting for the country, given the circumstances.

The headline caught his attention—CAN THE NATION SUSTAIN THOUSANDS OF RELOCATED CLIMATE REFUGEES? That's what he was now, he thought. *A climate refugee.* Seemed like back in 2021 he was reading articles about climate refugees, but they were on other continents. A completely different world from Floyd. Couldn't happen here, people said. Politicians pointed to snowstorms, rainy seasons, how could climate change be real? But when the Colorado River started to evaporate, pockets of angry Americans started shouting at town halls. The pundits and politicians made them out to be agitators, America-haters, unpatriotic. Now that the shit hit the fan seven years later, they still somehow managed to control the narrative. Either the Gulf being swallowed up wasn't a terrible situation, or Floyd and the other climate refugees were just another nuisance to be dealt with. So sorry to be a hassle, I just pay my taxes.

The news program moved on to breaking footage of the President, oranger and meaner than Floyd remembered, taking time out of his busy day to inform legions of Americans that the ongoing situation in the southern Gulf, tragic though it was, would be a beautiful opportunity to create a new Atlantic City. A reporter asked him what about the thousands of citizens displaced by the rising oceans swallowing up the South, and the President nodded, and security removed the reporter. The President said thank you, God Bless America, and returned to the comfort of his White House. The television focused on the talking head pundits, who changed the subject to another conflict in the Middle East. Enough about Americans like Floyd, who broke their backs their whole lives just to be patted on the shoulder, given lunch money, and told to get lost, the rich want this land. Let the climate refugees eat cake.

The one percent wouldn't care until the whole country was eventually swallowed by the sea, and even then, they'd probably find a way to make a buck off it.

Somebody in the bar shouted to turn that shit off, and the bartender changed the channel to a baseball game. People had gotten too good at showing outrage on social media in the comfort of their La-Z-Boy recliner, arguing with bots about climate change, only to tune out when it was happening.

Floyd crushed his beer can, cut his palm on a cracked edge of aluminum. Least he still felt something. He sucked the blood mixed with beer and ordered another one. The thought of where to go next kept him drinking.

He dipped out on his tab by crawling through the bathroom window, clinging on to his dollar scraps. The southern summer humidity didn't bother him. Figuring out where his next home would be took up plenty of worry.

❖

A week wandering around Memphis, stealing copper wire from a condemned trailer park. Sweat-stained shirts he washed in park bathrooms. Ducking cops rounding up other vagrant climate refugees like they were invaders, undesirables, fugitives. Floyd clung to the walls and balked into the shadows. The President and his cronies preached a Christian nation, and now that Floyd was the hungry refugee, he was looked down on like the unwelcomed cockroach. Very Christian.

He learned to recognize fellow refugees by the bags under their eyes, the tightness of their faces. Hunger was the mutual friend between them. Floyd would give a nod in solidarity as he walked past one, each fending for themselves. It was a hell of a way to live. Last year he had a job, friends, a home. The insurance companies had stalled, pulling Gulf residents under the rug by ending policies for ocean damage.

Graffiti started going up around Memphis, a globe with a red X crossed over it. Each morning, Floyd watched city workers quickly paint over it, but someone would come along in the shadows of the night and recreate the image. Then Floyd noticed flyers nailed on utility poles everywhere, with the same X'd over globe. At the bottom were two-inch strips segmented for taking—half were gone already. The strips featured crude sketches of a snake, the words JOIN OR DIE written in its body, and an address below.

Floyd grabbed one of the strips and looked at the address closer. It wasn't much to go on—it just said, "five blocks past the river and I-55." The vagueness intrigued him, and maybe that was because wandering the streets was becoming boring, a haphazard type of existence when all he wanted was a job and a bed. Whenever he went somewhere asking for work, he felt the eyes of desk clerks and managers on him, as if "climate refugee" was tatted on Floyd's forehead. Just another bum trying to take jobs from hard-working Americans. Like all of this was his fault.

He pocketed the strip and figured he'd work his way up there. The evening was young and one thing he had learned lately was how to stifle the pain of blisters. Be like a politician. Ignore the problem, and surely it will go away. He hoisted his bag over his shoulder and headed towards the interstate.

◆

Gusts of wind from each passing car and truck and semi felt strong enough to throw him over the sidewalk, but Floyd kept walking. Head down. The moon cast an eerie glow over the Mississippi, and the tent cities thrown up on the Arkansas side went on for miles. There was the small glow of campfires and flashlights, people just scraping by.

With his head on a swivel, he made his way down to the road by the river and walked east five blocks. This was stupid, he thought, coming down here with no concrete address, probably some scam to rob and maim and take whatever meager earnings he had. He'd stolen for less since getting here. But the snake, and the words on the paper, the X'd out globe, kept him going.

Streetlights became few and far between during the last two blocks, the buildings spread out like the teeth in an old man's mouth. Dilapidated, rotting from the inside. Weeds reclaiming cracks in the pavement. If someone was going to knife him in the kidney for ten bucks, this was the place. He stopped and checked both ends of the streets. There was nothing out here. He waited for ten minutes before bouncing back toward downtown to find a park to sleep in.

By the time he heard footsteps on concrete, it was too late. He went to turn around but lost his vision through the thick fabric of a black hood. Someone grabbed his arms and held them behind his back.

"What the fuck," he said, his words muffled. Nobody said anything back, but he heard others say to hurry to get him off the streets before the heat came.

They dragged him, his feet treading the concrete, but they carried him in a way that didn't hurt. These weren't thugs, gangsters, meth-heads looking for some easy cash. Maybe that Porsche owner hired some private company who tracked Floyd down to bumfuck Memphis, in the weeds by the riverfront. Soon he'd be bloated and floating down the river back into the sea. It took every ounce of strength not to piss himself.

He heard the knocking on a metal door, locks clanging, the screaming of rusted hinges. Then the footsteps started echoing, and the coolness of air-conditioning calmed him. Fluorescent lights blurred through his covering, and he was sat on a metal folding chair. Someone zip-tied his hands behind his back.

"Sorry for the scare," a voice said. It echoed in the large room and sounded like a god. "We just have to make sure you're not law enforcement. They don't take kindly to our sort of thing."

"Where am I?" It sounded stupid when he said it. His words lingered in the air for a while.

"How did you find the paper?"

The snake. The globe. Join or die.

"On a powerline pole downtown," Floyd said.

"You weren't staking out the place?"

"I didn't even know what to look for."

It was beginning to feel like an interrogation. Floyd wondered when they would bring out the torture tools to really get him singing.

"Are you now, or have you ever been, employed by any law enforcement agency? Or the DMV?"

Floyd shook his head.

"Are you now, or have ever been, a registered Republican voter?"

He shook his head.

"Have you ever willingly posted misinformation concerning climate change on social media?"

"Never."

"Have you been affected by the recent events in the Gulf?"

"They evacuated me," Floyd said. "They wouldn't let me take anything except clothes and cash."

There was a moment of silence and then the footsteps came closer, and someone pulled off the face cover. After a minute of blindless from the lights, Floyd blinked and squinted at the ragtag group of people.

They were dressed in frayed and faded military fatigues, pistols on their hips, a few had machine guns strapped over their chests. They wore balaclavas.

Floyd heard the sound of a pocket knife and then felt the pressure of the zip-tie releasing from his wrists. He rubbed them.

"The one-percent and our fascist government denied climate change," one of the people said. "They let corporations take home a few bucks at the expense of the planet and its people. And now those bastards are getting richer while thousands of Americans are homeless, penniless, aimless. We aim to bring them to their knees with the time we have left."

On the shoulders of their camo jackets, the American flag was stitched upside down. There were maybe sixty people in the building.

"The influx of Gulf residents into our area is concerning. The indifference of our tyrannical president and his cronies in Congress makes us angry. People see refugees as beggars, asking for handouts. Help us make the rich burn, or forget you saw us. The choice is yours."

Floyd thought about the condos and the high-rises and the mansions erecting from the ruined landscape of his home, the eight-thousand dollar check to piss off, the people in power praising a new vacation spot. He clenched his hands on his knees. The answer was so simple.

"I'm in."

❖

Two months later, they sent Floyd and a few others down to the Gulf for recon on the construction. There were new developments. A casino. A yacht club. Tennis courts and a golf course. All built upon the devastation and pain of ruined American lives. Floyd wanted to shoot the billionaires all right there. But there was work to be done.

His training had been intensive—hours spent at shooting ranges, poring over instructions to make pipe bombs and car bombs, ways to make the rich and politicians understand that some people weren't going to sit by and let their world be changed without a fight. The group had robbed banks in Memphis and Little Rock, refugees pooling their government checks to buy needed resources—vans, ammo, dynamite. Floyd was told something major would happen soon that would force those in power start to listen.

Sitting in a van in New Gulfport with three other men, Floyd watched. His old stomping grounds held no resemblance to his home—it was like stepping into another country. Some of the mansions were already up, big boats skidding on the new coastal line, the rich tanning themselves and eating caviar. They would never have to worry about becoming refugees, Floyd thought. And the thought made his insides boil. When the coastline kept moving up, they would just rebuild and displace more and continue to say that nothing was wrong, poor folks. Keep working.

It was Floyd's plan to bomb the casino. Over the weeks he had impressed the Refugee leadership, led some funding expeditioners without a hitch. Deep down he thought he was blinding himself with his own rage and fury, his disgust at his country for letting this happen to him and so many others, but maybe that rage was a necessary evil. This movement wasn't any different from the revolution against England. This was a revolution against those in power.

The casino was a hotel hybrid, the structure already eight stories tall, the tallest building on the new coast. A perfect vacation spot. A source of pride for the rich.

The plan was simple enough. In the middle of the night, Floyd and the others would load a van to the brim with dynamite and park it at the casino entrance, set a timer to go off the next morning, and watch their work unfold in real time.

Mitchem had gotten ahold of blueprints, showing the best blast location to bring down the support beams. When the dust settled, the refugees would celebrate. The pundits and politicians would talk about the bombing for months.

"The security guards step away between eleven and midnight," Floyd said. "I want Mitchem and Davis on lookout detail. Shoot only if necessary."

"What if some rich dick prowls around?"

"I'm not worried about that," Floyd said. "They'll be asleep or partying on their yachts."

"Any exit plans?" Davis asked.

"I've been living on the streets for months," Floyd said. "They won't find us."

Everyone nodded.

"Davis and I will bring the van up tonight. Meeting place is the Shell five blocks north. Good view from the diner next door to watch this go boom."

Floyd looked around the van. They all looked tired and older than they were. Climate refugeeism aged them all, as they fended for food and money, foraging their way back into an existence in a country that abandoned them. It was only a matter of time before Los Angeles sank, and Manhattan was swept away. The Great Lakes were starting to lower. The walls were closing in, and the climate refuges were the wake-up call to the nation.

"Once that van blows up, there's no turning back."

Floyd waited for someone to voice concern. That the plan was too risky. Too destructive. But they were ready to show the rich how the country felt about them.

Balaclavas over their faces, Floyd and Davis drove to the coast at the speed limit. The half-moon made things a little clear, and they drove with the headlights off. Floyd's stomach did backflips as the structure of the casino came into view. They stopped fifty yards away, and Davis scanned the area.

They eased the van closer and closer.

When the red and blue lights flashed, Floyd's mouth went as dry as the Colorado. He turned to Davis. "Mask off. Turn your safety off. *Be cool.*"

Floyd rolled the window down, felt the breeze from the ocean. He pulled out a pistol and put it under his leg.

A flashlight beamed into the cabin, like looking into the sun.

"You gentlemen lost?" The cop moved his light between faces.

"We're on a delivery," Floyd said.

"It's almost midnight."

"We're just doing our job."

"This is a no trespass zone," the cop said. "Construction site."

"We know."

The cop stepped closer. He put his hand on the windowsill. Floyd noticed skull tattoos on his knuckles.

"Lemme see your license."

The cop had one hand on his holster, ready to quickdraw like a cowboy. A soldier-boy for the rich.

"We don't need to do that," Davis said.

"I'll say what you need to do."

Floyd looked at Davis. Be cool.

The cop leaned into the cabin, the flashlight moving from Floyd to Davis, the dash, the back. All he would see was blue tarp. "What's back there?"

"Equipment," Floyd said. His heart was going as fast as a Mustang engine. His palms sweat.

"Step out of the vehicle slowly."

Floyd looked at Davis. He felt sweat wash down his forehead. It stung his eye. They could hear the waves of the new gulf crash against the shore. Floyd turned back to the cop.

"I can't do that."

Floyd heard the button snap of the holster, and stared at the barrel of a gun.

"I'm not asking," the cop said, fixing his greedy smile on them.

It happened so fast.

Floyd exited the van, brought his pistol to the cop's stomach and pulled the trigger.

The gunshot must have echoed across the Gulf. Gulls took off in excitement.

The cop staggered back into the flashing blue and red lights that illuminated his expression of contempt and surprise like a concert. He gurgled through his mouth and tried to lift the gun up, but his hands went to his gut instead and squeezed.

"We have to move fast," Floyd said. The adrenaline had replaced the tension. He would see this through.

Crawling back into the van he felt the pain, like Superman punched his kidney, before he heard the shot.

He collapsed over the seat, and when he reached behind him, felt blood. He turned, wincing, and saw the cop sitting up holding his pistol.

"Officer requesting backup, officer down!" the man yelled.

Floyd emptied the clip of his pistol until the cop fell back onto the pavement. Sweat fell down Floyd's face like a sweet summer rain. He could taste the salt on his lips.

He turned to Davis. "Get the hell out of here. Go to the Shell. Tell the others it's happening now."

"What about you?" Davis asked.

"I'll be fine. Now go." Floyd could already hear sirens blazing down the road.

Davis got out and hightailed it back the way they came.

In the driver's seat, Floyd felt the pain from the gunshot. Felt his body fighting against it in a vain attempt to keep going. Everything was sticky. His mind was as light as a helium balloon. It had to be now.

He pulled the timer from the glove compartment and placed it on his lap. Then he put the van into drive and slammed the accelerator. Here he was riding the bullet, just a climate refugee returning home.

He didn't see the flash when he rammed into the front doors of the casino and pushed the button. He half expected the dynamite not to work, one last laugh in his face. A mechanical failure, some small oversight, fate. But soon he felt warm, as warm as the earth had gotten in the last three years. He closed his eyes and heard the roaring of a million angry people sweeping up into a fury of unfathomable rage.

It is estimated that 1.2 billion people could be displaced globally by 2050 due to the rise in extreme weather and natural disasters.

-IEP, an Australian think tank

"Becca seethed as she poured Grossman the coffee's bitter dregs—he was too distracted by her sixteen-year-old ass to notice."

Ice Out

Priscilla Paton

In 1972, ice-out on the six-thousand-acre Maine lake happened on May 23.

In 2010, ice-out happened on Becca's birthday, April 16.

Last year, ice-out happened on April 23.

The plaque displaying the dates hung by the wood-pellet stove in the host cabin of the rustic resort, a homemade chart that had become citizen science. This winter, Becca decided, was a game of ice-in, ice-out, ice-in, ice-out on the lake. A hard freeze and thaw in December, a hard freeze and thaw in January, a bone-chilling blizzard to open February. Climate havoc killing how her parents made a living from the waterways and mountain ridges, killing their future, degrading Nature into a lawless destructor.

The squawk of a chair behind Becca broke her chart reverie and she recalled her mission—coffee—and grabbed the percolator from the stovetop. The squawking chair's occupant, Mr. Grossman (*the leech*), pulled forward to rest ham-like arms on the kitchen table, his jacket a Filson, her dad's a Carhartt.

Mr. Grossman spurned the big lodge for the host cabin with its family feel and birddog Coop snoring by the stove. Using slight pretenses, he'd barge in on their breakfasts; lately, he dropped the pretenses and plopped himself down at the table like the relative who ignored that he'd been banned from Thanksgiving. Becca figured Grossman wanted to be up-close-and-personal and have the first crack at the apple pie. A client for over a decade, he'd asked on his first fishing trip how Dad became a Maine Guide. Dad replied, "passed a test," and Grossman belly laughed. He'd picked Dad, at the moment benignly sipping coffee across the table, because of his online reputation, *that man knows how to hook'em*. Grossman (*the lech*) also got off on arguing with Mom in a perverse flirtation. A danger today—Mom was ornery after Coop had tripped her last week and put her in a knee brace. She limped around banging pans back into their places, a hint that backfired when Grossman squinted his eyes to track her.

"Look, Jen, I'm out of the PFAS biz so don't hold *that* against me. And PFAS, so you know, put out fires and waterproofed your old rain gear in the entry there. I could walk into your bathroom and find PFAS in your cosmetics. Except you don't wear makeup. You're a plain people up here."

Mom flushed so scarlet she'd need PFAS to douse it, and Dad jumped in to avert an eruption. "We're for natural beauty up here. Like our website says, we focus on serving clients while honoring the outdoors."

Coop thumped his lab tail in agreement.

Becca seethed as she poured Grossman the coffee's bitter dregs—he was too distracted by her sixteen-year-old ass to notice. There were those who felt born to be wild, born to be free, born to run. Mr. Grossman clearly believed himself born to have more. He scarfed up triple food servings in the lodge dining room. He ignored fly-fishing etiquette—*Respect the Resource, Respect the Space of Others*—until Dad threatened to drop him as a client. Grossman insisted on using their heavy utility snowmobiles when ice fishing rather than the sleek new models because "a man of substance deserved a machine of substance."

Grossman slurped the coffee with a grimace. "Instead of freezing my heinie for a fish I'll throw back, I mean to ratchet up my snowmobile skills, ride across the lake, and check the trails into the forest."

"The woods," Mom autocorrected.

"Yeah, your trees are *woods* and your lakes are *ponds*. Get over yourselves and that fake aw-shucks stuff."

"*We're* the fakes?" Mom flamed. She seemed too flustered to catch Dad's deadpan, *no fakes from New Jersey*, and Grossman was busy hyping himself.

"Look, I'm doing you folk a favor. You know those paper company lots for sale around here? I'm the chair of this conversancy that has enough bucks, not deer bucks, and I know you're good at bagging those, Jen, to protect your 'woods' and make the tree-huggers happy." Grossman hee-hawed. "Too bad your son took off. I liked Ethan. He knew all the shortcuts until he got too caught up with those ski-bunnies on the slopes to mind me." He winked at Becca.

"He's a mathlete." Gritted teeth contorted Mom's smile as she snatched the men's not-yet-empty mugs to put them in the dishwasher. Ethan had accepted a scholarship and a spot on the ski team at the University of Maine. "Has a talent for it, like his father."

"Good at math, Will? What the hell are you doing here shivering through the ice age? No you don't, Jen. You've told me already that your winters are two weeks shorter. You should like that."

"It's more complicated—"

Grossman talked over Mom. "Becca here, knows the ropes, right? Did you drop out of school? It's a Tuesday."

Dad's turn for gritted teeth. "School's on February break, and Becca's baking today." As he said that, Becca retrieved the pans that her mother had just banged away.

"Little woman in the kitchen, huh?" Grossman leered.

Becca could bake gluten-free like nobody's business for her mother, and doofuses like Grossman never caught the difference. An idea made her stagger. By state law, she was old enough to work a hazardous job.

"I can take you out. Baking I can do later." She inhaled to squash rising nausea, and her parents stared like she'd turned into a rabid bat.

❖

Becca's dad was a poet of the outdoors. As a registered Maine Guide, he knew the ways of fish the way some knew the stock exchange, and in ruffed grouse season, he stunned clients with how easily he found the game birds. The deer hunters he left for sharpshooter Mom, also a guide, and the moose for Mom's crazy older brother, Madman Thibodeau.

Eight years back, Ethan and Becca had been excited kids when the parents bought side-by-side cottages on the coast. Surf, beach, fried clams! Oh, it was a rental, a money-maker, available to family rarely. If global warming screwed Northwoods jobs involving fishing, hunting, skiing, snodeos, and ice tournaments, the ocean stayed the ocean, forever dramatic. The weather mattered less when visitors loved watching water pound rocks, loved eating lobster, loved waiting for a local to say *ayuh* or *wicked pissah*.

Last winter, fierce January storms—nor'easters with record rains, tidal surges, and winds—wiped out the cottages, the dock, and their ocean frontage. The nearby beach might be restored through a scheme which involved laying conifers along the seafront to catch the silt brought in by tides. But the twin cabins, busted up and flooded, were beyond salvation, and the insurance coverage a joke.

As Becca went upstairs to change into snow gear, she grabbed the banister to stop from shaking. Over her shoulder she saw Mom limp out for grocery shopping, and Grossman pull Dad into the mudroom for a talk. He'd yack that his conservancy would save them, it was a done deal, and if Dad knew what was good for him, he'd make sure it happened.

Becca's breakfast oatmeal churned in her gut like liquid cement, and she dashed to the bathroom, turned on the shower to cover the noise, and puked into the toilet. She was out of her bleeping mind, and she needed to check her computer, provided rural broadband delivered.

Her dad came from quiet people. Words a molasses drip on a cold day, infuriation signaled by a lone *damn*. When clients asked Dad how he learned his field skills, he'd say, "time outdoors, mostly." He released his taciturn eloquence for cronies and clients when hanging around the dock or snowmobile shed. Arms crossed, he'd look to his feet, look to the crown of a pine, then turn piercing eyes on his audience. His stories would stretch like fishing line caught on a snag. The only real fight Becca had overheard between him and her mother happened over a year ago when Grossman and his companion Kingery, smooth moleskin to Grossman's bristles, came for grouse hunting.

Grossman used to amuse, like a belligerent red squirrel. That trip, he transformed into a skunk setting up shop under the porch. Through Dad's real estate bud, Grossman found a hillside woodlot that could be permitted for housing—he wanted a "personal" lodge, a minimum of 6,000 square feet. He came by to tell the family when they were clearing leaves from the lodge porch, and he bragged that he'd have the best effing panorama of the lake when he removed the effing trees, like hundreds or more.

Dad said the State would fine Grossman effing thousands or more for removing that number from a watershed.

"So, I'll pay the fine," Grossman snorted, "You got trees coming out of your—"

Becca's Mom quickly ordered her inside.

Becca figured that Grossman was like a couple of out-of-staters in Camden who poisoned their neighbors' oaks to improve their own ocean view—they were fined and the incident made national news. The poison that denuded the trees also leached down to the community beach which spoiled it for the summer.

When Mom tried to warn Grossman with this cautionary tale, he huffed, *don't get in the way of determination*. Later that fall, his lodge deal fell through because of a hitch with the local permitting (Dad knew those guys too), and the trees stood their ground.

Grossman returned to his New Jersey business while local soreheads suddenly had the funds to sue the realtor and the permitting agents on other trumped-up grievances.

Mom and Dad assumed they'd lost Grossman as a client, but since he booked his trips years ahead, he stuck to his schedule.

He returned last summer, smug Kingery with him, and talked up his new conservancy, insisting Dad grease the wheels and bragging that Kingery supported it.

"I do?" Kingery had smirked.

The next day, the two men canceled the rest of their trip without warning. Mom had repeated, *blackmail, it's blackmail*, and accused Dad of caving (*caving to what?*), and Dad tightly answered that he was *not* caving, that he'd never cave.

So yesterday, when Grossman drove up in the Land Rover he kept stored in Portland, he and Dad had gotten into it in the lodge driveway.

Becca spied, spying a skill she developed through time hanging around, mostly. From behind the lodge's curtains, she saw Grossman lean in, Dad lean back, Grossman grab Dad's upper arm, Dad turn stone-faced. A stand-off that seemed an agreement to resolve 'this' (*what was 'this'?*) later. The thing about Dad was that stone face.

Back to her snowmobile plan—Becca rinsed her mouth in the sink. There had been a rule, *never google clients*. Yeah, right. Mom did it constantly, and Dad had the "ins" for background checks beyond the usual vetting for hunter safety courses and licenses. Guide Rule No. 1: never go in the woods or a boat with a nutjob. Uncle Madman Thibodeau, as proof, bragged about birdshot in his butt from a client who was an (Becca in her head inserted forbidden expletives) idiot.

For the second time this morning, Becca jumped in the shower and prayed the heat would stop her trembling.

Kingery—into investment banking, private equity, whatever—had not joined Grossman this time. Kingery was canny, and by assuming he hid his air of superiority he revealed it. After he and Grossman stormed off last summer, he returned by himself. Then a thing happened between Kingery and Dad when the two fished.

Dad came back fine, if wet from the beginnings of a downpour, but Kingery was a stringy thing the cat dragged in. His irony drowned and his bulging eyes pearl white, he thanked Dad profusely. Had Kingery been sucked beneath a current to suffer a lake change?

Yesterday, as Becca scrubbed potatoes for the family supper, Kingery had called the landline. She said "hello," and, mistaking her for her mother, he blurted, "Jen, I need to speak to Will. Don't tell Grossman I called."

She stammered, "it's, uh, Becca," and Kingery, not his suave self, stammered back, "Oh, hello. Ask your father, em, to call me when he can. No word to anyone." At her silence, he added, "a personal matter, everything's safe."

Safe—who said anything wasn't safe? Ice came to mind, where a fishing shack broke through last week because an [*insert expletives*] idiot left a faulty propane stove burning. She told Dad about the call the second he returned from checking in the day's ice-fishers. Her voice hitched on the "don't tell Grossman" part. Dad hmphed, hung up his coat, kissed her mother as she glazed landlocked salmon for the oven, and sat down with the local paper. He'd call Kingery back in his own good time. Most likely. Becca texted her brother Ethan anyway.

Stepping from the shower steam, Becca cocooned herself in a towel, toddled to her room, and wriggled into layers—the snowmobile onesie would come later. She checked her computer. Ethan had messaged back at two a.m. and again at seven when she was eating oatmeal—*don't think about eating*. Links of what he and his hacker friend dredged up about Grossman. Investments in oil companies, donations to anti-green superPACs, an investigation of his current company underway, and the lowdown on his new bailiwick, the conservancy.

It was a shell-game, Ethan reported. The conservancy's backers were developers that under the pretense of being a nonprofit bought big parcels then subdivided them into housing and commercial lots. Density spoiling the North Maine Woods. Might as well be in Ft. Lauderdale on spring break.

The morning shone crystalline with fresh powder glistening on the firs and creating pinpoint sparkles across the frozen lake. So brilliant it could blind, like in Becca's favorite Dickinson poem, *Too bright for our infirm Delight*. She adjusted her goggles, and the opening line came to her, *Tell all the truth but tell it slant*. Suited, gloved, helmeted, she waited on her machine for Grossman to clamber onto his clunker mobile.

He'd signed a waiver with a line inserted about declining the snap-in Bluetooth audio for the helmet that allowed communication between riders. He preferred following Becca over listening to her "pretend to order me around." He had attached a GoPro to his machine because he wanted to "map the trails." He seemed antsy, like he was born to run after all. Or was he *on* the run and dreamed of making a break for Canada?

Becca, beset by a sudden chill, gave him a thumbs-up and rode down the bank and onto the ice.

She started off easy, trundling along the ragged shore where trees reached out over the point. Uncle Madman's warnings about riding the ice looped through her mind. Yes, he'd jumped ice breaks, tilted dangerously on one ski, and slalomed through trees, but he was "Madman."

Since Madman was nearly as big as Grossman and muscled, she considered telling him about the times when Grossman cornered her in the boathouse. (She was an escape artist.) If she told her parents and they kicked out Grossman, he could sue and murder their reputation online. Born for retaliation.

Becca understood the flags that crisscrossed the lake and ran into the trees, knew where the ice was solid at three-feet thick, where a stream rushing beneath made it unstable, where immersed rocks lurked under snow cover waiting to flip a machine.

"*Faster*," Grossman shouted. He'd flipped up his helmet's face shield. Not a face she ever wanted to see again.

Her snowmobile could reach 120 mph, except that speed equaled disaster on trails where sixty was chancing it. She pushed 55 mph, fast and light.

The man on his machine outweighed her unit by at least three-hundred pounds. He could mow her over, but the odds were in her favor.

You're the escape artist, she reminded herself, *so escape. Be the angel of death.*

She leaned forward and zoomed past the spot where three snowmobilers had gone under several winters back, their bodies not recovered until May. She saw ahead where the icehouse had sunk and recent snow appeared to heal the spot. Too soon for the ice to have thickened much, though it would hold for her.

Grossman's utility machine roared up behind her.

She accelerated, spit curdling in her mouth, and despite goggles her eyes stung so she saw nothing but the point of her aim—*it must done, it must done*. Becca tensed, ready to veer right at speed. His fault, all his fault.

Seconds away, she jerked the handlebars too soon, swerving left not right to spin out on the ice and do snowmobile wheelies toward the shore. The machine guttered out near a granite outcropping. She stopped and blacked out.

The rest of the day fever and chills kept Becca in bed, and her mom, not-a-doter, doted. "You lost control," she soothed, "because you were sick. We're so lucky other snowmobilers came along because Grossman was clueless."

Becca asked if Dad was furious at her. Of course not, Mom said. Grossman had pushed her, forced her to ride crazy. She kissed Becca's burning forehead and left.

Becca was too sick to feel furious at herself though she should be. But furious for concocting the ridiculous plan or furious for failing to pull it off?

Throughout the night fever dreams wracked Becca. She was the Cowardly Lion, Bambi in the fire, Mulan, Atticus Finch, Rex from *Toy Story*, and her monotone high-school principal. Insane or sane. She calmed and dreamed that Dad stroked her sweaty head, murmuring, *it's not on you, little girl. Not on you.* Or was it, *never use a hard sell on a Mainer*?

She must have fallen into a coma in the wee hours, not stirring until noon when she heard sirens and in the kitchen Uncle Madman's rumbling voice. Wrapped in a quilt, she made her way to the kitchen where her father, wrapped in a plaid throw, sat by the stove grasping a mug of tea.

Mom, white as a birch, guided Becca to a chair and murmured, "Dad had a scare. He'll be fine, you'll be fine. I'll get you tea."

"The man's own damn fault," Madman boomed. "The [*insert expletives*] idiot. If they can't pull him out, it's because he refused the flotation suit. Always thinking he knows better. Will says one thing, and the man does the damn opposite. And why [*brand new expletives*] was he wearing that backpack? Might as well have been stones."

Mom set down Becca's tea and again murmured in her ear. "Mr. Grossman broke through the ice on our utility machine. He demanded Dad take him out first thing, wanted to be on the path you were on yesterday, acted like you hid something from him. For goodness' sake, I can't think what! Dad nearly died trying to save him. He—he's still under."

Dad, eyes like a dead fish, tried to speak, couldn't. Only then did Becca notice the young game warden standing by the mudroom. The game warden, a cutie in his red wool jacket, checked his phone and walked up to Mom, who guarded Becca.

"Police'll want to chat with Will once he's warmed up and over the shock. He refused help from the EMTs, but they'll stop by to check on him soon. Don't worry, Jen." He patted her mother's shoulder. "Will's too damn smart to get himself in trouble. A real escape artist."

After the warden showed himself out, Uncle Madman ranted, his foul mouth and volume comforting in the moment, and Mom got into it with Madman, a familiar routine that pacified them all.

Dad, eyes clearing, looked a question at Becca.

She mouthed, "I'm safe."

He nodded, all he would ever say on the matter.

The woods were safe. Safe to shelter the lynx, safe to filter the water, safe to sigh out oxygen.

That is, safe for now.

If you're 32 or older, you've been alive for every one of the 25 warmest years on record (since 1880).

-Prof. Susan Solomon

"I've heard it all before. Greenhouse gases, feedback loops, tipping points. Meanwhile, my insurance company is already making noises about 'investigation' before they'll process my claim."

The Origin and The Truth

Christian Emecheta

"Another day without rain," I muttered, wiping sweat from my brow as I stepped out of my car. The thermometer on my dashboard read 108°F—a record for Clearwater in May. Not that records meant much anymore; we broke them weekly now.

I clutched my press badge in one hand and my notebook in the other as I approached the police barricade. Behind it, the charred remains of what had once been the Richview Estates subdivision smoldered. The air smelled of ash and detergent, making my throat itch.

"Press," I said to the officer, flashing my credentials. "Cassy Rigo, Clearwater Tribune."

He eyed me skeptically. "Another one? Haven't you people written enough about this tragedy already?"

"I'm seeking a different angle to the story," I replied, not bothering to explain further. The truth was, I wasn't entirely sure what angle I was looking out for yet. Just a hunch. A feeling that there was more to this fire than officials were letting on.

The officer sighed and lifted the tape. "Stay behind the marked perimeter. The structural engineers haven't cleared all the buildings yet."

I nodded my thanks and ducked under.

Three days ago, the worst wildfire in Clearwater history had torn through the eastern suburbs, consuming forty-two homes and displacing over a hundred residents. The official story was that it started from a downed power line after record winds—another symptom of our increasingly erratic weather patterns. But something about Editor Bill's behavior when he assigned me this follow-up piece had raised my suspicions.

"Find out who really benefits, Cassy," he'd said, his eyes carrying that intensity that only showed when he knew something but couldn't—or wouldn't—say it outright. "This isn't just about climate change causing another fire. There's more to it."

I picked my way carefully through the ash-covered street. What had once been a pristine, affluent neighborhood was now apocalyptic badlands. The skeletal remains of expensive luxury cars sat in driveways, their metal twisted and warped from the heat.

A man in a hard hat and reflective vest approached me. "You shouldn't be here," he called.

I held up my badge again. "Clearwater Tribune. I'm doing a follow-up on the fire."

"Not much to follow up on. Climate change is a bitch, right? Drier brush, hotter weather, stronger winds. Perfect storm." He gestured around at the devastation. "This won't be the last neighborhood we lose. Not even close."

"I heard it was a power line."

"That's the official cause, sure."

"You don't sound convinced."

He glanced around before stepping closer. "Look, I'm just a recovery worker. I don't know anything."

"But?"

"But I've worked disaster recovery for fifteen years. Been to fires all over the West. This one. . ." he hesitated, "this one burned hot. Too hot. And the spread pattern doesn't make sense."

I pulled out my notebook. "What's your name?"

He took a step back. "I didn't say anything. I've got a family to feed, and jobs like this are becoming the only steady work around here." He turned and walked away quickly.

I jotted down his observations anyway. It wasn't much, but it was something.

As I continued through the wreckage, I spotted a small group of people wearing identical blue vests with "Clearwater Insurance Assessment" printed on the back. They were clustered around what remained of a particularly large home, talking in hushed voices and taking photographs. I edged closer, pretending to examine a charred vehicle while straining to hear their conversation.

"—definitely going to be contested," a woman was saying. She was tall, with sleek dark hair pulled back in a severe ponytail.

"Can you blame them?" a balding man replied, kicking at a piece of charred debris. "Fourth major fire this year. We're losing money."

"I know, but still . . ." The woman trailed off, photographing what remained of a tree house.

"Still what?" The balding man looked up from his tablet. "Victoria, you are getting soft on me?"

Victoria shrugged. "These people paid premium rates. Top dollar for supposedly comprehensive coverage."

"And now they'll get what the policy actually covers, not what they thought it covered." He tapped his screen. "I already got three code violations on this property alone. Bushes too close to the building, outdoor furniture kept carelessly . . ."

"Jesus, Frank." Victoria lowered her camera. "My sister lost her life recently due to the frustrations she battled after the fire at Paradise Estates three years ago."

Frank's expression altered slightly. "That's different."

"What exactly makes it different?"

Frank didn't respond. Victoria was quiet for a moment then spoke, "Sometimes I wonder if we're still doing the right thing."

Frank glanced at her angrily. "Hey, we all got needs, Vic. World's changing. We either adapt or starve."

I'd heard enough. I made a show of checking my phone, then walked toward them.

"Excuse me," I gestured. "Cassy Rigo, Clearwater Tribune. I'm working on a piece about recovery efforts. Could I ask you a few questions about the insurance response?"

The balding man stepped forward quickly. "All media inquiries need to go through Mackenzie Insurance's corporate communications office."

"I understand," I said, "but I'm just looking for some background on how claims assessment works in disasters like this. Off the record, of course."

"Like I said—" the man began, but Victoria interrupted.

"Actually, I think it's important people understand the process." She handed me a business card. "Victoria Trudo, Senior Claims Adjuster. Call me this afternoon. I might be able to help."

The balding man shot her a warning look, which she ignored.

"Thank you," I said, pocketing the card. "I appreciate it."

As they moved on to the next property, I noticed someone standing across the street, watching the assessors intently. He was tall, with the tanned face of someone who spent a lot of time outdoors, and though he wore ordinary clothes, his rigid posture suggested military or a law enforcement background.

Our eyes met briefly before he turned and walked away. I made a mental note of his appearance and continued my survey of the devastation.

At the far end of the subdivision, where the houses backed up against what had once been dense woodland, I found a small crowd gathered. As I approached, I recognized Dr. Arushi Patel, a climate scientist from the state university who had been vocal about the increasing wildfire risk in our region. Getting closer, I noticed from her press badge that she had come with the news crew.

She was speaking to several former residents. "—tenth major fire in our county in just three years. The models predicted this acceleration, but even we're surprised by how quickly conditions are deteriorating."

A middle-aged man in a soot-stained T-shirt interrupted her. "With all due respect, Dr. Patel, we don't need a science lesson. We need answers. This wasn't supposed to happen here. They told us Richview was safe—built with fire-resistant materials, and defensible space around the perimeter. We paid extra for those perks."

Dr. Patel nodded sympathetically. "I understand your frustration, Mr.—"

"Cooper. James Cooper. Or I was, until two days ago. Now I'm just another climate refugee with a maxed-out credit card and a motel room that I can only afford for another week."

"Mr. Cooper, you're right to be angry. The developers of Richview made promises they couldn't keep. But I'm actually here because I noticed some anomalies in the satellite data from the fire. Patterns that don't match typical wildfire behavior, even under these extreme conditions."

"What kind of anomalies?" Cooper pressed.

Dr. Patel hesitated. "I need more analysis before I can say definitively, but the burn pattern suggests this fire may not have been entirely natural."

"Save it," Cooper cut her off. "I've heard it all before. Greenhouse gases, feedback loops, tipping points. Meanwhile, my insurance company is already making noises about 'investigation' before they'll process my claim."

I stepped forward. "Excuse me, Mr. Cooper? Cassy Rigo from the Tribune. Would you be willing to talk about your experience with the insurance company?"

Cooper looked me up and down. "Another reporter? What good did the last three do me?"

"I'm investigating potential irregularities in how Mackenzie Insurance handles climate disaster claims," I said, deciding to be direct. "I heard their adjusters talking earlier. They're looking for ways to deny coverage."

This caught his attention. "Yeah, that sounds about right. I've already gotten calls asking if I had done brush clearing recently if my smoke detectors were functioning if I had followed every single item in the fine print of my policy." He laughed bitterly. "As if any of that would have mattered against a wall of flame moving at forty miles per hour."

I handed him my card. "I'd like to hear more. Maybe your story could help others in your position."

As Cooper took my card, Dr. Patel approached me. "You're investigating the insurance company? That's important work, but there's more to this story."

"What do you mean?"

She glanced around, then lowered her voice. "This fire's spread pattern was unusual. I've been studying satellite imagery and ground reports ever since I saw the initial thermal readings. Something accelerated it beyond what even these extreme conditions should have allowed for."

"The recovery worker I spoke to said something similar," I replied. "You think this wasn't just a downed power line?"

"I think—" she started but was interrupted by a sharp call.

"Dr. Patel! A word?"

We both turned to see a man in an expensive grey suit approaching. I recognized him immediately: Lawrence Mackenzie III, CEO of Mackenzie Insurance and one of the wealthiest men in the state.

"Mr. Mackenzie," Dr. Patel acknowledged coolly. "I'm surprised to see you on the ground."

"I like to assess major situations personally," he replied smoothly before turning to me. "And you are?"

"Cassy Rigo, Clearwater Tribune."

His automated smile didn't reach his eyes. "Ah, the press. Always quick to sensationalize tragedy."

"I'm just looking for the truth," I replied.

"A noble pursuit. But sometimes, the simplest explanation is the correct one. Climate change creates conditions for fires, power lines might fall, and homes may burn. Tragic, but straightforward."

He turned back to Dr. Patel. "I was hoping to discuss your recent comments to the state insurance board. They weren't appreciated."

Dr. Patel stood her ground. "My testimony was factual. Insurance companies can't continue to collect premiums in high-risk areas while knowing they'll deny claims when disasters strike."

"Your 'facts' fail to account for business realities," Mackenzie countered. "If we paid every climate-related claim at full value, we'd be bankrupt within a year."

"Then perhaps your business model is obsolete in our new reality," Dr. Patel suggested.

Mackenzie's smile turned cold. "Careful, Doctor. Your research funding comes from many sources. It would be unfortunate if some of those sources reconsidered their investments."

Before Dr. Patel could respond, he nodded briefly to me. "Ms. Rigo, I suggest you focus your story on community resilience rather than looking for villains. We're all victims of changing circumstances." With that, he walked away toward a group of men in similar expensive suits.

"He just threatened you," I said to Dr. Patel.

"Not the first time," she replied grimly. "Mackenzie sits on the board of several foundations that fund climate research. He's been effective at directing money away from scientists who highlight insurance industry vulnerabilities."

I watched Mackenzie as he joined his group. "He seems awfully hands-on for a CEO."

Dr. Patel nodded. "Mackenzie Insurance has the largest exposure to climate disasters in the state. They've been lobbying heavily against new regulations that would prevent them from dropping coverage in high-risk areas."

I made a note of this while my mind tried to connect the dots. "Dr. Patel, you were about to tell me something concerning the fire's spread pattern before we were interrupted."

She hesitated. "It's just a theory. I'd need more data to confirm it."

"Off the record?"

She considered this, then nodded. "The fire moved too fast and burned too hot in specific areas—particularly here in Richview. And its path was oddly selective, focusing on newer, more expensive developments."

"You think it was deliberately set?"

"I think it's worth investigating whether someone helped the fire along. Especially given that Mackenzie Insurance's financial reports show they've been struggling to maintain their reserves after last year's hurricane payouts."

I stared at her. "Are you suggesting Mackenzie would deliberately aggravate a wildfire to have an excuse to deny claims?"

"I'm suggesting that desperate times make people capable of terrible choices," she replied carefully. "And these are increasingly desperate times."

The implications were staggering. If true, this would be far bigger than a local news story.

"I need evidence," I said, thinking aloud. "Data, testimonies, anything concrete."

Dr. Patel pulled out her phone. "I can send you the satellite imagery I've been analyzing. And I know someone in the fire marshal's office who might be willing to talk."

As we exchanged contact information, I noticed the same man I'd seen earlier, once again watching from a distance. This time, when our eyes met, he didn't look away.

"Do you know who that is?" I asked Dr. Patel.

She followed my gaze, composed her facial expression and replied "I've seen him around. He seems to turn up at a lot at events like this."

"You don't know who he is?"

"I'd rather not speculate," she said, but something in her tone suggested she knew more than she was saying.

My reporter's instincts were on high alert now. "I think I need to talk to him."

As I started toward the man, my phone rang. It was a number I didn't recognize.

"Cassy Rigo speaking."

"Ms. Rigo, this is Victoria Trudo from earlier. Are you still at Richview?"

"Yes, why?"

"I need to show you something. Meet me at the community center parking lot in fifteen minutes. Come alone."

The line went dead. I looked back to where the mysterious man had been standing, but he was gone.

Something big was unraveling, and I was getting closer to its roots. The question was whether I'd be able to actually finish the story before getting into major trouble with Mr. Mackenzie.

As I hurried toward my car, I couldn't help but reflect on how quickly our world had changed. Just five years ago, climate change was still discussed as a future threat. Now, it was reshaping our reality, forcing desperate adaptations, bringing out both the best and worst in humanity.

◆

The community center parking lot was crowded with emergency vehicles and relief worker vans. I spotted Victoria Trudo immediately, standing beside her car, nervously checking her watch. When she saw me, she motioned urgently for me to join her.

"Get in," she said, opening her passenger door. "We can't talk out here."

Once inside her car, she handed me a thick manila folder. "These are internal Mackenzie Insurance documents. Risk assessments, policy directives, and executive meeting minutes from the past two years."

I flipped through the pages, skimming the corporate jargon. "Why are you giving me this?"

Victoria's hands tightened on the steering wheel. "Because people deserve to know the truth. Mackenzie has been systematically redlining neighborhoods based on climate vulnerability while continuing to sell 'comprehensive' policies they have no intention of honoring."

"That's illegal."

"It's all carefully worded to stay just on the legal side of fraud." She pointed to a specific document. "But this . . . this crosses the line."

It was an internal memo dated three months ago. The heading read "Operation Firebreak" and detailed a plan to create "strategic documentation" of policy violations in high-risk areas before "anticipated climate events."

"What does this mean exactly?" I asked, though my stomach was already tethering with suspicion.

Victoria lowered her voice. "It means they've been sending teams to document minor violations—unkempt lawns, branches too close to roofs, improper storage of flammable materials—in neighborhoods they expect to burn. Then when disaster strikes, they have pre-built cases for claim denial."

"That's . . . predatory, but still technically legal."

"Keep reading."

I turned the page and froze. There was a list of "priority neighborhoods" for documentation, with Richview Estates at the top. Next to it was a handwritten note: "Expedite—forecasted incident window May-June."

"They knew," I whispered. "They knew Richview would burn this month."

Victoria nodded grimly. "Every climate model showed this would be a dangerous fire season. But the specificity of that timeline . . . " She hesitated.

The implications were too monstrous to contemplate, but I had to ask. "Are you suggesting Mackenzie Insurance knew about—or even arranged—the fire?"

"I don't know," she admitted. "But I do know I overheard Lawrence Mackenzie himself say to our CFO last week: 'After Richview is resolved, our Q2 losses will be manageable.' Past tense. Before the fire had even started."

I felt cold instantly, despite the heat. "Why are you telling me this? You could lose your job."

"My sister lost her home in the Paradise fire three years ago. Last month, she lost her life to suicide after fighting the insurance denial for years. She couldn't take the stress anymore." Her voice broke. "I've been part of the problem, Cassy. I can't do it anymore."

I placed my hand over hers. "I'm so sorry, Victoria."

She composed herself. "There's more. The mysterious man you've probably noticed watching the scene? His name is David Rider. Former arson investigator for the state, fired last year after he started asking too many questions about these insistent wildfires."

"And you know this how?"

"He approached me six months ago, asking questions about Mackenzie's claim denial patterns. I didn't help him then. I should have."

My phone buzzed with a text from Dr. Patel: "Satellite analysis complete. There is a definite accelerant signature at three points surrounding Richview. Call me."

I showed Victoria the message. "Evidence is mounting."

Victoria looked terrified now. "You need to be careful. Mackenzie isn't just wealthy—he's connected. State senators, judges, even the governor attended his daughter's wedding last year."

"Truth is still truth," I said, though my confidence faltered. "And people have lost everything."

"People lose everything every day in our new climate reality," Victoria replied bitterly. "Most never find justice."

As if to punctuate her point, a convoy of black SUVs pulled into the parking lot. Lawrence Mackenzie emerged from the lead vehicle, flanked by security personnel.

"He's here for the town hall meeting with victims," Victoria explained. "Promising support while his adjusters build denial cases." She reached for the folder. "I should go. If they see us together—"

"No," I said firmly, clutching the documents. "I need these. And I need you on record."

Fear flashed across her face. "I can't. Not yet. I—"

Her words were cut short by a sharp tap on the window. We both jumped. A security guard in a dark suit gestured for Victoria to roll down her window.

"Ms. Trudo? Mr. Mackenzie requests your presence at the briefing."

Victoria was still visibly shaken, but she managed to remain professional. "Of course. I'll be right there." Once the guard stepped away, she turned to me. "Hide that folder. Meet me at the Wine Place on Main Street at 9 PM. I'll tell you everything then."

I slipped the folder into my bag as Victoria exited the car. Through the windshield, I watched her join the procession of Mackenzie employees entering the community center. Lawrence Mackenzie himself stood at the entrance, greeting each with a practiced smile. When Victoria approached, he placed a proprietary hand on her shoulder and whispered something in her ear. Even from a distance, I could see her stiffen.

My phone rang—my editor's number.

"Cassy? Where are you?" He sounded agitated.

"Community center. Following a lead on Mackenzie Insurance. Bill, they knew about the fire before—"

"Get back to the office. Now." He cut me off.

"But I'm onto something big—"

"That's an order, not a request." His voice dropped. "We've had visitors. Men asking about your whereabouts. They didn't leave cards."

Fear gripped me instantly. "I'll be there in twenty."

I started my car and pulled out of the parking lot, checking my rearview mirror obsessively. As I turned onto the main road, I noticed a black sedan pull out after me. It maintained the same distance behind me for several blocks.

I took a sudden right turn down a residential street. The sedan followed.

I knew I was being tailed.

I called Dr. Patel while making another random turn.

"Arushi, it's Cassy. I need a safer place to meet than my office. I'm being followed."

She didn't waste time with questions. "The university research station on Lake Road. Use the service entrance at the back. I'll be there in thirty minutes."

I made a series of erratic turns through neighborhood streets, finally losing the sedan by cutting through a shopping center parking lot and doubling back in the opposite direction. By the time I reached the research station, my shirt was soaked with nervous sweat.

Dr. Patel was waiting by the service door, a concerned expression on her face. She ushered me inside, through a labyrinth of corridors lined with scientific equipment, to a small office in the back.

"You've stirred something up," she observed as I collapsed into a chair.

"Mackenzie Insurance might be involved in deliberate fire acceleration to avoid paying claims," I blurted out. "I have documents."

Instead of looking shocked, she nodded grimly. "My analysis confirms it. The fire pattern shows clear signs of intervention—strategically placed accelerants that ensured maximum spread through Richview while largely sparing adjacent neighborhoods."

"Those neighborhoods aren't insured by Mackenzie," I guessed.

"Exactly." She brought up a digital map on her computer. "Look here, here, and here. Satellite thermal imaging shows three distinct ignition points, all starting within minutes of each other, all in areas where Mackenzie has high policy exposure but can claim 'brush conditions' as cause for denial."

I pulled out Victoria's folder. "This confirms it. They called it 'Operation Firebreak'—identifying neighborhoods they expected to burn and documenting policy violations in advance."

Dr. Patel examined the documents, her scientific instincts firing up as the details connected. "These people lost everything . . . by design."

"We need to go to the authorities," I said.

"Which authorities?" Dr. Patel asked quietly. "Mackenzie funds half the politicians in this state. Their foundation sponsors the police department's climate preparedness training."

"The FBI then. Arson is a federal crime."

She considered this. "There's someone you should talk to first. That man you've been seeing at the fire scenes—I wasn't entirely honest earlier. I do know who he is."

"And who is he?" I asked like I hadn't been told who he was.

"David Rider. He's a former arson investigator, and he's been tracking these suspicious fires for over a year. I've been sharing my climate data with him."

"Why didn't you tell me that before?"

Dr. Patel looked uncomfortable. "Because he asked me to be careful about who I trusted. The last reporter he worked with had their investigation killed by political pressure before it could be published."

"The former arson investigator? I've seen him watching the burn site."

She nodded. "He's been investigating a pattern of suspicious fires across three states—all in areas with high insurance exposure, all with similar accelerant signatures. He contacted me for climate data last year."

"Why was he fired?"

"Officially? Budget cuts. Unofficially? He started looking into political donations from insurance companies to officials who then cut funding for arson investigation." She checked her watch. "He should be here any minute."

As if on cue, there was a soft knock at the door. Dr. Patel let in the strange man I'd seen at the burn site, David Rider, who looked even more haggard up close.

"Dr. Patel," he nodded, then turned to me. "Ms. Rigo. I've been hoping to speak with you."

"You know who I am?"

"I make it my business to know which reporters care about the truth." He sat down heavily. "I understand you've connected some dots regarding Mackenzie Insurance."

I slid Victoria's folder across the table. "More than dots. We have internal documents suggesting they anticipated—maybe even facilitated—the Richview fire."

Rider examined the documents with the methodical care of a career investigator. "This matches the pattern I've been tracking. Insurance companies facing climate-related bankruptcy, creating their own 'acts of God' to avoid payouts."

"How widespread is this?" I asked, dreading the answer.

"I've confirmed similar operations in seven states. Always the same M.O.—neighborhoods with high policy values but vulnerable to climate disasters. Always with corporate vocabulary that provides plausible deniability. 'Firebreak.' 'Surge Protection.' 'Watershed Management.'" His face dimmed. "Pretty names for manufactured disasters."

Dr. Patel leaned forward. "Do we have enough evidence for the FBI?"

Rider looked grim. "The FBI has had my evidence for eight months. No action. The political pressure is too intense—no one wants to be the one to suggest that respected American corporations are deliberately exacerbating climate disasters."

"So, what do we do?" I asked, while my frustration mounted.

"What you do best, Ms. Rigo. Tell the story." He tapped the folder. "With these documents and Dr. Patel's analysis, you have enough to publish. Once it's public, the FBI will have to act."

My phone buzzed with a text from Bill: "Where are you? The men came back. More official this time. Said they need to speak with you about 'national security concerns.'"

I showed the others the message.

"They're moving quickly," Rider opined. "You've spooked them."

Another text from an unknown number: "Wine Place meeting canceled. Not safe. They know. –VT"

My stomach became heavy. "Victoria Trudo is in danger."

"Your insurance contact?" Rider asked. I nodded. "Where is she now?"

"Last I saw, with Mackenzie at the community center."

Rider stood up. "I know people who can help her—former colleagues who aren't compromised. Give me her details."

As I described Victoria, another text came through from Bill: "Don't come to the office. Go dark. I'll handle things here."

Rider noticed my expression. "Your editor's right. You need to disappear until the story breaks."

"I can't just hide while others take the risks—"

"You're the only one who can write this story with credibility," Dr. Patel interrupted. "I have a cabin near the state park. No one knows about it. You can work from there."

My mind raced. "I need to get to the Tribune's servers to file the story remotely."

"Too risky," Rider countered. "They'll be watching all your usual access points."

Dr. Patel smiled slightly. "This is a climate research station, Ms. Rigo. We have secure satellite uplinks that can't be easily traced. You can file from here."

Decision time. I thought about James Cooper and the other residents who had lost everything. I thought about Victoria Trudo's sister, who was driven to suicide after fighting a corrupt system. I thought about the countless other communities that would burn if this practice continued unchecked.

"I need a few hours to write," I said finally. "And I'll need to call Bill to warn him about what's coming."

Rider nodded. "I'll handle Victoria's extraction and get my contacts to secure protective details for both of you."

"And I'll compile all my scientific data into a format you can link in your article," Dr. Patel added.

As they left me alone, the weight of the responsibility motivated me to write. This wasn't just a career-making story; it was potentially life-saving information for communities across the country. And it would make very powerful people very angry.

I opened my laptop and began typing: "THE ORIGIN AND THE TRUTH: How Climate Disaster Became Big Business"

The words flowed as I detailed the evidence, the pattern, and the human cost. Three hours later, I had a draft that would shake the foundations of the insurance industry and expose one of the most callous corporate schemes in modern history.

As I prepared to file, my phone rang—it was Victoria.

"Victoria, are you safe? I got your text—"

"Listen carefully." Her voice was strange, sounding manipulated. "I've reconsidered our conversation. The documents I shared were taken out of context. If you publish anything suggesting Mackenzie Insurance had foreknowledge of the Richview fire, you will face serious legal consequences."

My skin prickled. This wasn't Victoria speaking freely. "Are you alone?"

A slight pause. "I'm with colleagues who have helped me understand the gravity of making false accusations."

Colleagues. She was with Mackenzie or his people.

"Victoria, cough twice if you need help," I said, trying to inject some levity into my voice while confirming my suspicions.

Another pause. "Very funny. I'm serious, Cassy. Retract whatever you're working on. For your own good."

The line went dead.

I immediately called Rider. "They have Victoria. She just called to warn me off the story, but she was clearly under duress."

"Damn it," he muttered. "My contact spotted her leaving the community center with Mackenzie's security detail. We lost them on the highway."

"We need to help her."

"The best way to help her is to publish. Once the story breaks, harming her becomes a liability rather than an asset for them."

He was right, but it felt terrible. I was about to press "send" on the article when Dr. Patel burst into the room.

"New thermal satellite images just came in," she said breathlessly. "There's another fire starting—northwest corner of Jasper County."

"Another Mackenzie neighborhood?"

"Worse. It's directly adjacent to the Westwood Chemical Storage Facility."

It's going to be bloody. Westwood was the largest chemical repository in the state, storing agricultural pesticides and industrial solvents. If it caught fire . . .

"They're escalating," Rider said grimly. "Creating a distraction big enough to overshadow your story."

I added a final paragraph to my article, detailing the new fire and its suspicious proximity to the chemical facility, then hit send. The satellite uplink indicator flashed green—article transmitted.

"Now what?" I asked.

"Now we evacuate," Dr. Patel said. "If those chemicals ignite, the toxic plume will cover half the state."

As we hurried to her car, my phone rang—Bill.

"It's live," he said without preamble. "Front page digital edition, being picked up by wire services now. FBI just arrived at my office."

"To shut us down?"

"No." I could hear the smile in his voice. "To take my statement. Turns out they've been building a RICO case against Mackenzie for months. Your article just gave them the public pressure they needed to move."

Relief flooded through me. "What about Victoria Trudo?"

"Found by state police twenty minutes ago at a Mackenzie property outside town. Shaken but unharmed. They were apparently trying to get her to sign a retraction."

As Dr. Patel drove us away from the research station, I watched black smoke begin to rise on the northwest horizon—the new fire gaining strength. Even with Mackenzie potentially facing justice, the environmental damage was inevitable. Another community would be devastated. More lives upended.

That was the cruel reality of our warming world. Even when we caught those making it worse, we couldn't undo the harm already set in motion. The carbon already released, the ecosystems already destabilized, the communities already destroyed—these were permanent wounds on our collective future.

My phone lit up with notifications—news outlets requesting interviews, social media shares of my article multiplying by the thousands, texts from James Cooper and other Richview residents expressing gratitude and shock.

"Will it make a difference?" I asked nobody in particular as we drove past evacuation traffic heading in the opposite direction.

"It already has," Dr. Patel replied. "Truth always matters, even in a burning world."

Perhaps especially in a burning world, I thought, watching the smoke plume grow darker against the unnaturally blue sky. Perhaps truth was the only thing left worth fighting for when everything else was turning to ash.

"Everything caught in the rush will eventually flow
out to sea."

Ban Yuh Belly

Raymond J. Brash

Two nights of downpour flood village runoffs and storm drains. They clog with dirt and leaves and clumps of hill until it all plows into the Diego Martin River. The river's deep rapids propel dead palm branches, rusted galvanize slats, and clusters of torn bushes downstream.

Everything caught in the rush will eventually flow out to sea. Especially dead things.

Before light breaks the horizon, I borrow a pirogue and head for the river's outlet. The morning wind cools my face, but once I ease off the throttle, the humid air stills, waiting to be broiled by the sun. As I approach my destination, I lift the pirogue's propeller. A torn palm trunk bumps against the hull, and the boat slows to a lapping glide. The current here pulls south. It won't be long before the debris is swept out into the Gulf of Paria.

I smell the body before I see it. At first, it's like hot garbage left to boil in the afternoon heat. As I drift closer, an unnatural sharpness catches the breeze. I stifle a gag and tie a bandana, stained with fresh-cut ginger and soaked in lavender oil, around my nose. Spotting something small and metallic in the debris, I give the engine a quick spurt of gas and aim the bow at what I see. A silver wristwatch, tightly bound to a swollen wrist.

The body, dressed in a stained polo shirt and torn jeans, floats face down. If there were shoes, they're now gone. I grab my bamboo stick and slide an end into the body's jeans' pocket. I drag the body to the boat and tie a rope through a belt loop. My bandana struggles to stave off the rot. I hold my breath in intervals as I lean over and unclip the watch.

Some bodies are so bloated and blackened, skin peels off like squeezing an old mango. This one isn't there yet, so the watch doesn't take any of the wrist with it. I dunk the watch in the ocean, rub grime off its face like the skin of an apple, then do the same with fresh water from a plastic bottle. The minute hand moves and softly ticks. I pop the crown out and manipulate the time. No damage. I clip it around my wrist. Nearly a perfect fit.

A square shape bulges under the drenched and torn pants. I slip the wallet from the back pocket and spread its center flap. Wet cash sticks to the leather. Maybe four hundred in total. I peel each bill off, flap them in the air, and stuff them into my own back pocket. In the wallet's center, I find a driver's license, a bank card, and two credit cards. I dig around some more and unfold a tucked away picture.

A young mother holds a child on her hip. They're posed in front of a small house flanked by bright greenery, likely up in the valley. They're both smiling. I fold the picture and shove it back inside the wallet. I don't read names on cards or stare too long at pictures. It's easier that way.

I dial 999 from my cellphone, tell the police what I found and my location. I return the wallet to the man's pocket, untie my rope, and push the body with my bamboo stick. It drifts away in silence.

By the time a small, gray Coast Guard vessel arrives, the sun crests the horizon and bakes the sticky air. I wave them down, point to the body, but they approach too fast.

The captain yanks the two outboard engines in reverse. They growl and gurgle like awakened sea beasts and churn brown water into dirty whitewash. Pieces of chopped trash bubble up from the propellers. A few of the men onboard lose their balance and grab onto the metal poles supporting the boat's hardtop. The vessel quickly turns to avoid hitting the body. A floating cooler thuds off the red, white, and black stripes along the boat's hull. The sudden turn rocks the boat, and its wake lifts the dead man in a lapping wave.

Three of the four uniformed men lean over the vessel's rail and stare at the body. The captain, older with a graying mustache, stares at me.

"Jeffrey Perrera, how I know is you to find a next body?" The question sounds rhetorical, but I answer anyway.

"Came to fish for tarpon by the outlet, sir. Find the man just so." I point at the body and my skin turns frigid. The dead man's watch is still on my wrist.

"How many is that this month? Four?" He folds his arms and frowns.

I shrug and wrestle the instinct to hide my arm behind my back. A sudden but small rogue wave tilts our boats, mine more so being half the size.

The captain sucks air through his teeth, glances at the body, and shakes his head. "Rainy season getting worse and worse by the year. And they say God is a Trini."

I lower my arm to my side and clear my throat. "I live up the valley," I say. "Dry season make everything brittle and loose, and when rain come, hill does break away easy, take everything down with it."

Two of the men use a long pole with a looped rope to drag the body towards the stern. The captain keeps his eyes on me as they struggle to lift the body out of the water. Another man unfurls a long black bag and bends down once the body is onboard.

From my angle, I can't see what they are doing. "I remember when the river used to be small eh, but every rainy season it does flood half the valley, pull in all kinda hill, and last year it take a big tree." I continue, trying to ease my nerves. "Hadda wait until February for the police and them to drag it out."

The one who attended to the body hands the dead man's wallet to the captain who opens it, slides out the driver's license.

While he's distracted, I hide the watch behind my back, try to slide it off my wrist. It stubbornly catches against the width of my hand.

The captain parts the center of the wallet and lifts his eyebrows, returning his focus to me. "Did you touch this body before we arrived?"

I freeze.

"No sir."

He slaps the wallet against his hand. "Seaman Burton." One of the men snaps to attention. The captain doesn't shift his piercing gaze. "You were here when the last body was reported by Mr. Perrera, correct?"

Burton's eyes whip to me and back to his commanding officer. "Yes, sir."

My stomach knots.

"How much money was found on the last body reported by Mr. Perrera?"

"None, Captain."

I scratch at each length of the bracelet until my fingernail finds the clip.

"And the body before that?"

Sweat streams through my eyebrows and burns my eyes. The bay is quiet save for the *blub blub blub* of their idling engines. I find the clip's release, but my damp fingers slip.

"None, sir."

I press the watch against my lower back and finally pinch the release. The watch slips down my wrist and into my hand.

"Curious, Mr. Perrera. Don't you think?"

"Are there bank or credit cards in the wallet?" I point with my free hand.

He considers the wallet long enough for me to drop the watch in my pocket. He tilts his head. "How you know he have credit card?"

"Everyone-man-jack does have a credit card. If I was a thief, why I didn't take all of them?"

I never take the credit cards. Too easy to track who used them.

"Mmmhmm." He slaps his palm with the wallet again like it's a stick he wants to beat me with.

A long zipping noise comes from somewhere on their boat and a seaman stands upright. "Captain, body secured."

The captain opens his mouth to speak but is cut short by a panicked voice crackling over their radio. They crowd around the center console and turn up the volume.

I can't decipher the entire transmission, but three words are clear: MAYDAYMAYDAYMAYDAY.

The seamen hop in their nearest seats while the captain grabs the helm, quickly stowing the wallet in a lockbox on the center console.

"Boy, if I see you again out here, you going and have problems. You hear me?" Without waiting for my reply, he shoves the throttle control forward and the engines roar. The bow lifts and water sprays across my pants. The pirogue bucks from their wake, and I grab a cleat to steady my balance.

The coast guard vessel speeds towards the western horizon. When they're out of sight, I take the watch from my pocket and clip it around my wrist.

I start up the engine and head south along the shore. The sounds of the morning commute which runs parallel to the curving coast grow louder by the minute. Traffic clogs the Western Main, clumps near Hasley Crowford Stadium where maxi-taxis plow through the clutter of Wrightson Road. I slow by each outlet along the way.

Fields of rubbish float in the brackish water, but there's no stench of bodies. I come to a stop just before the Port Authority, where diesel exhaust coats the air and the morning light sparkles the water in slick silver streaks. Container ships with propellers twice the size of a car crowd the shipping lane, commercial giants inching their way to dock. If a body had floated into those waters, there wouldn't be anything left to find.

I head back to Carenage around midday and drop anchor near a jetty. A strong breeze cuts across the bay and the rope pulls taut. I hop into the waist deep water, warm from the beating sun. I trudge onto shore and give some wet money to the old fisherman who let me borrow the pirogue.

He searches the boat. "You scare the fish with that face of yours or what?"

"Nah, boy. Fish not biting."

He laughs. Air whistles between his missing teeth. "Not for you. Fishing like that, best had ban yuh belly."

The Carenage Fish Market bustles with fishermen back from their morning hauls. Spanish mackerel, snapper, tarpon on ice or filleted. My favorite stall sells fish sandwiches and fresh cuts, fried in cassava flour and ginger powder between two warm and fluffy coconut bakes. I use the wet money in my back pocket to buy two to go.

A loud metallic groan shudders the stalls. Everyone stops or hurries to follow the noise.

The derelict aluminum transfer station, built half a century ago beside the fish market, creaks and rumbles. A strong gust causes the empty holding tanks to thrum and flutter. A rusted rafter, high above the containers, aches and leans before snapping free. It tumbles thirty meters to the sea, slaps the face of the bay with a lighting like crack. The rafter floats for a moment, bouncing on the bubbling water, before the ocean pulls it under.

"Thing falling apart for decades now." Ignoring the show, an elderly woman cleaning fish behind a stall throws chum in a bucket. She pulls on a cigarette and shakes her head. "Rainy season, dry season, worse rainy season, worse dry season. No one minding it. Is dead. Government might as well put it out its misery."

I leave the commotion and slosh across the submerged road before heading uphill. The small valley's slope spares the inclined street from waterlog. My legs roast as moisture broils off the asphalt. My worn rubber slippers burn like they're going to melt into the road. I pass the village football pitch. Frustrated children try to kick a football to one another, only for it to skitter and splash to a stop. It could take days for the pitch to dry out, but by then it'll flood again.

Further up the valley, thick bush cools my ascent. The winding stone path home is littered with fallen palm and withered fern.

The constant trickle of leftover rain caught by leaves and canopies resembles a constant light drizzle.

"Jeffy, that's you?" Denise steps onto the path's crest, my niece Hazel on her hip.

A breath catches in my chest. The picture from the wallet flickers in my mind.

She frowns and bounces Hazel. "What happen to you?"

Shaking off the vision, I hold the plastic bag of food out. "I come bearing gifts."

She takes the food and, eyeing me with suspicion, kisses my cheek. I follow her inside to the kitchen.

She sets the food on the counter and pinches off some fried fish. Murmuring in soft tones, she feeds the fish to Hazel. My sister's voice hits the same song-like quality of Mumzie, our mother, had when we were young.

"The runoff fail." She continues to feed Hazel, smiling the world over, although her tone is not a happy one. Hazel absently opens her mouth and bites down. "Wall looking like it go bust, Jeffy."

She leads me around the back of the house. Half the yard is underwater.

I pull the money from my back-pocket and give it to Denise. "Run out and buy more PVC. I go and widen the runoff, cut down more bush."

"Uh huh. You feel that's enough? You done try all that at your place and watch what happen." She sucks her teeth, giving me the same look the Coast Guard captain had before she looks over the money.

Hazel's wide glistening eyes catch mine. The way they're standing. It's a familiar pose I want to forget.

Denise flaps the money at the air between us. "Where you get this?"

I try to focus on the worn retaining wall. It's old and needs work. The rain tank by the wall overflows even with daily use. The runoff further up the hill helps, but it's not a long-term fix.

Denise clears her throat, expecting an answer.

"Don't worry, nuh." I say.

She steps into my view, free hand holding her free hip, and cranes her neck like I muttered an insult. "It best be legal." Her accusing gaze waits for an answer.

I wave her off. "Tarpon was biting. Sold a few. Relax yourself, jeezandages."

Her gaze falls to my wrist and darkens.

I move the watch behind my back, a childish instinct when faced with the spitting image of my mother.

She huffs a disappointed breath of air and holds the money out to me like stinking trash. "I don't want any kind of criminal money in this house."

"Denise, why you getting on so?"

"Go and buy the *flipping* PVC yourself."

She tosses the money on the ground and stomps away. I can't argue with her. It's her house. I lost mine last rainy season. She only lets me stay because I do yard work.

I pick the money up from the wet dirt and yell behind me. "I could borrow your car, then?"

"Is supposed to rain again later, you know." Her voice carries through an open-slatted window. "Big storm coming through."

I pocket the money and watch her feed Hazel in the kitchen. She's tired. Tired of the rotten stench from the clogged runoff, tired of the festering mosquitos after the rain. "More of a reason to go quick. Hadda head up the next valley."

She watches me from the kitchen and rolls her eyes. "Go and bathe first. You smelling like a dead fish."

I quickly wash the itchy salt off my body under the rain tank's spigot. The watch slides up and down my wrist but doesn't slip off. My usual finds are useless. Car keys, empty wallets, shorted phones. I never find anything I can wear, especially something I could never afford. It's no Rolex, but it's not a cheap watch by the looks of it. I drop my arm, and the band holds snug around my wrist. Bit loose, but a lucky fit. I throw on a fresh jersey and shorts, snatch the car keys off the kitchen counter.

Denise doesn't say anything before I leave, but my mumzie's disappointed face is on full display.

The car is a black Nissan Sunny parked down the road, uncovered and roasting hot. I inch my way into the driver's seat, but the burning pleather sears my exposed legs and arms. Before heading into town, I crank the car and roll down the windows.

One lane is flooded. Traffic compacts the other. Impatient drivers ride the grassy shoulder, flicking mud along the car's side and across the windshield. I hit the wipers, but it makes things worse. As the bustle crawls, rain drizzles from darkening skies. The storm might reach quicker than I had thought.

I head up the valley to a supply store. It's a long, winding drive but cheaper than the shop in town. I park on a steep hill, set the emergency break, and head inside. The AC in the store sends a tingling shiver down my back, a cool relief to the stifling humidity.

I approach the counter manned by a cashier. "Need plenty PVC, boss."

"How much?"

"Thirty meters total. Cut in six lengths. The big ones, two-inch diameter. Need some elbows too. Oh and a roll of netting."

He taps lazily at the register. "Six hundred and eighty."

I pull the wet money out of my pocket and count it in vain. "Only have two-eighty."

He shrugs like it isn't his problem. It's not enough for even half of what I need. I should have gone past the Port Authority this morning, along Beetham, or followed the current further out to sea. Maybe I'd missed a body or two. They might have had the cash.

I grab my hair, trying to pull money out of my scalp since I have nowhere else to get it. The watch clinks and scrapes my temple. I twist my wrist up to the store's fluorescent lights. No Rolex, but probably worth something.

The cashier catches me staring at the watch and his eyes go wide. "Eh eh. Where you get that?"

"A gift," I quickly say.

He stares like I had just asked for directions to the sea. "Who give you that, Jack Warner?"

"Why?"

"You know how much it worth?"

"No."

He pulls out his phone and types something into a search engine. He turns his phone and shows me the drowned man's watch. Underneath the description is a dollar amount. Two thousand USD. Over six thousand TT. My throat tightens, and my heart leaps.

"I can sell it for so much?" I ask while my eyes remain locked on the large, impossible number.

He shrugs again, putting the phone away.

"As long as it working properly. Depends on who want to buy it. My father know all kind of thing about timepieces. That's why I realized is a real nice one, but he don't have money to spend so. Pawn shop in town might give you half price, three-quarter if you lucky."

I jiggle the wristwatch. The face glistens. The casing shines. I rub the smooth bezel and shift it's fit. It is the nicest, most expensive thing I've ever owned. "What can I get for the two-eighty?"

I carry the lengths of PVC to the car, pop the trunk, and lay down the backseat. I slide the lengths through and tie a red flag to the end poking out from the trunk. A chilling breeze whips through the valley as I bungee the trunk down. The sun is gone and clouds churn the color of burnt wood. I head down the valley just as the storm hits.

Thunder shakes the hillside. The world is a soaking blur. Windshield wipers do nothing in the deluge. I turn on my hazards, barely hearing the *tickticktick* while rain batters the car. The hazard lights dance off the valley's sharp incline to my left. I round a curb and a form swims by outside. I slam my brakes, skid across the road to a jolting halt in a grassy curb by the river. Did I see—a person? They looked completely soaked through. What were they doing out in this storm?

I throw the gear in reverse, hit the gas, but the engine only screams while the tires spin. As I open the door, the rain pours over me like

I'm standing under a waterfall. I move around the car. Two tires are halfway submerged in mud. I glance uphill and squint. Nothing but downpour.

I trudge back uphill to where I saw the figure, a person holding—something against its side. I block the rain with my hands, otherwise it's like opening my eyes underwater. Eventually, the shape of the figure begins to come into view, standing on a slick slope by the river's edge. I yell for them to step back, to follow me to the car, but my voice is the soft patter of a raindrop in a violent storm. I continue to shout as I approach.

I come close enough to reach out, grab the figure, and haul them to safety, but stop. The figure isn't a person. It's a short tree, branches broken from a previous storm, a small trunk split from the side of the taller one. A transparent plastic tarp covers the tree, fluttering around its trunk. In the torrent, passing in a car, it had been the mirage of a person holding a—

A shuddering crash cleaves through the storm. The ground quakes. I twist and squint up the hill. Canopies shake and disappear. Trees buckle and snap. The hill breaks loose, bulldozing a small shack and dragging its corpse along with it. The valley barrels towards me.

The world crumbles at my back.

The river roars at my front.

I jump in.

I'm immediately yanked under water. I try to open my eyes, but the pressure forces them shut. I swim for what I think is up, but a sudden pain jolts my arm. I involuntarily scream.

Earthy water shoots up my nose and chokes my throat with grit. A sudden metallic grip squeezes my wrist, and a sharp sting digs into the length of my arm. The river runs over my body and forces my pants down my hips. I feel like a piece of bait trolling behind a speeding boat.

When I'm thrown against something pointy and hard, I push my freehand against the torrent and feel along the hefty branch of a sunken tree. I follow the branch and find my problem. The branch hooked the wristwatch, half a meter down the limb.

I grab the branch, pull and bend, but it's too thick and pliable from being submerged. My lungs are set ablaze as I try to pinch the release. My fingers bend back against the water's force.

If I can pop the release, I'll take the watch straight to the pawn shop, sell it, get whatever I can. I'll use the money to buy more equipment, the best, fix the overflow for good this time. After this storm, I'm sure Denise will have plenty work for me to do.

I try again. My nail catches the metal strap but rips and slips. Flecks of rock and dirt pelt my body. White light flickers behind my eyes. I wriggle my numb hand, twist and flail and kick. The watch is a vice around my wrist.

I'll break the clasp, rip my hand from it, tear off my skin. I'll leave the watch for the river, for the Gulf of Paria. I'll fish more, all day if I have to, sell whatever I catch, every dollar legitimate. I'll go home, hold Hazel, tell Denise I'm sorry.

If only I can just get free of this blasted watch, I'll swim to the surface, take a breath, grab onto dead palm branches or a rusted galvanize slat, something, anything, and just float down river.

Everything caught in the rush will eventually flow out to sea.

Carbon Dioxide (CO₂) is at its highest concentration in 2 million years.

-earth.org

"And then the phone rang, and he knew it was time to run."

Marching to Jerusalem

Edward Barnfield

T hey've changed the station, he thinks, as the crowd stumbles out through the exits, clutching luggage, and children, and low expectations. It feels cleaner, brighter than it used to, once the people have left. Didn't there used to be a taxi rank there, in the concourse?

Outside has been upgraded too. There's a water feature (empty for now) and some twisted steel sculpture representing brotherhood or togetherness or European bureaucracy. It happens in rundown localities like this—the council exhumes an obscure grant from an ambiguous authority, and a prominent patch of land is blessed with foliage and effective lighting. When you walk out of the train station, you can convince yourself for a brief shining moment that the place will survive, that evolution is possible.

It doesn't last.

They offered to send a car, of course. A sleek grey limo with an unsmiling Croat in the driver's seat. But where would the fun be in that? How much nostalgia can you absorb through tinted windscreens?

He wants to live in this moment. Standing here, thirty years later. Anonymous but empowered, still able to tap into the buzz of his twentysomething radicalism. I helped shape this city, he thinks. The things I started, the things I stopped. It's fitting that he's been invited here to talk about his work, to defend his actions to a preselected audience of third-year Politics and Economics students. It's a chance to confirm his place in the historical record. An opportunity to speak after being silent for so long.

Park Hill Flats are still there, squatting on the ridge above the station, secured by a preservation order. They were dilapidated when he was last here and must be tumbledown by now, but the high ground has done them some favours.

And just like that he's back, in a dark council flat plotting ecological rebellion.

Thirty years ago.

❖

There was never enough furniture at the meetings. People pretended it was a sign of success, that the movement was outgrowing the space that capitalism made available for them, but it was mostly a reflection of poverty.

The first session he attended was at Julie and Rob's place in Park Hill. Activists who arrived early were sitting cross-legged on the carpet, waiting. There was a three-bar electric heater burning in the corner, and one of the women, Shaz, kept leaning over to relight her roll-up on it.

Jess introduced him. "Guys, guys. This is Darren Matthews. He wants to help us."

He knew for a certainty that she'd phoned ahead, that she'd told Julie and Rob all about him, but activists always made a show of making things look organic and unplanned. He got used to it over time—the comrades who sat on the same panel discussions pretending not to know each other, the differences in the way they acted in public and private—but it always seemed an affectation, like they were roleplaying radicalism.

He'd met Jess in one of the Broomhill health food shops. She been canvassing in the local halls of residence and was trying to lift her spirits with organic carrot cake. He noticed her eyeing the badge he was wearing—'Nuclear Power? No thanks!'—and smiled.

"It's getting worse," she said, as he switched seats and bought her a soymilk latte. "The new thing is genetic splicing, messing with animals in the womb to make them better test subjects. Have you heard about this company, Monsanto?

He liked her, liked her dyed red hair and nose ring, and she seemed relieved to meet someone, anyone who seemed to give a shit about animal testing. She told him about a protest taking place in the peace garden later that week, and he asked for her number in case he couldn't make it. Somewhere, somehow, the spark was lit.

◆

He's not more than a hundred steps out of the train station before the wreckage from last summer's heatwave becomes evident. A tram has been abandoned in a siding, windows smashed, pen and paint tags all along the sides. 'Cooked' someone has sprayed in metre-high letters. 'Frying tonight.' The tram lines are buckled and bent, the steel warped by record-setting temperatures, and the asphalt pavement has cracks and gullies running like rivers all the way up the hill.

Most of his fellow train passengers are wandering around in a daze. He had travelled first class to avoid the sight and smell of the masses, but they're hard to ignore in the aggregate.

"Excuse, please. Excuse." A big man with a Slavic accent stops him. "You know where Flood Centre is?"

He shrugs, points up the hill. The man goes to ask again, so he says, "No English," which seems to do the trick.

Sheffield has always been a welcoming place. Open to immigrants, friendly to other cultures. 'The Socialist Republic of Yorkshire' they called it when he lived here. He wonders how far such tolerance will stretch in the current conditions, as people move in ever greater numbers from the flood-hit south to the remaining dry spaces. When everyone is basically one rainstorm away from becoming a refugee.

◈

Julie and Rob were suspicious, he knew that. Rob made a point of asking the same questions over and over, on protests and at planning meetings. It was always friendly, always conversational, but he knew that they were trying to catch him out.

"Darren, did you say you were vegan or vegetarian?"

"Were you on the miners' march in '93?"

"What does your dad do? What does he think about the protests?"

There was an element of envy in the interrogations. Rob was the aging punk type, shaving his head to disguise a receding hairline. He'd been convicted of criminal damage over the summer, so he had to avoid any fieldwork that could lead to another arrest, which opened the door for someone younger with more energy. Someone like Darren.

"I'm just saying, I think we can be more radical," Darren would say at every meeting, like a mantra. He'd catch the eyes of people like Jess and Shaz, and they'd nod in affirmation.

It helped that he'd arrived with Jess. People liked her. "She's one of the good ones," they said. She had baby sister energy and had gotten into activism for the right reasons. She didn't give her comrades a hard time if they skipped a meeting or sneaked a bacon sandwich. Darren became one of the good ones by default.

◈

Most of his time in Sheffield was spent in pubs, in clandestine meetings of one sort or another, and they're all closed now. He never drank but would buy cider for the others and give them space to talk about a better world. Part of him is a little sad that the city has lost so many of these third spaces, shut down so many opportunities for socialisation and gossip.

'The Lion and Unicorn' used to be here, on this corner. Gone now, shutters over the windows, brickwork covered in grime. There's a faded plastic sign that says, 'Sky Sports Here' in fake chalk writing. The pub wasn't one of the traditional activist hangouts, so was useful for those meetups you didn't want other people knowing about.

He's surveying the abandoned pub, looking up at the second floor, when a ghost taps his shoulder.

"'Scuse me. Are you Darren?"

The woman is short, broad, wearing big hoop earrings and one of those shiny jackets that young people seem to covet so much. Late twenties or possibly older, already worn out. There's something in the face . . .

"I think you knew my mum. I've seen your picture."

Shaz. He sees it in the woman's eyes, and the anger that's blazing out from behind them. This must be Shaz's daughter.

"Sorry," he says, "no English," and turns and moves up the hill at a quicker pace than he's comfortable with in the heat. He knows not to turn round, knows that further eye contact will only add to the evidence she's accumulating.

"Cunt," she screams as he reaches the brow of the hill. "Lying cunt!"

◈

It didn't take long for him to clock that 20th century activism recreated the drudgery of wage labour, only without the salary and social status. There was a clear hierarchy and a tendency to delegate the grind work to the youngest and most impressionable comrades. Collections, petitions, Saturday paper sales—Jess and a few others put in long hours for limited results, subsidising the fund drives with their own money, preferring to tap their student loans rather than disappoint Julie and Rob.

"I'm just saying, we should focus on direct action," he'd tell Jess as they slipped exhausted under the covers in her bedsit, with its Nicaragua posters pinned over the damp spots on the walls. "The world is in danger now. We can't wait."

Most people paired up with someone from the movement. It was the easiest way to avoid having to deal with a civilian partner's scepticism or scorn. He and Jess were roughly the same age and sexually compatible. It made sense that they were together.

"That's lovely. That's lovely," she slurred in his ear, as their bodies made a particular type of music.

Even if they weren't going to save the planet, they could save a part of themselves. At least for a little while.

❖

By the time he reaches Fargate, he's winded and damp. The heat is getting worse, abandoned office blocks trapping humidity between their concrete and steel, creating stifling pockets that make it almost impossible to breathe. The old Peace Garden is brown and dead, tree stumps degrading into dust, and the shops that remain are makeshift affairs, collectives offering jumble sale stock and salvaged clothes.

All the time he spent talking about environmental crisis never really prepared him for this. When they discussed a warming world, he never pictured places like Sheffield falling so far. Disaster was always something that happened somewhere else, somewhere hypothetical.

This is where the protest was, right where he's standing now. It was a big one, populated by anarchists and green groups, swelled by the remnants of the labour movement and a thesaurus of Trotskyists—the RCP, the SWP, the SO, the WL. A meeting of a subgroup of the World Bank was taking place in City Hall, and even though it was ceremonial and mostly meaningless, it was prominent enough to attract the attention of the city's activists. Flags were waved and people chanted, and the atmosphere was more like a carnival until a small group tried to break through the blockade and charge the City Hall steps.

He remembers locking eyes with a copper on the frontline on the police cordon, a boy about the same age as him, before slamming into his riot shield, screaming. Jess was with him, trying to protect him, pull him back. He didn't know—how could he?—that she was carrying their first child at the time. He didn't think through the consequences until it was too late.

❖

Ironically, people were more receptive to his arguments after Fargate. They felt bad about Jess, obviously, and carried bruises and sprains that morphed into longer held resentments. Talking about state power was one thing, but having it slam you into the pavement was something else entirely.

Julie and Rob tried to calm everybody down, spoke about the importance of passive resistance, but they only succeeded in making themselves seem old and out-of-touch with the needs of the movement and the moment.

Darren spoke over them both. "We need to do something to show them"

It was easy to convince Shaz, and Sally, and Steve to join him. They assembled at the station to catch the first bus of the morning, waiting in separate locations in case they were being watched. At that time, the station was an unoccupied zone for the two main cultures of Sheffield: club kids trying to get home after a long night of MDMA and factory workers rolling out for a dawn shift. You could sense the reciprocal waves of envy and resentment that floated between the two groups, both so alien to the other—the club kids in face paint and Lycra, the proletariat in overalls and reinforced footwear.

His team were young enough to be part of the clubbing crowd, although they didn't have the accessories, so no one stared at them. (The woman on the front seat, with a pink silk wig and baby's dummy in her mouth, attracted a lot more attention). No one cared about the sports bag he was carrying, or the way it clanked every time the bus went over a bump. The passengers were all in their own little worlds, likely thinking about the beats they'd been lost in, or the overtime they were expecting, or anticipating the bed they would climb into at the end of the journey or the end of the day.

No one gave any thought to the quiet young man and his friends, or the bag full of pickaxes on his lap.

❖

He looks back. For a moment, he thinks that the woman—Shaz's daughter—has followed him, but it's just another lost looking kid in a shiny jacket pushing a pram. He thought he'd have enough time to stop for a pint, read through his lecture notes, but none of the places he remembers are open anymore. He's winded after all the exertion and worried he might have sweated through his suit.

It's been a long time since a woman screamed at him in anger. At least in his earshot. He associates the experience with the passions of his previous life, when it seemed like all the rage had some direction, some purpose. Nowadays, everyone's a cynic in person, and they reserve all their fury for the internet.

"Cunt," she'd called him. "Lying cunt!"

He never did think through the consequences until it was too late. Maybe he should have asked for a limo after all.

❖

Hillsborough Golf Club was more than seventy years old. He learned that from the local newspaper, which ran a frontpage story the day after their early morning pickaxe landscaping. 'Eco Loonies Trash Historic Course' was the headline.

It took a few paragraphs before the report covered the slogans they'd sprayed onto the course or the holes that they'd hacked out to plant seedlings in their place. He didn't get a chance to read the rest before Rob threw the paper in his face.

"Happy now? We're going to have the cops all over us," Rob screamed.

"Golf courses use gallons of water every day. Water that's needed in the wild. All so that rich pricks in polo shirts can ride around in those stupid little buggies. It's a legitimate target," Darren fired back.

"You don't get to decide that. We're supposed to be a collective."

"Sally agreed. Shaz agreed. Steve agreed. We didn't want to sit around waiting while the old folks took another vote."

"You little prick. You even wrote Jess's name on the clubhouse."

It was true. He'd sprayed 'For Jess' as a final fuck you. She'd been out of hospital for a few weeks but was still wounded and raw. He felt guilty, not least because he'd started seeing Shaz on the side in the interim. He could taste the tobacco from when they'd kissed before the meeting.

"You might as well have signed it," said Julie, in her best disappointed tone.

But her anger wasn't about the activity. Even when the police announced the formation of a special task force to investigate green groups in the area, and Rob was pulled in for a long night of questioning, it was never about their actions. Julie and Rob were losing their group, and they knew it. The future belonged to people like Darren.

❖

There are little pockets of affluence as he gets closer to the campus. He stops outside a chain coffee shop, scans the people inside. This time of day, the only occupants are either noticeably young or old, alone, and all but one on screens.

He keeps expecting to run into people he once knew, as though the city has stayed locked in time waiting for his return. It's an arrogant instinct, but a human one. He's not interested in furious strangers like Shaz's daughter. He yearns to see his contemporaries again with an intensity that surprises him.

His reflection in the window quickly corrects that old instinct. The eyes are still sharp, bright, but the flesh is grey, dripping from his face. A ruin of a man. A young woman looks up from her latte, red hair, tattoos. She shudders when they lock eyes.

He moves on.

❖

Back then, he had a true talent for organisation. He divided the group into cells and tasked each one with a particular mission, a particular target. The older generation, the minute takers, were relegated to raising funds and assembling kit. The younger crew—his people—were unleashed.

It helped that his life was compartmentalised in other ways. Nobody asked him where he was spending his nights or questioned if he disappeared for days. He could stay with Jess—soft, comfortable Jess, who probably knew more than she let on—or go on the run with Shaz. He even spent a couple of nights at Julie's place in Park Hill. Rob had gone into a kind of internal exile at the time, and she was up there on her own.

Over the course of the year, they ran up quite a bill. Other parts of the movement were focusing on high profile public protests—treehouse occupations, road blockades—but Darren Matthews preached a gospel of silent sabotage and property crime, hitting back against global destruction with a series of clandestine counter-strikes across the North of England.

Vandalizing machinery at the quarry, shutting work down for a week.

Hitting a supermarket, smashing the meat aisle, flooding the floor with spilt milk.

Setting light to parked cars at the life sciences laboratory, the most expensive vehicles catching first and exploding in showers of sparks.

After each operation, he waited for the local news. He was polarising opinion, he knew that, but he was proving that environmental outrage didn't have to go unanswered. He personally recruited thirty, forty people in that period, all young and committed. Student types, certainly, but also a couple of homeless kids that had trekked down from Scotland after hearing about their exploits, and a lonely German girl on the run from her dad. He was the only thread connecting them all, inspiring them. It was the best time of his life. His own private army.

And then the phone rang, and he knew it was time to run.

❖

Shaz accepted his decision. Julie seemed almost relieved. She was 'having talks' with Rob, looking to get back together. Jess surprised him with the extent of her anger.

"You coward," she said. "You fucking coward."

"I'm leaving the country to avoid life imprisonment, Jess. There's an informer somewhere, and the police know my name. It's only a matter of time before I'm arrested. They're out to make an example of me."

"Bullshit. You're running out on me. On us."

"Don't be selfish, Jess. There's a whole world that needs protecting. The Amazon. The rivers. I can't do any good inside a cell. Think about the movement."

He'd always seen her as passive, accepting. That was what people really meant when they said she was one of the good ones. That final night together, when everything he said only made things worse, exposed a whole new side of her.

He remembers how cold it was when he finally got out of her flat, his meagre few possessions in the same sports bag he'd carried the pickaxes in. It would be a long time before he was as cold as that again.

◈

His feet hurt by the time he reaches the campus, but it's worth it. He can see the tops of the buildings he remembers from his time here—the Arts Tower, the library—but they've been joined by a whole new cityscape. There's a huge slab of flood wall, and a run of wind turbines and solar panels, a series of checkpoints with security guards. Someone is trying to build an ark, he thinks, to ensure that even if the city sinks, they will be able to salvage something from the university. It's a kind of optimism, he supposes.

"What's your business here?"

The guards wear body armour and mirrored face visors. He sees his own expression glare back at him.

"I'm a guest of the Vice Chancellor," he says. "Special lecture."

"What's your name?"

And in that moment, nostalgia traps him. A guard holds a scanner to his face, and he's so deeply enmeshed in the past, so lost in his memories, that he says the cover he used back then. "Darren Matthews."

The machine squawks in disagreement.

"Sorry, sir," the guard says, reaching for the baton on his belt. "We don't seem to have you on the system."

Stupid. Stupid. He hasn't been Darren for thirty years. And if Sheffield is dying, then Darren, who did so much to shape this city, has been dead for much longer.

"Sorry. My mistake. Try again. Try Charles Cromwell," he says.

The guard's grip on his weapon doesn't relax. "Would you mind telling me why you gave us a different name, sir?"

He sighs. "Force of habit. I was an undercover officer in the environmental movement, you see. Here, in Sheffield, before you were born. That was the name I used. My real name is Charles Cromwell."

It feels strange to say out loud. His handlers stole the 'Darren Matthews' identity from a kid who'd died in childbirth, which made it easy to fabricate a full paper trail. He wonders whether any record of that remains in the system.

It doesn't matter to the guards. They make a phone call, speak to the Vice Chancellor's office. They let him pass.

◆

They called him 'Undercover 24' throughout the trial. His testimony was delivered on camera, with features blurred, voice disguised. Rob got the worst of it, ironically, because of his previous convictions and his status as a 'leader' in the organisation. The German girl was deported back to her abusive parent, and the homeless kids sent to a young offenders' institute. Shaz got a suspended sentence, likely because she was pregnant.

None of his handlers seemed too concerned by the romantic entanglements of the operation. It made it easier to find information, padding round bedsits in his boxer shorts, going through bank statements and confidential reports while his lovers slept. Learning every possible detail of their lives and then typing it up, handing it to his handlers in the upstairs room of 'The Lion and Unicorn.'

The fuss only came later. There had been other operations in other parts of the country, other partners, other babies born out of undercover investigations. The 'Spy Cop Scandal' became a short-term obsession in the more liberal sections of the media. Apparently, the team left behind enough fatherless kids to fill an orphanage. Jess did a television interview about her experiences. She argued that she'd been 'raped by the state.'

He didn't watch.

❖

The vice chancellor greets him in his office, sits him down by a pompous little bookshelf that doubles as a marketing display for the university press. He calls him 'Charles', like they're old friends.

"Of course, Charles, the great mistake the environmentalists made was letting that little girl front them," the VC says, by way of conversation. "What was her name? Peta? How could someone like that persuade someone like me?"

Charles smiles, nods. He's comfortable in this kind of company. The VC's attitude—that the generational failure to confront environmental change was a failure of communication on the activists' part—was one his intelligence unit had been careful to cultivate. Men like the VC (and they are mostly men) assume their attitude is the default position, and it's the job of the world to conform to their preexisting prejudices or convince them otherwise. No one was able to persuade them, so they never had to advocate change.

"And how should I refer to you in the introduction? I was going to say something like 'highly decorated policeman,' but is there an official term you prefer? I'll mention you've been awarded the MBE for services to the crown, obviously."

Heh. Charles considers for a moment. He likes the words that his opponents throw at him—'spy cop,' 'agitator,' 'infiltrator,' 'Judas.' Call me by those names. See what your audience does, he thinks.

"Undercover officer is fine," he says at last. "Although, I'm really a freelance academic these days."

"Yes. I saw that you'd been lecturing at Hendon. That must have been interesting."

"It was a few years ago. They had to abandon the centre when London's flood defences failed."

"Yes. Yes. Bad business."

The VC starts rattling through the purpose of today's presentation, about how they're trying to provide context for the current batch of students, help them to understand the mood of the time.

"I don't think they'll be much controversy or too many difficult questions," he says. "We chased the activists out of universities long ago, so this class are all ambitious little strivers. Most of them are from China, so they'll probably consider your undercover adventures a little tame."

Heh. Tame. He's not thinking about the lecture anymore. It can wait on the flash cards inside his jacket. He's thinking of Jess, and Shaz, and Julie. All the activists he got naked with and made promises to, back when his body was worth a damn. It's a crude sort of victory, but there's still some pride in how easy it was to seduce them all into prison.

He's never worried about the ethics of the situation or made space to consider that maybe the environmentalists had a point. Even now, when it's clear the world is warming beyond repair. He had a job to do and a clear target, and he nailed it. He nailed them all.

❖

He never really recovered his fluency after Sheffield. There was talk of other undercover roles, some wild-eyed plan for him to pretend to convert and set up in a radical Mosque in East London, but he mostly just filed report after report.

There were promotions, and teams of eager young coppers wanting their chance to go out into the field. In some ways, the atmosphere was the same as Park Hill Flats all over again, only with nicer rooms and better coffee.

The environmental movement recovered, after a fashion. They still do stunts and acts of public protest—throwing paint over masterpieces, disrupting West End plays and dual carriage motorways with equal conviction—but he notices that they mostly hang around afterwards to get arrested. Maybe they know that their movement is riddled with informers and agitators, that tabloid journalists and spy cops stalk every meeting. Maybe there's no point in trying to keep things secret anymore.

As he's grown older, he has learned to minimise the impact of his actions. He never married; never had any kids he acknowledged. His sex life became globalised, with increasingly frequent trips to Thailand. It lacks the emotional and professional satisfaction of his undercover work, but it means he doesn't have to care about the longer-term impact of global warming. He only needs worry about the next ten, twenty years at most.

The lecture hall is cool, its temperature controlled by a large air conditioning unit at the back. He thanks the VC for the kind introduction, spreads his cards out on the podium. He scans the faces of the crowd, looking to see if Jess, or Shaz, or Julie have sneaked in, their aged faces streaked with tears as they seek out a final confrontation.

Or maybe Rob, or one of the homeless kids, hardened by prison and ready for revenge. Or even Shaz's daughter. Or Jess's. Desperate to connect with the father who never bothered to visit.

Perhaps there's someone undercover out there, a radical in a borrowed suit and tie, waiting for an opening to seek payback, a knife slipped between the lecture notes. Someone looking for the justice that the courts will never offer.

But no. He looks hard but sees nothing. Even though he's trained to look for anomalies, he sees only the audience the VC predicted. Docile, distracted. A few yawns. A couple talking at the back.

After all these years, it's impossible to uncover the secrets in people's hearts.

At least from this distance.

In 2022, Bitcoin consumed as much electricity as Maine, New Hampshire, Vermont, and Rhode Island put together.

-Earthjustice

"Angel knew what would come next. Blood and a lot of it."

Bad Egg

Kendall Brunson

Moonlight glistened off Angel's titanium hunting blade. It could pierce the head of a gator like it was slicing through butter, but she wasn't here for gators. She secured the knife to her thigh and breathed in the hot night air. Sawgrass swayed even though there was barely a breeze. After sunset, the swamp was a symphony of cicadas screaming, crickets chirping, frogs grunting, and gators croaking.

A sea of stars cloaked the Everglades, though there weren't as many as there were when Angel was a girl. More and more builders encroached on the protected wetlands. She worried that soon, the stars would be drowned out by the bright lights from thousands of matchstick McMansions with expensive green lawns that required too much water and too many chemicals to maintain the unnatural façade.

With her flashlight, she skimmed the surface of the water. Gator eyes gleamed back at her. She swatted at the mosquitos swarming and applied another coat of deet. Clouds of the annoying insects were impossible to escape in mid-August. While it was the worst time to be outside, it was the best time to hunt pythons. Without a natural predator, the invasive snakes were destroying the fragile ecosystem. Kay deer, marsh rabbits, bobcats, and opossums had all but disappeared thanks to the constrictors.

Angel's brother, Marlin, fueled the larger airboat that belonged to their dad. The three of them spent their days on the water showing tourists the dangerous and delicate beauty of the swamp.

"I thought we were taking Birdie," she said to him. Birdie was the smaller airboat in their fleet, perfect for two people. It was more agile and easier to navigate through the smaller crevices of the glades, which usually meant more luck finding pythons.

Marlin ignored her, as he often did these days, but Angel brushed it off. They needed to go tonight. Late summer was blazingly hot, each day more blistering than the one before. Even the pythons, hating the heat, hid in the water until after sundown.

There were only two more days left in the state's annual python competition, and so far, she and Marlin had only bagged half of last year's catch. She blamed the tropical storm and relentless August rain, which forced them to stay home for almost a week. She hoped their other competitors were having similar luck.

In the distance, she heard the hum of an engine approaching their dock.

"You expecting anyone?" Angel asked, but again her brother didn't answer. The car roared into view. She shielded her eyes from the obnoxiously bright headlights. After the lights turned off, it took her eyes a few seconds to adjust to the darkness.

"You ready to fucking go?" Spider stomped onto the dock. He reeked of weed and cigarettes. She looked her cousin over. He didn't really think he was going out hunting with them, did he? Spider wore work boots, not waders, and she doubted he was wearing ankle protectors in case of strikes from moccasins.

"Tell me this is a joke," she said to her brother.

Marlin shrugged. "Can't hunt tonight. Spider and I need to go check our traps." Her brother and cousin had set traps for wild hogs, another invasive species.

"You're not seriously leaving me to hunt by myself. We signed up together. We hunt together. That's what a team is, remember?" Angel tossed the bottle of deet into the boat.

Spider lit a cigarette. "Aw, ain't that so fucking cute."

"We'll be on the radio if you need us," Marlin said, referring to the walkie on his shoulder. Angel had an identical one. "You've hunted by yourself before. What's the big deal?"

"Yeah, cuz. What's the big deal?" Spider slugged her in the arm, middle knuckle out so it would leave a nice bruise. Some things never changed. "You ready to wrestle with some giant anacondas? I bet you've had a lot of practice." He grabbed his crotch and flashed a row of pointed teeth, sharpened during his last stint in prison.

Her dad hadn't told her what Spider had done, and Angel hadn't asked.

Her father often described his nephew as a "bad egg." Even Spider's mom had discarded him early, leaving him with Nana for a weekend while she went apartment hunting. What she failed to mention was that the new apartment was in Mobile, Alabama with some guy the family never met. Spider spent his youth bouncing between Nana's, Mobile, juvie, and a few months on their couch here and there.

Unlike the animal kingdom, humanity didn't take care of the "bad eggs" early or often.

Angel didn't like how easily influenced her brother was by Spider, and he'd gotten Marlin into a lot of trouble over the years. It had started early with skipping school, smoking pot and taking Dad's beers. It eventually escalated to stealing their neighbor's Camaro. Their dad didn't let Spider stay with them after that. Dad spent every penny he'd saved, which wasn't much, to hire a lawyer to keep Marlin out of juvie. There was no money left for Spider's defense.

Angel couldn't understand how Marlin still loved Spider, visited him when he was locked up, and went out hunting and drinking with him. Recently, she'd really begun to feel Spider's influence on Marlin, missing work, cancelling tours, and even no-showing without so much as an apology.

"You've got Birdie. I even fueled her for you. You happy?" Marlin said, not a question.

"We've only got two more days in the competition," she reminded him.

Marlin rolled his eyes. "I don't need to waste time losing."

"Yeah, Fish," Spider said, calling her by her nickname since she had been named after the angelfish. Likewise, she only referred to him as Spider and not his birth name. Like spiders in real life, no one wanted them around, but they were impossible to get rid of.

Marlin tossed Spider a headlamp, and he placed it proudly on his head. "Losers go in the little boat. See ya, Fish."

"Just radio if you need us," Marlin said.

Angel secured her own headlamp. "Won't do, brother."

Angel navigated the boat to a group of islands a good hour ride away from the dock. Bright white floodlights mounted on the boat lit the dense scrub and brush. The electric green bodies of iguanas glistened among the tree leaves. Yet another invasive species. Not as harmful as pythons. In winter, when it got cold enough, their bodies would freeze, dropping to the ground like fruit. They were collected and sold as cheap bait to fishermen.

She pulled up to a small break in the scrub. There, on the edge of the island, a bush of white flowers had bloomed. Her father considered moon lilies good luck.

As she slowed the boat, the quick tail of a gator whipped wildly and disappeared into the murky water. She considered returning to the dock. Her dad wouldn't want her hunting alone, and once he heard about the night's details, both she and Marlin would get an earful. Not that Marlin would care. He did less and less these days. But Angel had been looking forward to hunting after the storm passed, and she wasn't going to let her brother—and especially not Spider—take that away from her.

She parked the boat.

◈

Angel illuminated the flashlight that hung around her neck like a horseshoe, giving her extra visibility, and jumped off the boat into the wet marsh and up to dry land, which was still mucky from the storm. The thicket was dense, and she wished she had brought her machete. In addition to the ten-inch titanium blade on her thigh, she had a sidekick diving knife on her left arm, a bolt gun with ammo secured to her waist, a metal spike, and the long tongs needed to catch pythons.

Using the light as her guide, she took careful steps forward, but that didn't prevent her from walking face first into spider nests and the wrong end of a cockspur bush. This used to be one of her favorite times of the year, out here with her brother, working intuitively together, spending hours in the Florida wilderness. It wasn't about winning—at least not to her. It was about trying to make her corner of the world a little bit better, even if most days it felt like throwing a bucket of water on a wildfire. It was better than doing nothing.

A creature slithered near her foot. Not a snake but a blue tailed skink. "Good to see you, little friend." She watched it scurry away from her light. Lizards had moved in and feasted on the little creatures. Just another loss in a series of losses.

After only finding a gator and narrowly avoiding not one, but three moccasins, Angel headed back to the boat. She hated moccasins, but they belonged here more than she did, so she let them live. She was almost to the boat when she noticed something glistening on the ground—a hundred pounds of tight coiled muscle.

"Finally." She planned the python's capture. Yes, she'd caught pythons on her own before, but they were giant, nasty creatures.

Slowly, she pulled at the python's tail, unwinding the serpent.

It lifted its cantaloupe-sized head into the air, opened its unfused jaw and struck at her.

She reached for its head with the tongs but missed. Angel kept her cool, but the snake was faster than she expected, shifting the center of its body close to her and then striking at her again. She lost her balance and stumbled over a log.

Before she could right herself, the python struck again. Its milky white fangs pierced her arm.

Her arm lit up in pain, like a thousand giant needles had been plunged into her skin at once. She fell to one knee and let go of the tail.

Angel knew what would come next. Blood and a lot of it. But she couldn't focus on that yet. She forced herself to stand. The worst thing that could happen now was losing focus and allowing the snake to wrap itself around her. She'd seen these constrictors strangle an alligator, and it would be more than happy to feast on her.

Blood poured from her right arm. While pythons weren't venomous, their saliva stopped blood from clotting. It was a good bite too, and if she didn't stop the bleeding, then . . . well . . .

She needed to stop the bleeding.

The snake bag.

It was in her back left pocket. She kept one eye on the snake as she pulled out the cotton bag. Using her left arm, she wrapped the bag just above the bite, tied it off with her teeth, and swallowed the pain.

Angel took a few deep breaths to collect herself and studied her opponent. The python, likewise, was studying her. It had already struck at her three times, but this one was feisty. She estimated it had another couple of strikes left in it before it tired out, which meant she needed to be extra cautious.

She held out the tongs, enticing the snake to bite. It struck with a nasty hiss. Angel pulled back and then made her move, clutching the snake tongs as close to the python's head as possible before hoisting the heavy creature into the air.

Angel estimated it at six, maybe seven feet, and thanked her lucky stars it wasn't larger. She crouched and anchored her elbows into her thighs to leverage her strength so she could keep the snake suspended as it writhed. She ignored the pain and focused only on letting the python exhaust itself.

After the snake struck the air a few more times, it went slack, too drained to keep moving its heavy body. She let it flop to the ground and put an air pellet through its head with her bolt gun and then scrambled its brains with a metal spike. Even snakes deserved a cruelty-free death.

Then she saw the nest it was protecting. She'd only found a couple of nests before. This was the jackpot. Twenty eggs. No, thirty. Maybe the moon lilies were a sign of good luck.

She found the largest tree branch she could and pounded the pile of eggs, crushing each one as brown slop poured out from the shells. Every egg destroyed was a victory. She sifted through the goop and crushed shells. Not a single python egg would remain intact on her watch.

❖

Angel felt joyous after dragging the snake onto the boat. In the distance, heat lightning flashed from large pillowy clouds. The night felt cooler. A breeze washed over her. Was it her imagination or were there fewer mosquitos?

The air boat churned amid the noxious acrid smell of swamp water. Tourists said it reeked like rotten eggs, but Angel didn't mind. It smelled like home, like where she belonged, even though the presence of humans did more harm than good.

The swamp had been altered too much by man. The government originally built canals and levees to drain the Everglades, and then allowed for endless construction in paradise, flooding the water with chemicals that caused algae blooms that choked and suffocated wildlife. Then there was the heat, which was more and more intense each year, drying out the glades in the dry season and flooding it in the wet season. The hurricanes were hotter and more powerful, each storm causing more chaos. She looked down at the dead python on her boat.

At least she'd made a dent tonight.

Angel wasn't ready to head back, not yet. She'd cleaned the wound with the first aid kit, and the blood was starting to slow. She wanted to keep going, just for a little bit longer.

Up ahead, a boat caught her eye. She turned off the motor as she neared it, letting the momentum push her forward to investigate. It was the boat Marlin and Spider had taken out to check traps. Slowly, she pulled up next to them, using the floodlights to guide her way in.

She couldn't see either of them on the boat or near the shoreline. Using a rope, she anchored Birdie next to them and noticed white plastic storage boxes. Weird. Why would they need those for killing wild boar? She strained to hear Spider or Marlin's voices but heard nothing.

"Hey boys. Where you at, over," she radioed.

In the distance, she heard her own voice come through Marlin's walkie, but he didn't reply. She jumped over to their boat. Something clattered inside the boxes, alive. Were they secretly out here catching pythons without her? Had Marlin switched teams to compete with Spider? Pathetic.

Angel wanted, no needed, to see their haul. Something moved inside the box again. Anything could be inside. Snakes. Spiders. Iguanas. But why keep them alive? They always killed them first before storing.

Carefully, she outstretched her hand as far as she could to open the lid. The last thing she needed was another bite.

But nothing struck her or attacked.

"Turtles." This couldn't be right. Dozens of mangrove diamondback terrapins squirmed in the box. Some tucked their light grey heads into their diamond-patterned shells, afraid.

With as much ease as possible, she moved the box to the side to see what was in the other one. Dirt. She shifted the wet earth to reveal tiny eggs that she guessed would soon be turtles themselves.

"You stalking us or something?" Spider shone his headlamp directly in Angel's face.

Angel shielded her eyes. "Lower your damn light."

"Not until you tell us what you're spying on us for."

Then she heard her brother's voice. "Just lower it," he told their cousin, who did as instructed.

For the second time that night, her eyes had to adjust after being blinded by Spider's light, and she saw them standing on the bank. "Just saw your boat and came to see how the hunt was going. I've had a pretty good night myself."

"Yeah? Your arm says you got had," Spider said.

"I got a momma and her entire nest," she answered, but this conversation didn't feel like a victory. Gone was her excitement from the kill. The swamp stilled. The breeze disappeared, and the swarm of mosquitos returned. "What are you two up to?" she asked, and then immediately wished she hadn't.

Marlin jumped into the boat and walked toward her. He studied her arm. "You need to go home. Have Dad patch you up." His voice was calm, but annoyed.

A year ago, Marlin would have been concerned, but none of that old Marlin remained. When exactly had he disappeared? There had been signs, but now she saw it so sharply. This was no longer the brother she'd been raised with.

"Are you two selling turtles?"

"It's not what it looks like," Marlin answered, a little too quickly.

Spider laughed and lit a cigarette. "Oh, it's exactly what it looks like."

Angel's heart dropped. "Why are you doing this?" She searched her brother's eyes for an answer. "You know they're endangered."

"Technically, they're vulnerable," Spider interjected.

Angel felt an animalistic urge to put out his cigarette in his eyeball. *Vulnerable* was one step away from *endangered*. Nests struggled to stay afloat, and there had been several black-market rings capturing and selling turtles to support the food supply in other countries. Most people took the turtles for granted, not bothering to think twice if they saw one killed on the side of the road. It wouldn't be long before these turtles were on the verge of total collapse.

"I got a good buddy who's looking to add to a shipment going out to China. Medicine or some shit. I don't really care. But Marlin and I are actually a team, aren't we, Mar?"

"Shut up." Marlin refused to meet her eyes.

She couldn't believe what she was hearing. "You two know you can get time for this if you're caught, right?"

"Why do you make such a big fucking deal about everything?" he asked.

"Because you were raised better than this."

Spider snorted.

"If you release them back into the water, we can all pretend like this didn't happen."

At this, Spider stepped into the boat. The bitter scent of cigarette smoke blew in her face. "See, we can't do that, Fish. There are roughly twenty-thousand dollars' worth of turtles in that box. Another two grand with the eggs. So no, they're coming with us."

"This is illegal," Angel said.

"This is the free market, baby." Spider flicked his cigarette into the water.

"Just go," Marlin told her.

Angel had a horrible thought—maybe her brother was a bad egg too. Even if they released the turtles, their illegal enterprise wouldn't stop. As their father often said, once a poacher, always a poacher.

Spider's fingers danced in the air. "Run along home to Daddy, little Fish."

She thought about the bolt gun at her waist. The knife that could slice like butter. The other diving knife at her side. How easily could she get rid of Spider? Leave him here in the Everglades? Bodies were dumped all the time. Many of them, she suspected, would never be found. Maybe it was finally time someone did something about this bad egg.

But she couldn't. That's not who she was.

"Fine, I'll leave." While she couldn't kill another person, she would protect her corner of the world. "But I'm letting them go first." She picked up the box of turtles.

Before she could release them into the water, her world went black.

❖

Spider went over the story with Marlin multiple times. They were all python hunting together, but then Fish insisted on going off on her own. They said it was a bad idea and tried to stop her, but by the time they found her boat, she was gone. They'd go back, report her missing to the sheriff, and stick to the story, no matter what.

Marlin looked a little pale, but Spider knew his cousin could stick to a lie. Marlin had shoved her, and then Fish lost her balance and fell against the edge of the boat. Her head had made a disgusting juicy *thwack* sound that made Spider want to throw up.

Besides, even if Spider did tell the truth, he'd probably get blamed for the shove anyway, even though it was Marlin who did it. Spider knew how that would go. His Daddy would just hire another lawyer, and then it'd be all on Spider, just like last time. After all, it had been Marlin who stole the Camaro, not Spider. He suspected his cousin spent a lot of time pretending to be a good guy. Spider found it much more freeing to just let the world know who he was up front.

But damn. He liked Fish. Sure, she was an uptight bitch, but she was cool in the end. He didn't know any other chicks that could kill a python, especially not on their own. That was pretty bad ass. But why did she have to make such a big fucking deal about the turtles? They were just stupid little guys. Not like they mattered, not really.

Marlin knew a spot to drag her body out where the water was deeper and high with grass, somewhere there was rarely traffic on the water and where he didn't think anyone would look for her. He was cold, cold in a way that made Spider nervous, especially when Marlin said that she'd probably be "taken care of" by the hurricane already headed their way. That was hard core.

Why did she have to be so righteous all the time? So filled with this need to fix what was broken? Even he was smart enough to see the truth—the glades could never be fixed. Not really. There was nothing anyone could do to keep it from being destroyed. Spider had no time for false hope. He'd accepted the truth a long time ago. So why not make a buck?

If global temperatures increase by 2°C by the year 2100, 18% of all species on land will face a high risk of going extinct.

-International Fund for Animal Welfare (IFAW)

"The pipeline had been buried in the ground so long
that it felt like part of the farm."

Burn

Michael Downing

Matty Crowe always played by the rules, even when it was a hard choice. Never took risks when he didn't need to. Didn't cheat. Knew the difference between right and wrong. Most times, that worked out okay.

This wasn't one of those times.

Tall, broad shoulders, hair cut short, skin tanned from years working in the sun, Matty stood still, his hands steady, eyes locked on six hulking yellow Caterpillar bulldozers. The bulldozers were parked at the Southeastern U.S. Oil Company's construction site, along with a massive front-end loader that was angled diagonally nearby. Grey silhouettes against a slowly darkening sky. The engines still had that sharp smell of oil, dust, and diesel, the heavy odor of raw, rich dirt clinging to the rollers and track train rails. It was quiet now. During the day, the site hummed with the sound of metal grinding against rock, the noise low, staccato vibrations shaking the ground. Matty had spent the last two weeks watching workers tear up the land—his land—digging trenches for the oil company's new compressor station. He didn't sell the land, it had been part of his family's livelihood for generations, but when the county played the eminent domain card, taking twenty-five acres they needed, he was out of options.

At least legally.

It was barely eight, still light, but late enough that none of the work crew were on-site. The world around Matty felt still, tense, with the kind of silence that would snap back when something broke. Matty could feel the anger in his gut, a simmering rage that had been building for days, weeks, maybe months now. Probably longer.

He lit the tail end of the rag stuffed in the closest bulldozer's gas tank. He didn't flinch, didn't hesitate. Felt the weight of his breath, a slow inhale that didn't settle the tension inside as the cloth caught. The flames spread quickly, faster than he thought they would, licking the metal, burning into the tank while simultaneously following the gasoline trail Matty had laid out between the machines. He backed up a step, then a few more before turning and running to his pick-up, watching over a shoulder as the flames engulfed the bulldozers. For a moment, everything stopped, then the sound of the world came rushing back, louder, sharper, clearer. The noise was a crack in the night, an explosion that twisted metal and steel, shredded rubber, decimated the machines, and swallowed the work site as dust rose from the dirt.

The roar of the blast sent shockwaves rippling through the air, triggering a memory from Fallujah: Matty's Hummer rocked by an IED planted in the desert dirt, flipping end over end like a toy, in slow motion. The noise reverberated, just like it did then. Smoke curled up in the air, thick and black, visible in the sky. Matty felt the weight of the fire as he raced away, glancing in the rearview mirror at the flames consuming the construction site.

He didn't slow down. Kept his eyes straight ahead with his hands fixed firmly on the wheel, his heart pounding in his chest.

He smiled. Felt whatever had been gnawing at him release. Not completely, but enough to make him feel better, at least for a little while.

There was no turning back now.

❖

The sun was still low, just breaking through the trees as Matty made his way towards the porch. Georgia in late March could sometimes feel like a hot August day. Sweat trickled down his neck, mixing with dirt, his shirt clinging to his back. Worn out, the kind of tired that came from too many sleepless nights, too many problems he couldn't solve. The soft red Georgia soil stuck to his boots, but he didn't mind. The land had never been pristine. It was a farm. If you didn't like dirt, you weren't cut out to be a farmer. He leaned against the porch railing, wiping his face with a sleeve, letting the stillness settle around him.

The smoke from the construction site fire was gone, but the smell remained, acrid and heavy.

The screen door slammed as Kayleigh stepped outside, barefoot with her skirt waving in the breeze, shaking slightly. It wasn't the cold making her shake. Her grandmother's old quilt was wrapped around her shoulders, pulled tight against her thin body with one hand.

She looked pale, tired, and weary. Her long blonde hair, once thick and full, was thinning, just like the doctors said it would, the streaks of gray more pronounced now.

The cancer was tearing through her body faster than the drugs could eradicate it. Optimism had disappeared from conversations with her doctors. Matty had been losing her for months, a little at first, then a lot. Watching her suffer, helpless to do anything.

It was a pain that twisted deep in his chest.

They locked eyes, sharing soft smiles. Matty felt his heart tighten, the same way it always did, even after twenty years of marriage.

Kayleigh handed him a steaming cup of coffee.

"Didn't hear you get up," she said. "Did you sleep?"

"Not much. Tossed and turned, then got up early. Didn't want to wake you," he said. "Figured you could use the sleep."

She smiled. "Could use a lot of things. Not just sleep."

Kayleigh eased back onto the hanging swing, tucking her feet beneath her as Matty slid alongside her. She leaned her head against his shoulder, taking his hand in hers.

"What happens next?"

Matty shrugged. "Guess we'll have to wait and see."

"Like everything else."

Matty didn't answer.

"They'll just bring in more machines."

"Probably. Just want to hurt them a little. Hurt them the way they're hurting us."

"I don't think they care," Kayleigh said softly, her voice trailing off.

"These oil company bastards don't see any wrecking balls coming their way. Think they have nothing to fear," he said. "If I keep doing this, maybe it'll change the way they look at things."

Kayleigh nodded, her eyes slowly closing.

Matty sipped his coffee, gently squeezing her hand. The sun rose higher, the whole morning slowing down. The only sounds for miles were the whine of cicadas and the rustle of leaves blowing through the yard. The farm wasn't a place for change, not in the ways that mattered.

But everything had changed.

That was the thing about change. It could creep up behind you, bend you over until you broke, or burn down everything that mattered before you could even blink.

Matty had lived his whole life on the farm, forty-three years wrapped around two tours in Iraq and another in Afghanistan. The land still clung to him like a second skin, and there was never any doubt he'd come back home when he was done. It was in his blood. Four generations of Crowes had worked the land. His great-grandfather started with five or six acres. By the time his father took over, it was two thousand. But then the Eighties hit, and everything burned.

It was all because of climate change. Heat waves. Droughts. Floods. Hundred-year storms that came too frequently, so often that the Farmer's Almanac was useless by the time summer rolled around. Crops failed, and the bills, along with loans, over-extended credit lines, and second mortgages, piled up. The farm couldn't catch a break. The weather was unpredictable, each season was a gamble.

Competition intensified. Costs and prices rose. The supermarket chains and Big Box retailers didn't care about "Made In U.S.A." They wanted cheaper produce and more profit from low-cost crops in places like Mexico and South America. Small farms like the Crowe's couldn't compete.

The business died.

As revenue spiraled downward, Matty's father was forced to sell off parcels of land, piece by piece. Each sale was a part of their history being chipped away. When Matty thought about his father now, all he could remember was a man who was always angry, always unhappy.

During Reagan's first term, Southeastern U.S. Oil showed up with plans to build a new pipeline running straight through the Crowe land, one that would take heavy crude from the north, bringing it south to the refineries along the coast where it would be exported overseas. A pipeline that would allow the American fossil fuel industry to double oil production, feeding an insatiable demand for oil around the world, even if it wound up contributing to climate change. The oil company downplayed those negatives, wrapping the positives of the pipeline in patriotism.

Matty's dad didn't care about the long-term cost of oil addiction. Didn't care about climate change. Couldn't think that far ahead. He just saw that monthly lease check the oil company promised and figured he could keep the farm afloat a little longer. So, he took the money.

The pipeline had been buried in the ground so long that it felt like part of the farm. Matty never thought much about it—even when his mother died young, then his father a few years later, both casualties of lives lived close to the land. It was the way things were—it was just life, the luck of the draw, he figured.

Then Kayleigh got sick.

That's when Matty finally started to see the chain, the way everything was connected.

He always considered himself an environmentalist, but took a couple of courses on Environmental Science at the community college. Learned about bitumen, the oil extracted from the tar sands, getting pumped through the pipeline, and how it needed to be diluted with chemical cocktails like benzene and xylene. Chemicals that cause cancer. Chemicals that leaked through the pipeline, seeping into the earth, into the water, into the air, into the crops. Chemicals that poisoned the land. Made it worthless, at least as a farm.

Matty read the papers. Saw the news. Southeastern was increasing production—the new administration in D.C. had killed the Green New Deal, calling climate change a hoax, even though fossil fuels were the largest contributor to global climate change. Increased oil production released carbon dioxide into the atmosphere when the oil was burned, worsening greenhouse gas emissions. It didn't matter. They wanted more.

The new compressor station would feed that worldwide lust for oil.

Nobody gave a shit about climate change. Not the politicians. Not Southeastern. Not the state or the county.

When Matty saw the bulldozers and construction equipment roll in, it changed everything. Made him angry. Made him want to make a difference. Made him want to take everything from them, the way they were taking everything from him.

He started with the bulldozers.

❖

A couple of days later, Matty's phone rang while he was tinkering with his truck. It was the St. Mary's County Sheriff's Office. Sheriff John Bishop had been around forever, long enough to know a few generations of Matty's family, long enough to be the kind of guy who'd turn a blind eye, until he couldn't anymore. Good ol' boy with a badge and a conscience that came and went in pieces, usually to the highest bidder. Matty and Bishop's son Tommy had grown up together. Played ball on the same high school team, drove down Main Street on Friday nights, the Allman Brothers blasting from open windows in their trucks, joined the Marines right after 9/11 like other kids in the county did, like they were invincible. Matty came back from the sandbox. Tommy never did. Something about that changed Sheriff Bishop.

Bishop's voice cracked through the line, rough and low, like it had been dragged across gravel. "Had an incident at that site over on Hog Mountain Road. Where they're building the compressor station. You hear anything about it?"

Matty let the silence hang for a beat. "What kind of incident?"

"Somebody decided they didn't like what was happening there. Burned everything to the ground. Machinery, tools, the whole damn place."

"Yeah, I thought I heard something."

Bishop's voice dropped. "Heard something?"

Matty gave a slow exhale, a slight edge in his voice. "Couldn't tell what it was. Figured it was just some kids screwing around."

Bishop's tone changed, and Matty could almost hear his jaw tighten through the phone. "This wasn't no damn kids. This wasn't vandalism. This looked personal."

"Lot of people aren't too thrilled about that compressor station. You know that."

Bishop's voice came back, cold. "You were one of 'em."

Matty let the words sit there for a second. His shoulders tensed, but his voice was slow and deliberate when he spoke. "I've got enough on my plate right now, Sheriff. If I hear anything, you'll be the first to know."

He hung up before Bishop could say another word, the call ending with a quiet click that spoke louder than either wanted to admit.

Matty jammed the phone in his back pocket, trudging back inside to be with Kayleigh.

◆

Matty walked into the woods, the same woods, same trees he played in as a kid. The stars were scattered across the sky, bright, lighting the night like the darkness had been sliced open with a knife. He walked a couple of miles through thick underbrush, maneuvering his way closer to the construction site. The backpack slung over his shoulder was filled with bottles wrapped carefully in rags, a five-gallon can of gas in his hand. Even with the light from the stars, it was dark, and Matty moved silently, cautiously, edging closer.

A row of new bulldozers filled the construction site.

Wasn't surprised by that.

Wasn't surprised by the chain link fence surrounding the site either. That's why he had stuffed a pair of heavy-duty bolt cutters in the backpack. What surprised him was the two F-150 extended cab trucks idling along the road, shadowy figures talking inside the cabs while another guard stood a few feet away. On the far side of the site, someone else patrolled the perimeter, his rifle slung across his body with the buttstock tucked under one armpit, the barrel pointing downward. Same way they carried rifles in Iraq.

Matty stood on the edge of the woods. He hadn't counted on Southeastern hiring a security team so quickly. Hadn't counted on them hiring pros.

He thought about edging closer, finding a spot farther away from the security detail, but stopped. Past the NO TRESPASSING signs nailed to the trees, a battery-powered outdoor camera was angled towards the fence. If there was one camera, most likely there were others. Matty got a tingling sense of déjà vu, like going through Baghdad , door to door, hunting for insurgents, eyes watching him as he moved.

Matty realized the depth of his miscalculation. Even if he burned up more machinery, Southeastern would replace the bulldozers. They could go on doing that for months. Matty torching machines, Southeastern bringing in more. More machines. More workers. More security guards. At least until the compressor station was finished.

It was pointless. Wouldn't change a thing. And like fighting in the desert, sooner or later, the odds shifted the other way and came back at you. Turned you upside down.

Matty slipped back into the woods, heading home.

He had to come up with a new plan.

❖

His phone buzzed again a few days later. Sheriff Bishop, like a ghost that wouldn't stay buried. "Just circling back on that Hog Mountain Road thing," Bishop said when Matty answered.

"Told you what I know," Matty replied, flat, like he didn't care.

"Southeastern's not real fond of watching their equipment burn, though," Bishop said. "They take that kind of thing seriously, same as I do. Got security now, cameras watching over the site. Making sure nobody tries barbequing their bulldozers."

Matty didn't respond.

"Here's the funny thing," Bishop continued. "A couple nights ago, those cameras caught someone hanging around the yard. Came out of the woods, looked like they were headed straight from your place. Watched for a while, then disappeared back into the woods."

"That so?"

"Can't say for sure, but it was a guy looked about your size. Coming from your direction."

"Could've been anyone. A lot of guys around here about my size."

The silence between them was thick. Neither of them spoke, letting the quiet sit there until Bishop finally broke it.

"If you think you're gonna change anything, make a dent in this, you're wrong. Same way all those activists whining about climate change aren't gonna make a damn bit of difference. Just wasting time and causing trouble. The world runs on oil. Always has, always will. Ain't nothing you can do to stop it."

Matty's voice hardened. "Seems to me, you're not the one with a pipeline buried in your backyard."

"That's old news," Bishop said, his voice a low growl.

"Old news?" Matty shot back. "That was my dad's deal, not mine. Nobody knew about greenhouse gas emissions forty years ago, and if the oil company knew, they didn't care. They still don't care. The thing killed my farm. It's killing my wife."

"Forty years, forty days, or forty hours, it don't matter anymore," Bishop said. "Nobody cared about what was buried in the ground then, and nobody cares now. Your old man took the money. No use crying over it."

Matty clenched his jaw. "Forty years ago, nobody knew what it was gonna do to the land. Or to the air. To any of us."

"Makes no difference. It's progress," Bishop said, tone flat.

Matty's breath came sharp. "It's the kind of progress that's killing us."

"Drill, baby, drill," Bishop said. "That's the plan. The country's gonna do everything it can to keep the oil flowing. All this talk about climate change? Just hot air. The lights stay on because of oil, not solar power or windmills or none of those things. Nothing's gonna change that."

"Even when it's wrecking the planet?"

"Small price to pay," Bishop said, like it didn't even matter.

The sheriff's voice softened, almost like pity. "I know you've got a lot weighing on you, Matty. Understand about Kayleigh. But torching bulldozers ain't gonna fix nothing. You can't change the world."

Matty squeezed his eyes shut, fingers digging into his palm, hand turning into a fist. "Maybe not. But I can try to fix my world," he said, voice a little broken, but steady.

❖

Days bled into weeks, then months, the heat of the summer blending into autumn.

Matty buried Kayleigh in October.

A week later, he put the farm up for sale. By early November, it was gone. Sold for cash to a real estate developer with a vision, a mixed-use development with retail shops, office spaces, and apartments. The pipeline wasn't an issue, at least nothing that would slow the build. Matty kept two acres for himself, parked a single-wide trailer on it, the kind of place he could leave at any moment. Threw things that mattered in a storage unit in town, then sold off all the rest.

Once he lost Kayleigh, all that was left were photographs, memories, and the farm. The land was a thing he had come to hate.

Now that was gone too.

❖

Matty stepped carefully through the mud, each movement slow and deliberate. The rain had stopped hours earlier. The night sky hung low and heavy. The air was cold, damp as he made his way through the woods, following a familiar path.

His truck was tucked away twenty yards down an old gravel road, just off Hog Mountain Road. The road hadn't seen a vehicle in years, thick with weeds and branches that scraped against the truck doors when he drove in.

Out of sight until he needed it.

Out of sight until he needed the ten propane tanks in its cargo bed that he was going to use to blow up the compressor station.

The compressor station was just ahead, a dark mass of steel, pipes, and humming machinery. Up and running a few weeks now, pushing crude faster down the pipeline. Matty caught the faint odor of diesel. His fingers twitched at his sides, the cold biting the skin through his gloves. It wasn't fear. He'd conquered his fears a long time ago. First in the desert, then recently, late at night, listening to Kayleigh drawing hard, raspy breaths, wondering if she would see the morning. Now it was just anger. An anger he had been living with for too long, now finally able to do something about it.

Matty crouched low at the edge of the road, blending into the shadows. The security lights buzzed and flickered, casting long, dark shadows across the ground. He had learned the rhythm of the place. Security was predictable: two men, neither armed with anything more than walkie-talkies, coffee, and cigarettes. No need for rifles anymore, now that the station was operational. The routine was dull, and nights were uneventful. They did laps around the perimeter for an hour, took a break, then did another hour, repeating the routine until their shift ended. Like clockwork, they were climbing into the company truck now.

Matty moved as soon as they slammed the doors shut.

He was fast. No hesitation. Knew exactly what he was doing. He had planned each step, choreographing the moves, practicing to perfection the same way routines had been drilled into him back in the Corps. He slid low alongside the truck, staying out of the driver's line of sight, hugging the blind spot on the passenger's side.

Matty yanked open the door, leveling his AR-15 inside the cab.

The guy behind the wheel sat up, startled, dropping his thermos of coffee, splashing it on his lap. The one in the passenger seat squeezed his eyes shut as Matty jammed the muzzle of the rifle into his neck, the silence of the moment suffocating. He could hear them each draw in heavy breaths. Neither let the air out of their lungs.

"Don't want to sound overly dramatic, but don't fucking move," Matty said, his voice low and hard. "Keep your hands where I can see them."

The driver turned, his face a mixture of surprise and disbelief. "You here to rob us?"

Matty spat a glob of phlegm on the ground, shook his head.

"Need you both to empty your pockets. Toss your phones in the backseat. Same with those walkie-talkies. Do it slowly. Give me your wallets, too."

The guards did as they were told, each of them moving in slow motion.

The guy in the passenger seat was braver, or just dumb enough to speak. "What'd you think you're doing?"

Matty opened the back door, slid into the jump seat, gun still trained on them.

"We're taking a little ride. You do what I say and don't get stupid, and everything's going to be fine. In a couple of hours, you'll be home. Sitting at your kitchen table. Eating corn flakes and drinking coffee, telling your wife about an incredibly shitty night that turned out lucky for you."

"I ain't married," the passenger muttered through gritted teeth.

"Well, be smart about this and maybe someday you'll find someone you can tell the story to."

Matty had them back out, driving slowly to the gravel turn-off where his pick-up was parked. Neither guard said a word. Matty could feel the air thick with their fear, both of them caught up in their thoughts, probably wondering how much shit they were going to catch. When they reached his pick-up, Matty had them haul the propane tanks two at a time onto the cargo bed. Then had them carry the ten-gallon galvanized trash can and carefully load it with the tanks. He zip-tied their hands in front, shoved their wallets back in their pockets, and prodded them towards Hog Mountain Road.

"Best thing you can do is move. Fast. Get as far away as you can. Don't stop and don't look back."

The driver was already walking. The passenger lingered, staring at Matty. "I know you."

"I'm sure you do," Matty said. "Saw your driver's license. Know you too now."

"You don't think they're gonna come for you?"

Matty smiled. "Figure they will."

"You ain't worried about that?"

"They can try."

"What's that mean?"

"Means spend enough time in the red zone, fighting a war against people trying to protect what's theirs, you pick up a few things," Matty said, his voice cold. "You might want to mention that when the cops start asking questions. Tell 'em not to come looking for me unless they're ready to find out what I learned."

It was risky, letting them go. It would only take one car passing by to change everything. Somebody might stop, pick them up, make a call to the Sheriff's Department, and that'd be it—his whole plan, everything he'd worked for, shot to hell. All the meticulous planning, all the hate he'd lived with for months, the anger that had burned inside, wasted. But Matty didn't want casualties. He'd seen enough killing, witnessed enough deaths firsthand. What he was going to do would be ugly – it didn't need to be complicated.

The EPA required shut-off valves in pipelines feeding into compressor stations and at various intervals in all pipelines to detect disruptions, automatically cutting off oil flow. It was meant to prevent catastrophic spills. Minimize damage. But that was before the new administration gutted the EPA, wiping away those regulations. At least the compressor station was built before the world shifted into something darker, when some politicians still viewed climate change as a serious threat and not a political football.

His tires screamed on the gravel as he pushed the truck deeper into the compound. The place was quiet, like the calm before a storm, the kind of silence that made his skin itch, his heart pound in his chest. He'd spent weeks before the farm sale gathering everything he needed—fertilizer, gunpowder, ammonium nitrate. Mixing it all in the trash can, piece by piece, carefully, like he was assembling a puzzle. His hands shook now, but it still wasn't fear. It was adrenaline, that sickening, familiar buzz that came with knowing you were about to cross a line.

Matty had crossed lines before, plenty of them.

He set the charge, slipped it carefully between the propane tanks in the back of the truck, his hands steady again, no hesitation. His breath was slow, measured. Controlled. Like he was fixing a fence in the middle of a hot summer afternoon, not planting explosives in the heart of enemy territory. Another flashback to Iraq—this time on the other side of the equation. But this was different. This was his fight now, not somebody else's. His fingers touched the detonator, the button hard, unforgiving.

He could feel it now, the weight of the decision, the weight of the power in his hand. The clock was ticking. His heartbeat in sync with the pulse of the earth beneath his feet. He ran out of the yard, down the road to his pick-up, the detonator pressed tight in his palm, like he was gripping the last thread of sanity he had left.

Matty didn't look back as he stood against the truck and caught his breath.

He pressed the button.

The explosion wasn't immediate.

There was a pause, a brief moment of silence, then a deep, violent tearing of metal and concrete, splitting into pieces. The roar of fire, a massive fireball mushroom cloud shooting straight into the sky, steel, wood, cement twisting apart like they were nothing, the earth screaming as everything burned. It was a sound that dug into Matty, familiar shockwaves finding a way into his gut.

He didn't flinch.

Matty wasn't close enough to see the debris raining back to earth where the compressor station had been, or the deep crater that would've been left behind.

There was no need to watch the flames licking the sky like something hungry. No need to track the fury burning at the edge of what used to be his world. Matty felt it all, felt the heat, the tremble in the ground as he slid behind the wheel, the way that everything had changed.

He took a deep breath. Thought about Kayleigh and felt the depth of that loss twist a little deeper in his chest.

It was done.

The road was empty, the pick-up's headlights cutting through the dark. It wouldn't be long until Hog Mountain Road was filled with police cars and fire trucks, cops combing through the wreckage, crawling with Feds investigating the explosion. Something like this would bring Homeland Security. The FBI. NSA. Any number of three-letter agencies from DC to investigate. Probably a good chance they would find their way to his trailer, although he hoped his threats would be taken seriously. That they would approach his property cautiously. He'd learned a thing or two in Iraq about burying IEDs in the road and booby-trapped houses.

A quiet settled over him, the kind that didn't ask for anything, that just *was*. The night stretched out ahead, cold and empty, just like the space inside his chest. His hands were still clenched around the wheel with the kind of calm that comes after doing something irreversible. His mind raced, but the thoughts didn't add up, just kept folding into themselves, over and over. There was no turning back now. He'd crossed the line, and maybe this was where it ended. Maybe this was the last time he'd ever do anything like it.

Or maybe this was the beginning of something else.

A lot of maybes. A lot of questions.

But for now, all he could do was drive, keeping his eyes on the road, letting the world burn behind him.

Recent research attributes 37% of heat-related deaths to human-induced climate change.

-World Health Organization (WHO)

"No one is allowed to be born on Svalbard and the dead are shipped immediately to be buried off-island. This place is a land of living, but not life, of dying, but not death."

Long Night of the Polar Bear

C.E. McKenna

Svalbard glows under the full November moon. It's early afternoon—only 1 p.m.—but the sun never even peeks over the horizon. There's just a hint of deep blue twilight before the island slips back into a generous polar night.

Atle Solås walks, headlamp pointed down, gloved and knit-hatted, in the darkness. Long, uneven brown strands push out at odd angles around his mouth. In his past, women called him hot—dapper, even—but since arriving on Svalbard seven months ago, he stopped cutting his hair or shaving his beard, and he's drifted from rugged to ragged.

The air is pierced by the long, throaty cries coming from the sled dog kennels, which are kept, by law, outside the Longyearbyen town limits. Even though it's dark, Atle can make out the twenty-foot-high chain-link fence, the fifteen-or-so dog houses, and a pack of pacing, panting huskies in the enclosure.

Like him, they've been relegated to the outskirts of society so their noises won't disturb the peace.

❖

It's been five days since Atle last went to town. In his cabin he keeps no vodka, no whisky, no K, no coke. When he was banished to Svalbard for accidentally killing an old woman during a job, he welcomed an escape from the Oslo nights, the parties and ekstase and waking up tangled in strange women's duvets, soaked with his own urine.

For the first four months, his employer rented him a house in Longyearbyen. Atle spent most of his time at Gruvehuset, a boarding-house-turned-restaurant up a narrow canyon on the southern edge of town, taking shots of Smirnoff Norsk and akevitt and being shouted at by the bartenders for falling asleep in the toilets.

There was a stuffed polar bear at Gruvehuset, posed on its hind legs, arms up, as if about to partner for a waltz. That's what happened on this island when bears were killed. Their skins were allocated, plaster-filled, positioned as if they were alive. Once, fearing the ire of a group of tourists with whom he'd gotten into a heated argument about the environmental effects of whaling, Atle curled up behind the taxidermy bear with a double vodka, waiting for them to leave.

They stayed for three more hours. He pissed himself.

That's where he is headed now, back to Gruvehuset. But not to drink. He left a package there when he first got to the island—a thumb drive wrapped in two plastic bags, which he stuffed into a small cavern he carved in the back of the leg of the dancing polar bear. Before his employer sent him to the edge of the world to "let things cool off," he'd copied the contents of a laptop onto that drive.

The laptop belonged to the daughter of the CFO, or whatever one would call the equivalent in a Nordic crime syndicate: "Lead debt collector;" "The hammerhead;" "Vidlitsa Vlad." Vlad was a Russian, a black stallion of a man who smiled all the time, as if he owned the world. Using a symphony of violence, he brought rivals and debtors to the dirt—their noses stone-broken, arms hanging from sockets, teeth shattered on the ground. Sometimes still breathing, often not. And he brought his daughter along on all his dark errands. Whether she was shield or apprentice, everyone was too afraid to ask.

Vlad's laptop held proof of where he'd gone and who he'd killed. Before leaving Oslo, Atle snuck into Vlad's house to copy it. But it was encrypted, and Atle was not technical enough to know how to duplicate the hard drive without knowing the password.

In the same room, there was another computer. That one belonged to Vlad's daughter, a fourteen-year-old K-Pop superfan who always wore purple cat ears and was far less security-oriented than her father. Her password had been "BTSARMY." On it, Atle had found a trove of sociopathic videos the daughter had recorded and dubbed over with cartoon noises. In one, a man, his broken leg dragging behind him, eyes wild, flees as Vlad pursues, set to the South Park theme song. In another, the daughter's face appears, wide-eyed and excited, before the camera jerks around as if it it's being shaken, occasionally catching glimpses of golf clubs and bright red blood and purple fur, sped up to 3x time and backed by *zings* and *bonks* and *whees*.

Those videos are Atle's ticket out of here.

He is going to retrieve that thumb drive and send it to a broker, who will verify the contents and transfer kr 22,000,000—roughly €2 million—into his account. By this time next week, Atle will be reconfiguring his sober life on a beach in Thailand, sunny and safe and far, far away.

Chalk-like snow. Dry cold squeaks. His heart beats fast as he considers all the different ways his plan could go wrong. Wishing his thermos contained vodka, Atle takes a sip of coffee and his breath blooms in a dense cloud, like the exhaust of a diesel truck. He grounds himself with an exercise his geologist mother—the person he will miss the most when he goes dark—taught him. He thinks of his heart, pumping blood to his extremities. Arms, legs, feet, toes. And those toes are in shoes, and those shoes are on the ground. Beneath him is the permafrost—frozen for millennia and hard underfoot—and below that, Earth's mantle, its four-and-a-half-billion-year-old outer core, its inner core. He is connected in a straight line all the way to the center of his existence.

On the road, he passes a polar bear warning sign—red and black. "Gjelder hele Svalbard," it reads. Polar bears are everywhere on Svalbard. And they've been acting strangely, these last few winters, the locals say, spending more time on land instead of hunting seals from the sea ice. He hitches the strap on his long rifle so the gun hangs flat against his backpack. These bears are protected so, in the event he's attacked, he's supposed to shoot in the air above the bear's head to scare it off. Only if that doesn't work is he allowed to aim for the animal's body.

Just last week, his neighbor, Dasha, a gruff redhead who often brought Atle warm pretzels, accidentally left the back door of her cabin unlatched while she went to town. She returned to find a gigantic white-and-red bear chuffing and grunting. Jaw-chopping.

Her dog—a malamute—had unfortunately found it first.

❖

It's twenty minutes of snuffling in the darkness before the lights of Longyearbyen glint white and yellow. Simple, rectangle buildings are arranged in rows between the steep, barren bluffs of a narrow box-canyon. Atle passes the North Pole Expedition Museum and turns left at the spaceship-looking building that houses the small university, then trudges down Vei 500, the main street.

In the distance, at the other edge of town, are the rotating blue and red lights of Emergency Services. The sight unnerves Atle, even though he hasn't been arrested in over two years. Things change when those lights make an appearance.

No one is allowed to be born on Svalbard and the dead are shipped immediately to be buried off-island. This place is a land of living, but not life, of dying, but not death.

Like Atle, everything here exists in a tentative balance, easily rocked by surprise.

❖

His first stop is the grocery store. He needs enough to get him through a few more days before he can board a southbound plane. Whether that plane goes to Tromsø or Oslo, he doesn't care, as long as no one stops him en route to Bangkok.

Atle enters through the automatic doors and swings his rifle into the umbrella stand that's been repurposed to hold everyone's guns. The overhead lights are blinding after being so long in the dark. It takes a second for Atle's eyes to adjust, but the moment they do, he spots Jarl, a guy he used to watch football and drink with at Gruvehuset. Jarl—one of those men whose hair receded in his late teens but he still has too much hope to give up and shave it—is heavyset, like a rugby prop. The bottom half of his face is covered in a neatly trimmed black beard, and he's judging loaves of pre-packaged bread as if they're vintage oil lamps and he's looking for one with a Genie.

The moment he spies Atle, Jarl grins wide.

There's a resemblance between Jarl and Vidlitsa Vlad that Atle had never recognized when drunk. Atle shivers and the hairs on his arms and neck stand on-edge. He gives his drinking buddy a quick nod, then heads to the other side of the store. Maybe, by the time he's finished shopping, Jarl will be gone.

Brown eggs, five spiced sausages, half a kilo of coffee. All go into his basket. The only other thing he needs is a package of wheat rolls.

"Out of your cabin, eh?" Jarl says as Atle approaches the bread.

"Errands," Atle mumbles.

Now that Jarl is closer, the similarity is uncanny. Atle wonders if Jarl and Vlad might be brothers, or son-and-father. How many children does Vlad have? Atle never asked.

Jarl peers into Atle's basket. "Rather light on the groceries. Going somewhere?"

"No. No." Atle shakes his head. That came out too quick, as if he were lying. He is lying. He needs to deflect. "I never asked. Are you Norwegian?"

"Конечно, моя мать была норвежкой," responds Jarl with a side-pulled smile.

Atle makes out the final Russian word, "Norvezhkoi," which he takes to mean Norwegian. And 'mat—' 'mother.' His heart clenches. He imagines he's a field mouse being toyed with by a barn cat.

When Atle and Jarl were charging through the long days of May armed with a handle of vodka and the yellow jerseys of Foballklubben Bodø/Glimt, was he being watched? Had Vlad sent Jarl here? Did Vlad know that Atle had proof of his and his daughter's crimes?

Even if Atle succeeds in his escape, it's only a matter of time before Vlad and Atle's employer know what he's done. Before they declare him a traitor, a dead man. Atle's chest hurts. He stopped breathing for a moment.

Jarl picks up a new loaf without so much as glancing at it and places it in his empty basket. "What have you been up to in there, all by your lone-wolf self?"

Atle definitely can't say that he's been using an encrypted messaging system to broker the sale of the flash drive. He can't come up with a lie fast enough, so he tells the truth: that an addict can't just stop, they can only shift focus. "Poker, mostly. Online."

"Not much new, eh?" Jarl claps Atle on the back fraternally. "Nothing else planned?"

Atle's heartbeat quickens. "My neighbor's dog was attacked by a bear last week," he says, unable to come up with anything else. "Came in through the back door. Killed him."

"I heard," says Jarl. "It's all anyone can talk about. She shot it?"

Atle shakes his head. "Scared it off." He swings his basket back and forth and gestures with his thumb. "I should get back. I'm up kr 3000." He tries to smile convincingly.

"We miss you at the bar," says Jarl. "You must come back up to Gruvehuset. We will play poker there. None of this online bullshit."

It sounds more like a command than a request.

❖

The emergency lights on the far side of town have multiplied. Something awful is happening on the southern end of the main road. It reminds Atle of a murder-suicide in Oslo a couple years ago that attracted a large crowd. The murderer, whom Atle knew in the vague, excited way he tended to make friends while partying, had stabbed his wife in the neck with kitchen scissors before jumping from a fifth-story window. Perhaps this emergency is like that.

Whatever it is, it will make a good distraction while he slips behind the polar bear and retrieves his package from its leg.

One more stop first. Atle looks over his shoulder for Jarl. His backpack, heavy with groceries, clunks against his hip. Funny. He never checks for polar bears when he is walking alone outside, but now that he's afraid of Jarl, he's checking behind him all the time.

◆

At the post office, the rifle stand matches the one in the grocery store. On the door is a circular sign: a red slash through the picture of a rifle and a handgun. They're not allowed inside Atle hesitates for a moment, thinking of Jarl. But no, that's just anxiety. Ice, frozen soil, mantle, core. He swings the rifle in.

He's at the post office to pick up two things: a return-addressed, padded envelope, shipped to him by the broker who will assess the contents for the anonymous buyer; and an Amazon package that includes a second—blank—thumb drive.

In his messages, Atle assured the broker that he had the only known copy of the laptop, which was true. But he still needs to protect himself. He'll make one more copy to keep. Then, once the deal is done and he has clean papers and a Cayman Islands bank account and an apartment overlooking the Chao Phraya River, he can retire in anonymity and peace, and maybe he'll destroy it.

Atle gets in line, jittery. There are two people in front of him, an older woman with her silver hair held in a bun by a disposable pen and a man wearing the orange-and-gray jumpsuit uniform of a coal miner.

If Atle was wearing a jumpsuit, he would stick the envelope against his back and the new thumb drive into the ankle, so if Jarl forced him to strip and prove he wasn't smuggling anything, he could at least shake the thumb drive into his shoe before handing over the envelope.

Then again, he could outrun Jarl, couldn't he? At least far enough to get behind a building and shoot. Yes, that will be his plan if he emerges from the post office to find a receding hairline bowed in his direction.

"It's terrible," the miner says to the woman.

Atle internally agrees. This situation with Jarl is terrible. How did the miner know?

"They got everyone out, though, yes?" says the woman.

"Barely."

The two people must be talking about Dasha. Her poor dog. Atle is overwhelmed with the relief of thinking about something other than Jarl and Vlad.

"She was able to scare it off," Atle interrupts. "No evacuation necessary. It's too bad about the dog, though. He was sweet. Loved to bound through the snow drifts." He gives the woman a half-hearted smile and is calmed, for a quick moment, because her eyes look like his mother's.

She squints. "We're talking about the landslide." The woman's gaze jolts quickly towards the miner, then back to Atle. "The one today? An hour ago? It took out Gruvehuset."

"They're going to happen with more frequency, now. That's what the scientists say," says the miner.

Atle blinks dumbly. A landslide. Gruvehuset. "It's gone?" His mouth hangs open. He can't find more words.

"It's the permafrost," says the woman.

"It's the permafrost." The miner shakes his head.

"Good God," says Atle.

The woman frowns. "God had nothing to do with it."

◆

Atle shoves his two packages into the backpack with his groceries, sprints past the outer room of the post office, and charges onto the street, aiming for Gruvehuset.

His breath comes out in rhythmic pants and his nose hurts from the afternoon air.

A landslide. It makes no sense. Not with this snow on the ground, so cold it squeals under the balls of his feet.

Ice, frozen soil, mantle, core. Hardened and certain. The calming mantra does nothing for Atle now. He's too focused, too scared that his ticket off this island has just been buried. He doesn't even consider that if Jarl didn't know about the landslide, he must have been in the grocery store, waiting, for well over an hour.

❖

High-vis jackets and flashing lights. People cluster and clump. The air shivers with murmur.

"Will there be more?"

"It sounded like a freight train."

"It's a one-off. Don't panic."

"They shouldn't have built here."

A black river of earth engulfs the wooden boards and shattered windows of Gruvehuset. Four brick chimneys are broken and half-buried, mixed with familiar detritus: carved wooden chairs, the sharp corner of a picture frame, silver glints of forks and knives. And there—an unmistakable tuft of white fur.

Atle rushes towards the beacon of his taxidermy polar bear. He paws at the cold dirt with gloved hands, digging. The ground is heavy and it moves when it shouldn't. He pulls off his gloves. He makes deeper grooves and pressure builds underneath his nails. Still, he searches. Somewhere in this pile is the only thing he needs in the whole world.

He uncovers more of the polar bear's ear. Instead of feeling stiff, it's soft to the touch. Shouts and chatter build around him but Atle hears none of it. It is almost as if he is deep underwater and his only focus is swimming to air.

A young woman drops to the ground to his right and starts digging, too. Then a boy steps across and pulls dirt from the other side. A broken vodka bottle catches Atle's sleeve and he grabs its handle, using it as a shovel. A sharp edge nicks the bear and a small red trickle appears.

"Is it still alive?" Tears stream down the young woman's face.

"We have to get it out," says the boy. "Quick!"

Atle doesn't meet their eyes. They're wrong. This bear is the one from the lobby, the one that has guarded the thumb drive for months. The drive is small but salvageable, safe in its double-bagged plastic, housed inside the bear's leg. He will find it. He will leave this place.

Atle comes at the cold earth from the side, digging with the jagged edge of the bottle and throws the dirt to his left.

Another person dives in, pulling muck and rubble away from the bear. The bear's head is half-unburied, now. Dark globules mix into its fur. Eyes open but unblinking. It's not breathing. Inside Atle, the ground shifts.

"Help, there's a bear in here," someone yells. More people rush over.

It's clear, by now, that this isn't the taxidermy bear from the lobby. This one had been alive—caught in the same torrent of nature that ripped through wood and stone, dirty wine glasses and stew-scraped plates, the floorboards where Atle sat in urine-soaked pants, the air ducts, the plumbing, the trash cans, the warm-and-pungent compost bin in the industrial kitchen. The humans escaped, but this giant, violent animal couldn't outrun its fate.

Atle wonders if this is the beast that killed Dasha's malamute.

Even if it is, he can't stop. He's too far in. He is overwhelmed by the feeling that if he can just free the bear, it can be resuscitated. If he can extricate this bear from the trap no one knew was set, it will have a chance at life again. He's digging with more intensity now. Dirt flies. It's all over his clothes, his hands, his unkempt beard. He grabs huge armfuls of soil and pulls it into his lap. He uncovers a wide fur shoulder from the earth.

A woman across from Atle looks up and gasps.

"Get up," says a deep voice. It's Jarl. He's holding two rifles. One is Atle's, which Jarl must have taken from the post office stand. It's clear now who Jarl is. He knew where Atle went after grocery shopping, what he got in the mail, why he sprinted towards the rubble of Gruvehuset.

Everyone digging scrambles backwards, their eyes on the barrels of the newcomer's guns, but Atle goes back to digging. "Shoot me," he dares the larger man.

"Where did you put the copy of her hard drive?" Jarl's tone is angry.

"Inside the bear." It's not a lie and not the truth.

Jarl hesitates for a moment. "How—что ты делал?" Then drops to his knees. He tucks one gun underneath his armpit and begins pawing around the carcass with his left land, keeping his right index finger close to the other rifle's trigger. Around them, the crowd pulls back, eyeing the scene.

"Пьяный мудак," Jarl spits. "I should have dealt with you when you hid from those tourists like a child." He is referring to the long evening when Atle crouched in the corner, drunk, and decided the dancing polar bear could protect his secret.

The crowd's whispers build into yelling.

"He's going to shoot—"

"Stop, get back."

"Run!"

Atle can see in his peripheral vision that the commotion upsets Jarl. If this large man were a dog, his hackles would be up. He tucks his toes under his ankles and rocks back off his knees and onto his feet in a fluid motion, rifles splayed out for balance.

"Put down the guns," a man commands. "Now."

Jarl spins around. One rifle cracks with a shot. It echoes, followed by the screams of the crowd. Atle throws his hands over his head, then peeks through the crook of his arm when he realizes he hasn't been injured. People rush in every direction, twisting orange and gray. The ground shudders.

Three yards away, someone lies in the dirt. From where he's kneeling, all Atle can make out is the silver top of the person's head. A disposable pen pushed through a bun. Silver hair. He thinks of his mother's face when he lied to her, said she shouldn't worry but he had to leave Oslo for a while: *What have you done?* Of the old woman he killed, the confusion in her eyes when she couldn't make sense of the blood pouring from her stomach. The question in her eyes: *Why did you do that?*

Atle leaps to his feet, the broken vodka bottle still clutched in his hand. Pouncing on Jarl's back, he swings the weapon around to connect with the large man's face. Jarl's rifles fall to the ground as he pitches forward and roars. Blood spurts onto Atle's fingers. He gouges everywhere he can. The dark, wispy crown of Jarl's head, the bulging side of his neck, the hard muscle of his chest. Arms, torso, eyes, hands. Skin, tendon, muscle, arteries.

People are screaming, but all Atle can make out from the din is, "She's dead."

Atle isn't sure if they're talking about the woman or the polar bear. If it's the silver-haired woman, her corpse will be flown to Oslo. But the bear's body will stay. It will be hauled from its grave and filled with plaster. Fur cleaned and brushed. Posed as if it were alive, as if it were in the middle of a joyful afternoon, prancing across the sea ice, sated with seal blubber.

Jarl drops to his knees, then falls to his side like a felled spruce. The ground glistens with blood.

"О, Боже," groans Jarl through the flaps of skin where his mouth should be. His breath is ragged. He only has a few minutes left.

"God has nothing to do with it," whispers Atle. He turns from Jarl and makes his way back to the dead polar bear in the ground.

He is digging around the bear's leg when a piercing *pop* ruptures the air. It dimly registers that Jarl has committed one last act of violence.

Atle's chest feels warm. He can't catch his breath. The air is heavy in his mouth but refuses to be gulped down. He collapses backwards. The dirt on his neck is freezing, but soft. Beneath it, mantle. Core.

The apartment over the Chao Phraya River is gone. So is the new passport, the Cayman Islands bank account, the version of Atle that might have been redeemed.

Overhead, the lights of the emergency vehicles interrupt the stars. Steam twists off Atle's body and gathers into a swirling cloud. The dead polar bear's uncovered head is bent towards the dying man.

Atle has no final questions, no confusion about why or how. Just one last wish: don't fly Atle's body off this island. Take his corpse away from the wreckage and the dirt. Fill him with hard plaster, cut and shampoo his hair, replace his eyes with resin orbs. Pose him with this bear, in the moment he realizes they are the same. Both caught in a trap neither knew was set, swallowed together by the long polar night.

"The river's current is infamous, he explained. If you fall in, you die, and if you die, there are two places you end up: in the belly of a caiman, or on a beach at a bend in the river."

The Place Where The Dead Things Go

Jim Ruland

When Fiddler was told she'd be traveling to the coast with her supervisor, Mayne, she assumed there would be a beach, but that's not the case. It's been raining since they arrived at the hotel, but now rain falls in sheets down the windows and puddles on the ground. The sky is a great mass of gray and the wind has picked up. The palm trees sway and shed husks of dead fronds that litter the road like the carcasses of giant insects.

The city sits on the edge of a river that empties into an estuary carved up by shipping companies and petrochemical concerns before finally making its way to the Caribbean. She'd packed a bikini, but the actual coast is a long way away. The closest she's gotten was last night's dinner at a restaurant overlooking the river. The turgid, greenish-brown channel unnerved her. The river was so vast and wide she couldn't see the other side. It looked like pea soup lit from below.

After dinner, Fiddler and Mayne went out on the patio with the man who'd decide if he would renew the contract that would allow the company they worked for to continue drilling. He was a big likable fellow with a thick mustache and an easy smile. He pointed out something swimming near the riverbank. Fiddler didn't know where she was supposed to look, and she pretended she could see the thing in the river. "What is it?" she asked.

"That, my dear, is a caiman."

"A caiman?"

"A cross between a crocodile and an alligator. They feed on the dead things that float in the river."

Fiddler saw it: long and lean and dark. Swimming against the current. There and then not there.

"What kind of dead things?" She regretted the question immediately.

"Best not to find out, eh?" The man roared with laughter as he fed scraps from his meal to one of the stray dogs loitering on the patio.

Mayne shot her a look she found impossible to read.

When they were alone, Mayne was not shy about barking instructions at her: finish these slides, overnight that package, order the car. These tasks were essential but anyone could do them.

Fiddler has come to understand that her job is to make her supervisor happy, but happiness does not come easily to Mayne. In public he presented a version of himself that was even more uptight and inflexible than he was with Fiddler behind closed doors. He could be cruel and condescending, which made even the most casual exchange fraught with tension. The meeting they are going to now is anything but casual. The future of the company depends on it. What about the future of this country? No one is asking that question.

Fiddler waits for Mayne in the lobby. The hotel is neither near the airport nor close to the business district where they are headed. The hotel's chief attraction is that it is secure. Although kidnappings, carjackings, and robberies are no longer common in the city, they remain an unpleasant reality. Stick to the main roads, don't go swimming in the river. That was the advice they'd been given. Easy enough, she thinks.

Mayne has been complaining about the hotel since they arrived three days ago. Yes, she'd booked the hotel, that had been one of her many tasks while preparing for the trip, but Mayne had chosen it. The hotel doesn't have a porte-cochere and though Fiddler has secured a pair of umbrellas from the front desk, she anticipates Mayne will find a way to blame her when he gets wet in the downpour.

Fiddler's phone buzzes. The car is approaching. She texts Mayne to let him know their ride has arrived. As soon as she presses send she hears Mayne by the elevators, talking loudly to someone on the phone. Fiddler offers him an umbrella, but he ignores her. She stands in the lobby with both umbrellas, wondering what she should do. Sensing her distress, one of the doormen relieves Fiddler of the extra umbrella and holds the door open.

"Thank you," Fiddler says with pointless embarrassment, and is hit with a blast of wind and rain as she steps outside. Her foot sinks into a puddle and she never quite manages to get the umbrella all the way open before it's time to close it again. When Fiddler climbs into the car, she is soaking wet.

Mayne shakes his head at her, still on the phone, but remarkably dry.

"Terrible night," the driver says in English after confirming the address.

"Yeah," Fiddler replies, though it isn't all that different from the other nights they've been here, each day wetter and drearier than the last. She would like to ask if it always rains like this at the coast but doesn't know what she'd do with the answer.

"You here for the concert?"

"No," Fiddler says.

It's a question that every driver has asked since they stepped off the plane. An international pop star who was born in the city and whose parents still live here is performing a free show at the football stadium. The city erected a fifty-foot statue on the esplanade in her honor, which Fiddler wants to see, but the weather has prevented them from visiting it. Each night after their business meetings they go back to the hotel for a drink at the bar, but when they get there Mayne complains he has too much work to do, and they go up to their separate rooms on the fourth floor instead.

Fiddler would take a shower, put on her bikini, and dry her hair. Then the texts started coming in. Mayne's messages were phrased as questions but came off as demands.

Can you re-send the slide deck?

What time is our flight?

Is it going to rain tomorrow?

This goes on for hours.

But last night, Mayne sent her an unusual text: *If that fucker doesn't seal the deal tomorrow, she's dead meat.*

She assumed the man they'd been wining and dining all week was the fucker. Fiddler likes the fucker. Anyone kind enough to feed scraps to stray dogs can't be all bad. If anyone is a fucker, it's Mayne, who is rude to everyone.

It was possible Mayne sent the message by mistake. Fiddler thought that was probably the case, but she needed to know.

Who is dead meat? Fiddler typed.

You don't need to worry about that, Mayne responded.

The driver fills Fiddler in on the pop star's activities since her return to the city. Apparently, the pop star built several schools and is paying visits to all of them. Also, her father is ill.

"That's too bad." Fiddler makes a point to be polite to their drivers because Mayne is so dependably rude. He'll bark at them to turn off the music or get off the phone. There's a way to make these requests respectfully, but either Mayne doesn't know how or he doesn't care.

The driver is explaining that he can probably get them tickets to the concert tomorrow, when Mayne interrupts.

"Can you turn off the air? It's freezing in here!"

The drive scowls. Fiddler sits back in her seat, keeping her eyes on the app that shows the route to their destination. Mayne often asks for updates about their ETA, and it's always better to have the information ready. The rain is coming down with such intensity that it's getting difficult to see. The driver abruptly turns off the main road, and takes them down a side street, which is not the route Fiddler's GPS has mapped out for them.

"Where are we going?" Mayne asks the driver.

"This is a better road," the driver explains. "When there is a big storm, the main road floods, and it becomes dangerous."

This seems reasonable to Fiddler. Just the other day they'd driven down a road that was little more than a trench of gravel and dirt. Apparently, the two municipalities the road connected couldn't agree on whose responsibility it was to maintain the road, so it fell into disrepair and stayed that way.

"Bullshit," Mayne says as he snatches Fiddler's phone and studies the map. "Go back to the main road."

The driver glares at Fiddler in the rearview mirror, like he's reached some kind of conclusion about them, and turns the vehicle around.

Fiddler knows there will be no more talk of pop stars.

The driver guides them back to the main road, which does seem a lot worse. The wind lashes the car and flings rain down on the roof. With the air off, the windows have fogged up, making it difficult to see.

Fiddler recalls the story the fucker told them last night. The river's current is infamous, he explained. If you fall in, you die, and if you die, there are two places you end up: in the belly of a caiman, or on a beach at a bend in the river.

"So there is a beach," Fiddler said.

This beach, the fucker said, is a place where things wash ashore with such frequency that whenever someone goes missing, the police are dispatched there to watch and wait.

That's how this trip feels to Fiddler: waiting for something terrible to be revealed.

The car is going slower now and it's difficult to see more than few feet in front of the car. The water isn't draining quickly enough and still the water rises, turning the road into a straight, fast-moving river.

Up ahead it looks like cars have pulled over to wait out the rain. At least she hopes they've pulled over. It would suck to get stuck out here.

"Keep going," Mayne tells the driver.

"I'm trying—" the driver says, but Mayne cuts him off.

"Keep going!"

The car continues to slow and up ahead several vehicles block the road. Their hazard lights blink a hazy semaphore through the cloudy windows. Were people abandoning their cars? Fiddler thinks she can make out shadowy figures wading through the murk.

"What's happening? Mayne asks.

"We shouldn't have come this way," the driver says with what sounds like resignation. He didn't want to be right, not like this, but here they are.

"Fiddler," Mayne begins and stops. She guesses what Mayne wants her to do. Call ahead and let the fucker know they're going to be late? Order another car?

But Mayne just sits there with her phone in his hands like he's waiting for it to tell him what to do. Fiddler notices something she's never seen in her supervisor's eyes before: fear.

The car stops. She can hear voices shouting outside the vehicle, but can no longer see out the windows. The driver doesn't say a word. Fiddler locks her door just as Mayne's flies open. Hands reach inside the car. They pull on Mayne's arms and legs while the driver watches impassively in the rearview mirror. Mayne puts up a fight, kicking and punching, but he's overmatched. The seatbelt is all that keeps him from being taken. Mayne looks at her, his face twisted with panic, begging her to do something. Fiddler reaches over and presses the button on his belt, releasing him from his seat. Something clamps onto Mayne's arm and pulls him out of the car. She reaches over and shuts the door, catching a glimpse of the beast as it thrashes its great scaly body and drags her supervisor deeper into the mad green river to the place where the dead things go.

One email composed with ChatGPT uses a 16 oz. bottle of water.

-UC Riverside study

"What I really loved about *Climate Cops* was that I'd
get to save the planet—and shoot people!"

The Skies Are Red

Richie Narvaez

Criminal Takedown: Climate Change Cops: An Oral History

Exclusive to *Hollywood Variety Magazine*

Although Criminal Takedown *went ballistic in the ratings from the start, not even an Internal Affairs investigation could have foreseen the show becoming such a behemoth, a hit that would be on the air for four decades and launch twenty-seven spinoffs.*

The original show and all of its spinoffs became wildly successful—and many have had their own spinoffs (including the current number one TV show, Criminal Takedown: White Heat*)—with one glaring exception:* Criminal Takedown: Climate Change Cops.

The logline for the show read, "Each episode features gripping climate crime cases and cutting-edge science. At the heart of every story is a tenant of the planet seeking justice." The show followed an elite group of detectives who battle climate change crimes all over America. Three episodes were filmed. None were ever aired.

Rumors circled that there were tempestuous on-set arguments and that the studio was not happy with dailies. Then, on July 12, 2019, the show's star, longtime TV veteran Sal Cassady died under bizarre circumstances. That was it. The axe fell.

What really killed CT: CCC? *Was it a victim of internal storms, a dark cloud of tragedy, or changing political winds? In recent months,* Hollywood Variety Magazine *has spoken with many of the people involved—producers, writers, and cast members—in separate interviews, for an in-depth look at the never-seen series.*

Jerry Melker (owner, Melker Entertainment, exec producer): Listen, *Criminal Takedown* is a juggernaut. A juggernaut! We could do *Criminal Takedown: Clown Car* and it would make ducats. Hold on, that's not bad. Let me make a note. Just kidding. Or am I? Anyway, so Sal comes to me with this idea. My father worked with him in the Sixties, so I figure I owe him a listen. For me, it wasn't about the politics of it. I mean, can you really believe scientists? But we'd just had another show cancelled, *Criminal Takedown: Fed Reserve,* and I wanted to fill that slot before the network dumped another eighties reboot in there. So I said, "Yeah, why not?" And to this day I think we could've had another hit if not for what happened to my dear friend Sal.

Rollo Ansen (co-producer/head writer): I used to hang at Sal's house in the Palisades. Huge, rambling place, bought it when he was starring in hippy movies back in the day. Half the place was banged out of recycled material and everything he ate was organic and grown in his yard. We were always pitching his eco ideas, but nothing anyone wanted to buy. So I said to him, "What if we take our idea and tie it to a known franchise?" I mentioned *Criminal Takedown,* which to be clear he was no fan of. "Fuckin' fascist copaganda," he called it.

Melker: Sal's house is nice, really nice. But to eat—everything has fucking bean sprouts on it.

Edith Cassady (Sal Cassady's widow): Sal was a big man with big ideas. Sweetheart, when he talked people paid attention because what he said was smart, was eloquent. He loved this planet, loved all the creatures who live and breathe here. He went to every protest, testified before Congress. When he talked, people listened. And it didn't hurt that my darling was as tall as a redwood and had biceps like boulders.

Sophia Volpe (co-star, "Gina O'Hara"): I loved the concept of the show. It's so timely. I mean, there was something on the news today, I think. What I really loved about *Climate Cops* was that I'd get to save the planet—and shoot people! What could be more fun than that?

I played the half-Italian, half-Irish second in command. I was the love interest for Sal's character. It wasn't in the script, but that's how I saw it, that's how I played it. Sal loved it, and he said he was going to have it written into the show. I said I hoped his wife wouldn't mind!

Dave Diaz (co-star "Federico"): So, the show bible said I was a newbie detective and that I was ethnic. And that was it—that was all they had for the character. I didn't even have a last name because they wanted me to cover a bunch of groups, I guess. But I didn't care—it was my first TV job!

Hanna Goode (co-star "Ariel Jade"): Well, I played Ariel, the geeky misfit technician. I had, like, four lines in each episode, and it was the same four lines, "Guys, check this out," "And then I found this!" "You're right, chief. How did I miss that?" and, last but not least, "Anyone up for a coffee run?"

Thing is, I truly believed in the idea of the show. I knew it was going to be filtered through all these cop drama tropes, but there had to be some way to crack the zeitgeist. When you think about what people watch all the time—besides fake news and reality TV—it's crime dramas. So it was kind of a brilliant idea. That was, of course, before everything went south—in more ways than one.

Could we have made a difference? I don't know. I mean, there's a wildfire headed for my area right now. That's the third time this year.

Mel Norris (co-star "Steve Remington"): It was a job. I'd played cops before. I've played them since. I'm an ex-linebacker. I got that look.

Cassady: I want to say, what happened to my sweet Sal is still hard to talk about, and I'll never believe what the coroner concluded. Never.

Ansen: Sal basically had a board covered with hundreds of environmental issues, and he would tell me, "Pick one and write an episode," and he'd add in research later. That's all the direction I got. There were a ridiculous amount of choices on that board.

Illegal deforestation. Illegal mining. Illegal dumping. Overfishing. Greenwashing. Methane leaks. On and on and on.

I came back with some pitches, and basically he said, "So each week it's some exec or his assistant who gets the blame?" I said, "Yeah." He goes, "Isn't that a bit repetitive?" I said, "Have you not seen the other *CT* shows?" He goes, "Don't you think wildfires, food insecurity, and superstorms can make the point for us?" I told him it hasn't yet.

Volpe: Everybody was lovely to work with. What a joy it is to work with people who care about the craft. I still see everyone all the time.

Diaz: I don't think she knows my real name. That's okay. I had been warned about her. Widowed three times. Went through men like a shark through chum.

Goode: Sophia and I had lunch. The one time.

Norris: There might've been some hiccups on set. It's been overplayed in the trades.

Goode: First day on set was brutal. We didn't even get through a scene before Mel waddles out of his trailer saying we can't say climate change is real. And I'm thinking, *Did you not read the script before today?* So Sal asks him, "Why the hell did you sign on for something called *Climate Change Cops* if you're gonna keep your head up your ass?" Mel gets right up in Sal's face and gives him this stare. Total deadeye. Then these two big guys get chest to chest like silverbacks. Mel finally says, "Fuck you!" and stomps away. Rollo had to go over and talk him down. Well, we did the scene without him, and they edited his stuff in later.

Norris: *Bullshit.* Never happened. Nope. What happened was we had a discussion. What I said was that we should focus on is entertainment, not preaching on a soapbox. People turn on their TVs so they don't have to think. I do remember Rollo promising me I'd get to shoot at least two people per episode if I did the scene Sal's way. [Makes double-clicking sound]

Diaz: Oh yeah. It was one screaming match after another. Norris has that violent reputation, you know. And Sal was like a quiet volcano that you never want to see erupt. So, that pilot episode—it was something about a megachurch committing carbon emissions fraud—

Hollywood Variety Magazine: "Carbon Footprints in the Sand."

Diaz: Yeah, that was it—and Sal had all this environmental technobabble he had to say. He needed it to explain the concepts, which I guess has a lot of what they call "nuance." Ergo, he had a lot of lines. Like, *a lot a lot*. You could see Mel getting pissed about it, but he didn't say squat. But when I had a small scene with him the next day, just him and me on a stakeout, he ad-libbed this whole ten-minute speech about how global warming was a hoax and that weather was weather.

Ansen: He didn't ad-lib that speech. He had two of his own writers on speed dial.

Norris: Marc and Akiva are my go-to script guys. They're always there when I need to punch up a script, you know? I get a scene where I have to shoot a guy in the head, and I give it to them and tell them to make it more Mel, and that's how I got my famous line in *Lethal Business*. "Bullet points . . . made!" Yeah! "Bullet points . . . made!"

Volpe: Okay, okay, there were some quarrels. But Rollo always did whatever it took to get the shot in the can. He's a pro. The business is in his blood. Oh—here it is on the news. There *is* supposed to be another wildfire. Well, I do hope everyone stays safe. My doggos get so frightened. They can sense when people get upset.

Ansen: Sal had his brand and his style, and Mel has his brand and his style, and never the twain shall meet. Gasoline and a match, they were—I mean, oil and water. But the most important thing was the show, and they both knew that.

Norris: That old hippy got in my face every goddamn day. Evidence this . . . Future that . . . Yadda yadda yadda. I was like, "Go back to your trailer and smoke a spliff and then come out and watch me shoot someone."

Diaz: Matter of fact, I lived through the fires in 2020. I stayed put, pretty much hiding in my bathtub. I know, I know, that's for earthquakes. Lucky I survived then, I guess. But now, shit, it's looking like I'm going to have to evacuate. I can smell smoke everywhere, even with the doors and windows closed.

Cassady: I don't think my darling was happy. I mean, who would be? He was co-writing the stories, he was practically directing every episode, and he was in almost every scene. The man was just exhausted.

Volpe: We were filming the second episode, and the script called for Sal's character to pick me up at my house. I said, "Listen, why don't you just have me waking up at *his* house and we can save money on a set?" I even came up with this great bit. His line was something something sustainability. So I ad-lib, "You never have any problems sustaining." But for some reason they decided not to use it. Sal's wife probably complained. She knew she had to keep such a robust man on a short leash.

Ansen: Sophia's whole thing was to get more screentime at any cost. She basically wanted to turn her character into Sal's gal pal, and in front of everyone he told her their characters were not going to hook up. She threw her lemon water at his head. She looked ready to kill him.

Diaz: She was weird on the set after that. Smiling to your face, but it was like a switch had been flipped. When she wasn't on call, she was locked in her trailer, wouldn't even eat with us.

Norris: Okay, first of all, everything was fucking organic on the craft table. Like lentils and tofu and beans and shit. C'mon, I need protein! I need meat!

Goode: Well, by episode two, Mel was having Six Guys burgers delivered every day. You could smell the salt and the grease. I gotta tell you it's really hard to appreciate hummus when you're smelling that! The burgers made Sal apoplectic.

Melker: I remember watching the dailies of the second episode, "Always and Forever Chemicals," with one of the network execs and some of the lawyers. In one scene Sal had done this speech about PSAs—PFAs?—is it PDFs? Hah! Anyway, it was a good speech, gave the scene flavor. Real flavor! But one of the lawyers turns to me and says, "You can't use this. DooPont is one of the network's biggest advertisers." I knew it was going to be a headache telling Sal.

Ansen: Yeah, so Jerry calls me in and tells me I have to tell Sal to tone things down. You don't tell a guy like Sal to tone anything down. But we sat down in his office and had a long heart-to-heart and, you know, a few hours later we were on the same page.

Cassady: DooPont? No, I never heard any of that. My darling Sal told me everything, and he would have told me if they told him to tone it down. He would never have stood for it. The environment was too important to him. He knew he was finally going to get to a popular stage to say what needed to be said.

Diaz: I remember it was at this point that Mel's movie *Black Pill* came out and it blew up in the theaters. I mean, blockbuster with a capital B. So he started coming to the lot like a cock on the walk.

Goode: The dynamic on the set totally changed by the time we were filming the third episode.

Volpe: It was called "Frak This." Can you believe it? What's not to love?

Ansen: That was basically my idea, the title. Mel loved it. Sal did not. Matter of fact, he fired me because of it. Said I was being too glib. I said, people don't like taking serious things too seriously. He basically said I had it all wrong, said he would let me finish episode three. All in all, a very shitty time in my life for that to happen.

Melker: After they worked on the third episode, it was clear that Sal and Mel were not getting along, and I was going to have to do something drastic. One of them was going to have to go. I mean, there were millions of dollars on the line.

Diaz: Can we talk about the fight? I want to talk about the fight. Because it was nasty.

Volpe: It's sad when sad things happen, isn't it?

Melker: I'd rather talk about some of the new shows we have coming up. Lots of new stuff.

Goode: It started with Mel picking on poor Dave. Dave flubbed a line, and Mel exploded. I don't know what was going on with him.

[Cough] Anabolic steroids [Cough]. Mel turns to the director—Craig Kolakowski, who has since passed—and tells him to start the scene from scratch, to which Craig balks, understandably, and Mel screams at him, "I'm in command now!" Which then makes Dave start giggling uncontrollably.

Diaz: I giggle when I'm nervous. It's a weird habit.

Goode: Then Mel turns and slams Dave against a brick wall.

Ansen: Oh, I was there for the fight, all right. That was basically my last day on set. Next day I was going to have to start looking for work all over again. At my goddamn age.

So, yeah, Mel has Dave by the throat, and Sal runs out of his trailer and pulls him off. Mel then throws a massive punch that gets Sal in the face. Sal flies back and hits the push bar on the technocrane. Basically, I thought he'd snapped his neck. But then he pops right back at Mel and suddenly punches are flying everywhere.

Volpe: I grabbed Rollo's arm and said, "Rollo, go do something!" He's got lovely, thick arms.

Ansen: Before I could do anything, Sal tackled Mel and pinned him to the ground.

Norris: It wasn't a fight. Just some shoving. Guys being guys.

Diaz: And next morning, yep, they found Sal in his trailer. Single gunshot to the head, the gun there next to him.

Volpe: The poor man. What he must have been going through to do that to himself.

Goode: I heard the angle was all wrong. I heard they found . . . Never mind. It's all just rumors, right? The police declared it a suicide. End of story.

Norris: Let me say this. I was sad as anyone about what happened to Sal. Sadder. He was a good friend and colleague. I still think about him every day.

Cassady: Now, with time past, I wonder if the networks and the producers—I wonder if they never intended for the love of my life's point of view to make it on the air. I'm not sure it wasn't just a tax write-off for Jerry.

Melker: Absolute bullshit. Total BS. *Criminal Takedown* is a billion-dollar franchise, a gift that keeps on giving, a hydra that keeps on living. Even the cancelled stuff, like, *Criminal Takedown: ICE,* which premiered to fantastic ratings in 2021 and then there was all this kerfuffle. Now we're reviving it.

Hollywood Variety Magazine: Are there any plans to revive *Criminal Takedown: Climate Change Cops?*

Melker: Not at the present moment.

Ansen: Sal was the heart, soul, brains, balls of the show. Without him the whole thing would fall apart. And it did. And, oh my god, after all that, two days later, Jerry calls me into his office and asks me to take over *Criminal Takedown: Blue Lives Matter.* The irony.

Goode: I have to say, what is the deal with all these cop and murder shows? They're, like, the same show, and yet there's not one single program, not one single piece of news about saving the environment. Maybe Sal knew this was coming, see? He saw the writing on the wall. And things have only gotten worse since Herr Chancellor got elected.

I mean, yeah, Sal's death does seem suspicious. And if someone wanted to do something to him, we all had the opportunity, right? Let's face it, a lot of us had a motive. Not me, but a lot of us. Though if I had a motive, I certainly wouldn't say I had a motive! Eesh! But then—what if he really saw what was happening to his vision and he couldn't stand it. There's always tha—wait. Let the sirens pass. I've been hearing them all morning. It's fucking scary.

I'm looking outside right now. The hills are on fire. Fuck, the skies are red. Red as blood. If there were a god, this is what his angry wrath would look like, terrible and merciless and swift. It's basically the wrath of the planet, isn't it? Mother Earth. And she's coming for all of us. Oh shit, I gotta go before I miss Fire and Rescue. I gotta—

Given the devastation of the 2026 wildfires, a month after our initial interviews, Hollywood Variety Magazine *contacted all of the participants to catch up with them. Unfortunately, co-producer Rollo Ansen died of lung damage caused by prolonged exposure to smoke from the wildfires and so was not able to participate.*

Cassady: Everything is gone. The whole house, the garden. Everything my darling built with his own hands, it's gone.

Melker: No comment. Absolutely no comment.

Diaz: Yeah, I'm currently unhoused, living back with my moms in Humboldt Park. I just got my real estate license. Acting wasn't going so well anyway.

Volpe: My thoughts and prayers go out to everyone whose lost their homes. Me and the doggos are fine, but it was so upsetting to watch on TV, my husband and I flew our private jet halfway around the world just to get some healthy distance from it. The doggos love Norway.

Norris: Shit. Yeah. My house got toasted. It's kind of devastating. It's emotional. I've been relieved from the burden of my stuff since it's all cinders. But that's just the Santa Anas. You win some, you lose some. I'm not going to buy into the big con game to get us to send our money overseas and bail out all these third world countries that supposably suffer.

Goode: I actually evacuated right after we last talked, so I'm all right, sort of. I have friends who lost everything. It was so sad about Rollo. I'm glad Dave's all right.

You know, I've been thinking a lot about *Climate Cops,* and I wonder if our show would have made any fucking difference even if it had gotten on the air. We could have convinced every viewer that climate change was a bad thing, but that wouldn't stop it. Because we could never change the heart of a corporation. You can't stop something that doesn't have a heart.

It feels like such a lost chance. I mean, the people on the news don't even say climate change anymore. Did you notice that? Are they not allowed to? Holy shit, can I even say it? Are they going to Silkwood me now?

❖

Update 3/15/26: Actor Mel Norris will be headlining the latest *Criminal Takedown* spinoff—*Criminal Takedown: Campus Crackdown*.

Tragically, less than a week after this article was posted, actor Hanna Goode was killed in a car accident. Her body was found in her car in a ditch on the side of the road.

◈

Update 3/16/26. This article has been removed.

"Three years ago, Ivan had swamped them. Washed everything they had down the river. No pumpkins. What was left had just been bare sticks poking from the dirt. The whole town had come together, though. Everyone, dirty but happy. Grateful to be alive."

What You Lost

Meagan Lucas

She'd thought the mud would slide like a milkshake from a cup, thick and slow. Plops. A plodding march of mess. Instead, it was like those huge tipping buckets of water at kids' water parks: urgent and unavoidable. Coming, and then there within a second, within a blink. And then everything was buried. Not gone, that would be better, but hidden under the slurry of rock and trees. Every-damn-thing, now suffocated by a stew of mud.

The river was worse. What had once been a feature, the pride even, of their yards and their town, now carried the remnants of neighbors' homes, the bodies of their livestock, their pets, cell towers, power poles, and miles of electrical lines. Award-winning gardens. Chemicals from the plant. Beloved She-Sheds. Sewage and years of hard work. Although she couldn't allow herself to think about it, some of the neighbors, too. That's what happened in these emergencies, people were lost.

The hurricane had roared. The silence after, interrupted only by falling trees, had settled, and she'd grown used to it. Now, the *whomp-whomp* of the helicopter was an assault against her ears, the seatbelt a trap. Violence, not rescue. But from up here she could see where the river and the wind collaborated, laid all the trees down in the same direction, like God's hand smoothing the nap of a velvet forest. It was almost pretty, until she remembered what lay beneath, and it turned her already empty stomach. Her husband said she was a terrible navigator. Maybe he was right, because as they flew, she didn't recognize anything. Once she saw something yellow, floating, maybe? Clinging to a tree in the sea of brown. Her heart caught in her throat. She didn't know where they were until she saw the glowing white spire of the First Baptist Church like a buoy in what she'd thought was the river.

It was now, before it had been downtown Burnt Church. It was all so much worse than she could have imagined.

The Rocky Broad River, the gurgling backdrop of Applefest, Art in the Park, and the Garden Jubilee, had once been her favorite part of town. The daily joy of having her morning coffee on the back deck watching the water bubble and splash over the dead falls. The children next door on the banks with their rubber boots and nets, looking for the elusive hellbender and shrieking. But now the river was inside the elementary school, and the post office, and the corner store, and the town would never be the same.

None of them would ever be the same.

She put her finger on the window. Her wedding band loose and spinning. She should be relieved. She was alive. If she could live with the guilt, she could start over. The landscape below made her think of high tide destroying sandcastles at the beach. Washing everything, good or bad, out into the ocean. Beyond her fingertips something moved. She looked closer. A boy.

"Look, look," she said.

All was not lost. There were still people who needed help.

She couldn't remember how to work the headset. She touched the copilot's shoulder, pointed.

He turned, irritated, but then looked out, and then back at the already overfilled seats.

"Next trip," a voice said in her ears.

She watched as the frantically waving boy nearly lost his balance. She imagined she saw tears on his face. She shook her head dramatically, but the pilot wasn't looking. She fumbled for the button, remembering how to give herself a voice.

"No," she said. "No," she shouted, the pilots looking at each other as one flipped a switch and muted her. She looked down at her empty useless hands and then she ripped off her seatbelt and her headset, and stood, and then thankful for once for her shrunken frame, she squeezed between the front seats and bludgeoned the copilot with her headset.

"Fuck, lady," he said, placing her in a chokehold. "We're just trying to help you."

She knew what was coming next.

◆

Bunny couldn't take her eyes off The Weather Channel. "It's going to rain the next three days," she told Phil, refilling his coffee as he read the paper, and she watched the little TV on the counter over his shoulder. "One-hundred year flooding," she said, like he couldn't hear it too.

"They want you to be afraid. When you're scared, you're weak, and they can sell you more stuff," he said. "We got our hundred-year flooding three years ago with Ivan. We won't get it again so soon. We got ninety-seven more years." He didn't look up from the paper, but reached for her, his patronizing pat, his hand going to the one soft spot right above her hip, his fingers squeezing, reminding.

He finished his breakfast and put on his waders, grabbed his pole, and he walked down their little path to the river. He fished every day. It was why they had retired here, or why he had retired here. She'd grown to like the tiny grocery store, and the quiet roads, the river, and the way the postmistress knew her name, but still felt like an outsider every time she opened her mouth. It didn't help that Phil thought everyone here was a hillbilly and refused to socialize. Their life in retirement was much smaller than she'd imagined.

She watched him out the window and tried not to think about how she'd stood in the same spot, three years ago, watching the river rise and holding her breath. Silently pacing as the brown channels snaked through their yard. The grass had not yet taken hold after construction changed the lay of the land. How high would it get? Would it reach the house? Or maybe all the water rushing down the mountain would take them first? The neighbors' pool had been swamped in brown water, and while Phil said it was their own fault for building on the side of a mountain, it was Bunny's phone that erupted with angry texts.

Now their yard was plush with Kentucky bluegrass. She'd spent the time since preparing the yard, alone, because she couldn't tell Phil of her fear. He would tell her she was stupid and a spendthrift. She'd read and researched. Talked to experts, and then installed plants, beds, dry rivers and berms herself; protection for something she hoped would never happen. She could still feel the pain in her muscles from lifting bags of rock and mulch, the blisters on her hands from digging. Phil's jokes about her dirt manicure stung. She wasn't ready for her work to be tested. She cleaned up the kitchen, and let her eyes wander back to the radar map on the television, and the talking head in front of it. It had already been raining for days.

She showered but didn't condition her hair. It would be a little dry today, but less greasy tomorrow if they didn't have water. She couldn't sit still so she cleaned with the TV on, made herself a cup of coffee. The news said to expect twenty inches of rain. She couldn't stop thinking about how, last time, the neighbor's driveway culvert had dammed up with branches like beavers lived there and swamped their entire side of the road. And that wasn't twenty inches. She grabbed her purse.

Phil stopped her in the garage. "Where are you going?" he said, blocking her way with his rod and net.

"Groceries," she said, trying to squeeze past him. She didn't bring up last time, when they'd started running out of the things he wanted to eat, he'd blamed her, and she couldn't deal with the stress of that, too.

He pinned her against the wall. "It's not going to be that bad. You don't need to be spending money on food we don't need to eat. There won't be anything good left at the store now, anyway." He punctuated his opinions by waving his gear around, and Bunny couldn't help but think it looked ridiculous, while also praying it didn't hit her in the face. "I'm not eating gluten-free, or God-forbid, keto bread for the next week just because you don't want it to be wasted." He said, holding her there until she relented. She should have said they were running low on Buffalo Trace.

She put her purse away and made another cup of coffee. The rain came down in sheets. She felt like she was in a car wash. She watched Phil in his bright yellow raincoat pulling the patio furniture into the garage. His hood kept whipping off his head. He shouldn't be out there. Every time he pulled a new piece into the garage and disappeared from view, she hoped that she'd hear the overhead door close. That he'd see how dangerous it was and just forget about the stupid chaises.

A crack ripped through the air, and a branch crashed onto the driveway. Phil jumped when the branch exploded into a million pieces, but he still picked up another chair.

Bunny cursed under her breath. He was going to hurt himself and then they were going to spend this Goddamn hurricane in the ER instead of in their dream home that they'd worked so hard for. She wasn't going to think about all the times that she'd put the kids to bed alone over the years while he worked late. All the moves to cities that she hated, but coordinated and facilitated, so he could climb the ladder. Instead, thought how two sets of hands would be faster. She picked up one of the lighter chairs and was carrying it over her head when he stopped her.

"Go inside," he said.

"I'm helping," she said.

He grabbed her arm. "You're useless at this. You're going to—" he said, and then a crack ripped through the air, and they both looked up.

❖

At the dinner table Jupiter's mother specifically said to stay inside. She looked into Jupiter's eyes with her fork in her hand, waving, and said this was going to be the storm of the millennia, that the roads would be terrible, that the power would go out, and that she was going to take a Valium and didn't want to have to worry about where Jupiter was, not even once.

"Play Skyrim," she said. "Draw a picture, read a book, clean that nasty pigsty of a room."

Despite the fact that she couldn't seem to do anything right, Jupiter really did want to make her mother happy, so she played Switch with her little brother until the power went out. Then she used her camping lantern to try to read, but then Canyon was at her bedroom window with that Christmas morning look on his face and she was trying, but failing, to say no. Before she knew it, she was lifting the sash and sliding through. Landing on a little platform of concrete blocks that they had built just for this purpose, well half for this purpose. The other half of the time Canyon was sneaking in. Her mother made the best cookies.

The trees moved above them like some kind of animal, and Jupiter had never heard the rain sound like that before, moaning and screaming and whipping debris into them like dodgeball. So loud that they could only shout to each other, but soon tired of that. She pulled the hood of her jacket tighter to keep the bullets of water out of her eyes. He hadn't texted what they were doing exactly. They'd both been caught by parents reading their texts before, so now everything had to be in code or unsaid, but she knew what would beckon him. The old Shipman place. No power meant no alarm system, and a broken window could be blamed on a fallen branch.

The road was a mess, covered in a carpet of fallen limbs and sticks and power lines. They stayed in the trees, letting the trunks provide as much cover as possible. It was pitch black beyond the beam of her flashlight and at every roar of thunder, or crash of a tree, she would turn and look toward home, and wonder if she'd made a terrible mistake. If this was just another example of how she made everything worse. But occasionally Canyon would reach back to help her over a rock, or a stream, and every time her heart would thump in her chest, and her palms would sweat, and her tongue would become thick and heavy. He was the handsomest boy in the tenth grade, a cross-country and track star, an honor student, and not very nice to anyone but her. And even, sometimes not to her either. But he was popular, and she'd been chubby until last summer. She was clumsy and not good at anything that was important to teenagers, and she liked to read and was completely invisible to most people. Being with Canyon was so much easier than facing high school alone.

The mansion loomed above them. All heavy stonework and thick wood; a fortress. They tested all the lower windows, but nothing opened. She knew this was Canyon's not-so-secret hope: that he'd have to break a window. The Shipman's had more money than everyone in Burnt Church combined, and they were never here. Everyone in town had a story about them. About how they didn't actually exist, or there was a ghost in the house, or some tragic story about racism and a disinheritance. But Canyon had the closest connection of anyone she knew. His aunt redecorated a room for them, going on and on about their money and taste, but she never let him come with her. He'd called her a bitch when he told Jupiter the story.

Around the back of the house, they found a window off a small porch. Canyon went into the woods and came back with a rock. Jupiter rubbed her upper arms even though it wasn't cold. He screamed as he broke the window, and he couldn't stop smiling as he used the rock to smash all the little shards around the edge. He held her hand as she stuck her leg through and stepped inside. Jupiter was immediately hit with a smell that burned her sinuses. She gagged. Canyon climbed in, scrunched his nose and said, "something died in here."

❖

Lucille knew what Harry would say, "they're only seeds. They aren't worth your life." He would say that it was too dangerous sitting in this closet, with these boxes, in the dark. He would have packed her into the minivan at the radio's first mention of 1916, and they would have headed to her sister's in Columbia. Or maybe even to North

Charleston where his brother lived. Anywhere the land was flat, and the trees didn't tower a hundred feet over the houses. He would make a joke about finally getting a chance to golf. He would have packed the seeds in the van. He would have stopped at every house on their way down the mountain to make sure people were leaving. To offer rides and help. To make sure everyone was safe. What she would have said to him was less clear. She knew that she couldn't say babies, that would hurt him. Maybe, life's work. Maybe that's why she didn't evacuate, because she'd been living in Burnt Church for eighty years, and her father had survived the great flood of 1916 in this house, and there was nothing coming that was worse than that. That and, moving the seeds was just too much of a risk. Too much could happen.

All lines of communication were down except her battery powered radio, but she'd gotten tired of having to hold the antenna up in the air in just the right position to catch a signal. She liked the quiet, anyway. She'd had to move all the boxes into this closet because it was the only room without a window. In this old house, these single pane windows were no match for the trees. And she knew now that she should switch out these cardboard file boxes for something waterproof, at least. She had near 10,000 packets of heirloom seeds. From asparagus to zinnias. She thought of herself as an archivist. Protecting future gardeners, heck future eaters, from the short-sighted modifications that were so quickly filling the seed catalogs. She was lucky that she'd inherited her first five hundred from her father. But the rest was her tenacity. Her single- mindedness. She knew this was important, so there she was in the walk-in closet with her boxes instead of evacuating. She'd taken down her shower curtain and covered the tops of the boxes in case the roof started to leak, though.

She should have brought a pen and paper. She might be stuck in there for hours, might as well plan next year's community garden. The garden space was down by the river behind the elementary school and would likely need some clean up tomorrow. The low-lying garden was so fertile because it was ripe for flooding. How full of bounty it had been all summer, and even yesterday, with the pumpkins finally ready, and the students so excited to turn them into jack-o-lanterns.

Three years ago, Ivan had swamped them. Washed everything they had down the river. No pumpkins. What was left had just been bare sticks poking from the dirt. The whole town had come together, though. Everyone, dirty but happy. Grateful to be alive. Her fingers slid over the envelopes, her knuckles bigger and rounder than they used to be. Remembering each of the varieties and how they came to be included. Gifts from friends and neighbors, community members. She was lost in thought, and didn't notice that her feet were wet, until the water was an inch deep.

"Oh dear," she said, looking down at her soaked house shoes.

Lucille took a deep breath and pushed open the closet door. The water was even deeper in the living room. Immediately, she started looking for the highest surface. She carried the four boxes one at a time from the closet to the kitchen counter, then she pulled a chair over from the table and put her foot up on it. Her slipper squished and a puddle formed on the seat. The water was so deep and so dirty that she couldn't see her linoleum. She braced herself against the counter and used all her strength to pull her body up onto the chair.

It took three tries. When she was finally up, she was dizzy and shaking, and she grabbed the upper cupboards for a minute to settle the spins. An accidental glance out the window stole her breath. Her backyard used to have a porch, pots of geraniums, grass, and a brick path to the river where a set of stone steps that her daddy had laid brought one the eight feet down to the water's edge. It was now just a lake of gray-brown as far as she could see. Branches and trash floated where her flower pots should be.

She swallowed hard, reached down, grabbed the first box, and shoved it on top of the upper cabinets. *There*, she thought, *that one is safe*. The second and third boxes went up too, but she was going to have to get down off the chair and move it and then get back up to do the fourth. She knew that her knees wouldn't allow it. She would have to step up onto the counter. There wasn't much room to stand. She was glad that Harry wasn't there to see this.

She opened two of the cabinet doors to use as leverage; to yank herself up off the chair so she could kneel on the counter. From there she used them to pull herself to standing, and that's what she was doing when the little hinge on the old cupboard gave way, and Lucille found herself weightless. There wasn't enough water to break her fall yet, and everything screamed when her body hit the floor.

❖

A branch as thick as her thigh missed Bunny's head by inches.

Phil's face was purple with anger. He pulled her inside the garage by her arm. "What the hell," he said.

"I wanted to help," she said, rubbing the sting out of her bicep.

He wasn't listening. He was already back outside shaking his head and muttering about doing things right.

She thought, not for the first time, that he didn't actually like her all that much. She wandered around the house and then cleaned, because she didn't know what else to do. If he came in and found her sitting, he'd make a passive aggressive comment about her work ethic, and the size of her ass. She kept trying to turn the TV on for some noise other than the growl of the generator, forgetting that no internet meant no channels. She kept looking at her phone, dying for some news of what was going on, whether her kids were okay. Not knowing was making her crazy.

By the time Phil came in, the water had gone out, and he was pissed he couldn't shower. "If it's yellow . . ." he said with a smirk as she handed him some wet wipes, knowing it would get her going, all those germs lurking and stewing.

"I can't," she said, shaking her head. "I'll haul water up from the river."

"Have you looked at the river?" he said. "The hell you will." He rolled his eyes at the tears welling in hers. "You use the master," he said. "I'll take the one down here, and we can share the den when our options run out. But the river isn't a solution; it will take you."

She nodded to make him stop talking, but she kept thinking about how she could flush without him. And then about where the river might take her, and would it be worse than this walking on eggshells? It wasn't always like this, she told herself. High stress situations were hard on every relationship. No one is their best self.

After dinner she waited until he was in the den, incessantly scanning channels on his battery powered radio, before she used the bathroom. She hadn't thought about how difficult it was going to be without anything to cover the sounds. No fan. No water to run. She had a can of room spray to cover the sour smell, and she hoped that that would be enough.

At bedtime she reminded him not to use her bathroom. He sighed. His kiss goodnight felt sharp. His snoring, aggressive. She couldn't sleep. The rain had stopped, but she knew that the river would just get higher as the water from the mountain above them flowed downhill. She flopped back and forth. Dreamed that they would wake up down river. She wracked her brain trying to remember if there was a waterfall in the Rocky Broad.

After breakfast she had a difficult decision. She needed to use the bathroom, but their house was too small, and too quiet. They were both twitchy and tempers were scalding. She was sure he was following her around. How would she get privacy? *Maybe, I could just not do it*, she thought. But then Phil was putting his waders on she was so excited he was going outside, that she forgot to warn him about how dangerous waders would be in these conditions, and he was barely out of the house before she ran to the bathroom and stuck her fingers down her throat.

The relief she felt was short lived.

"Bun? You okay?" Phil hollered from the bedroom. And then burst in and found her on her knees in front of a toilet bowl filled to the brim with vomit.

"I knew it," he said.

She looked at the floor. She was dizzy with the idea that he was looking at her puke. That he could tell it was multiple trips over two days. Different colors and textures mixed together. That he knew her secret. That he knew her shame.

"Christ," he said his eyes were wide and all the color had drained from his face.

"It's not what you think," she said.

He looked at her sideways for a long time, his eyes narrowing. "How could you know what I think?"

She desperately wanted to get rid of the evidence. She pushed the toilet flusher, hopeful. It just flapped and clicked. Nothing moved. Her face got hotter.

"I'll go get some water," he said.

Alone, she could breathe again. She wiped her mouth with toilet paper and gargled Listerine. He wouldn't tell her to stop. He liked her skinny, weak. If he asked, she decided, if he said anything, she'd tell him that she had the flu and didn't want to tell him. She wouldn't admit anything. She couldn't.

She went down to the kitchen and made a cup of coffee and looked for Phil out the window. The water was high. He would barely have to step off their back deck now to get water. He would be back soon. She cleaned the already clean kitchen and made another cup and then looked in the backyard again and gasped.

The river was right at the edge of their deck now. Moving fast. Her Adirondack chairs were gone. She couldn't see the fire pit or her bird feeder poles.

And she still couldn't see Phil.

She checked the garage and the front yard; she looked in the bathroom to see if he was already inside, but the toilet was still unflushed. She stepped out onto the back deck, the stairs to the grass were underwater, but the boards were still sturdy. She walked to the edge so she could see around the corner of the house. The whole yard was a river now.

Her breath caught in her throat. The watering can that he would have taken to collect the water, bobbed on the surface, stuck in a camellia bush. "Phil," she screamed. "Phil."

But the only sound was the roar of the brown water, racing itself down the mountain.

◆

Jupiter looked at Canyon with undisguised horror.

"Possum," he said. "I bet."

A deep sigh came out of her. All of the talk and danger of this storm definitely wound her up.

"Come on," he said, eyes wide with excitement. "Let's go."

She thought they were doing this together, but he abandoned her. She didn't like being alone in there. The house really wasn't a house. Not like Jupiter understood the house to be, anyway. The rooms were four or more times bigger than the biggest houses she'd ever been in. The living room's huge stone fireplace was stacked to a ceiling that was so far away that she couldn't reach it with the beam of her flashlight. She thought about the tour she and her mom took of the Biltmore, or the time that her aunt brought her to the Grove Park to see the gingerbread houses. She knew then why Canyon had been so desperate to get in. He was hoping for treasure.

"What cool stuff do rich people have that we don't?" He'd asked her. It would take the Shipmans forever to notice anything was gone, if they ever did.

The house was nearly silent, the thick walls blocking the reality of outside. Occasionally she could hear him, but she knew that he was bored with her mouth-open crawl through the space. He probably already got all their jewelry. She just couldn't move her body faster. In the library she pointed her light at the thick leather-bound volumes, and the black and white photos on the wall. She recognized some of the older buildings from downtown. Apparently, the Shipmans had been important for a long time. Were they still? Was money like this important anymore? Or did that high school girl with the millions of Instagram followers have more pull? She guessed it didn't really matter. She didn't have either. Even in a town as small as Burnt Church, Canyon and her mom and brother were the only ones who paid attention to her. Her mother kept telling her to get more involved, join in things like the frisbee golf club, or the photography club, or the community garden. Jupiter said she didn't have time, because homework, but that wasn't the truth. She was just bad at everything, and she didn't need the whole town to know that. Didn't want anyone looking at her, noticing.

"Can?" she called up the wide staircase. The banister was shiny dark wood, and a patterned carpet on the floor muffled her footsteps. "Can, are you up there?" But there was no response. She kept climbing. The hall was long with many closed doors. At the end was a double set. One of them was open. She was relieved. He wouldn't leave without her, but still. It was creepy in here alone, and the smell of death that she'd almost gotten used to, seemed to be getting worse. She was afraid that she was going to stumble on a dead possum, or worse a family of dead possums. "Can," she said, pushing open the door. The room was bigger than any of the others. A big canopy bed with curtains and a sitting area on the far side.

She swore she saw something move, and she was thinking about a possum when she saw the back of Canyon's head resting on the armrest of a couch in the seating area. There was a glass of something golden on the table beside him. *That doofus would find booze and get drunk during a hurricane,* she thought as she tiptoed across the room. He must have fallen asleep, otherwise he'd have seen the light from her flashlight. She was going to sneak over and wake his drunk ass up by scaring him. She held her breath, leaned over the couch and said, "Boo!" into his ear.

But it wasn't Canyon's ear.

Lucille woke up with the water lapping over her face. It was colder than she could have imagined and gritty. She tilted her head up to get her mouth out, but nothing would move below her neck and everything hurt. She could see the sky through the window. It was no longer raining. She wondered how much higher the water would get, and if she could wait it out. They'd gone to Hot Springs for their honeymoon and considered it the height of luxury. She'd never been in warm water in her bathing suit before. She wished that this water in her kitchen was warm; it would make waiting a lot more comfortable.

For their tenth anniversary they'd gone to Niagara Falls and gotten soaked on that boat where they'd kissed beneath the falls. Harry had loved the thunder of the water, but she liked their falls at home better. She would never tell him that. The best part was the thrill of his arms around her with so many people watching.

For their twentieth they'd gone to Graceland and Lucille had gotten food poisoning from some seven-layer salad. It was the only time in her life where she'd wondered if she was pregnant, laying there on the cold tile of that hotel bathroom floor wishing for death. She would have put up with that pain to give Harry a baby.

Thirtieth was the Grand Canyon, and fortieth an Alaskan cruise. Both were fancy, the rooms and restaurants much nicer than their home, but it was their fiftieth, the week after Harry went into Carolina Villages that Lucille loved the most. She'd only been able to spend the afternoon with him, but they'd toured the gardens, smelling their favorite blooms, and watching the bluebirds flit. It didn't matter where they went, she only wanted to be with him. She imagined she was pretty lucky. Not everyone had that.

She couldn't get her chin out of the water anymore, and she had to keep her mouth closed. The flood water was full of poop and chemicals. Her shivering made the water around her splash. She tried not to move but her teeth chattered. Harry always said that she couldn't keep her mouth shut. *He should see me now,* she thought. And then was immediately glad he was not here to worry. She would tell him the next time she got over there. Maybe tomorrow. He'd have heard about the flood on the news and would be worried about her and their neighbors. All those folks who'd sold their land. It had been hard for her to break her daddy's dirt into pieces. But they didn't have anyone to save it for, Harry reminded her. Might as well use the money to enjoy life. And oh, they had. What a wonderful husband and partner he'd been. She'd stop at MacFarland's tomorrow and get him one of those sticky buns that he loved so much as a little treat.

The packets from the spilled box were floating and occasionally they would pass into her sightline. Lucille closed her eyes. She didn't want to know what box she'd lost. Which treasures were gone forever. Which ones should she have to try to find again. *Maybe I can get a helper,* she thought. *Maybe I can convince the Smith girl.*

Lucille thought about how Jupiter had seemed kind of lost since her daddy left, shrinking into nothing. Her mother was so worried she hadn't stopped baking. Lucille would call her in a couple of days when she'd had a chance to figure things out.

Soon the water was over her mouth and then her upper lip. *Tomorrow,* she thought. *I'll go see Harry tomorrow.* She kept her eyes focused on those three boxes that she had gotten above the cupboards. Someone would find those. The gardens would be safe. *Safe because of me,* Lucille thought, closing her eyes. *Safe because of me.*

❖

Bunny raced around the edge of the back deck hoping for a glimpse of Phil. He was going to be angry if she got in the water. She couldn't tell how deep it was. It lapped at the decking. There was what, five steps down to the ground from the deck? Or was it seven? She couldn't remember. It could be over her head. The water was coming up on the deck now. Her bare feet were wet.

She went back inside to grab her phone and call 911 but nothing went through. *Emergency calls only, my ass,* she thought and threw her phone at the couch. Outside became too much and she closed the patio door. Set the dowel that Phil had cut to secure the door into place. Would it hold? Or would the water just rush in anyway? Phil loved the mahogany floors. He'd be so mad if they got ruined. She'd probably left the watering can out by accident. He'd probably wasted time looking for it, and she was going to hear about that, too, when he came in.

He wasn't used to disappointment. He always got what he wanted. When they first got together, he'd told her that he bent the universe to his will. She'd loved it, because then his will was hers too. They had gotten tickets to concerts she'd never dreamed of, he got raise after raise and used the money to buy them a big house and a nice car and fancy vacations. But somewhere along the way, what he wanted stopped being what she wanted, and then she never got what she wanted ever again.

Bunny started picking things up, placing them higher. She pulled books from the bottom shelves and stacked as many as she could up high. She put the coffee table on top of the couch and her dining chairs the top of the table. Doing something kept her from thinking about Phil. About where he could be and whether he needed her.

"You're terrible in an emergency," he'd said to her in bed the night before when he'd found her crying, and she'd said she was scared.

She saved all of Phil's expensive shoes though, and all of her own. She pulled out lower dresser drawers and stacked them on the bed. The house looked ridiculous. She sighed. It was actually kind of nice being alone. When he got back in, he'd be pissed about the watering can and how much work it was to get the water to clean up her mess. And then, he'd lecture her about the puke.

She started working on the kitchen next, moving baking supplies to upper shelves. She was half done with her collection of Le Creuset and cast iron when a knock on the kitchen window startled her. It was Phil. She worked hard to keep the disappointment off her face. He motioned for her to come outside. *Here it comes,* she thought.

"Why the fuck did you build that berm right at the top of the bank?" He was screaming, and pointing toward the river, and yanking her toward the edge of the deck, and she had no idea what he was talking about. "You're so fucking stupid. You nearly killed me."

There was nothing wrong with the berm, and when she'd asked him about it before she built it, he hadn't cared. Apparently, he had forgotten about it and tripped over it on his way to the river, and that was her fault.

His hand was on her left arm, and he was pulling her toward the water to show her one of her many terrible landscaping mistakes, and she didn't want to get her feet wet.

She widened her stance and pulled against him.

His eyes narrowed at her resistance, and he gripped her tighter, and pulled her harder.

She clutched the cast iron pan that was still in her right hand and swung.

She made contact with his left temple and then lost her balance when he released her arm as he fell backward into the waist-deep, fast moving, water.

His eyes were closed as he bobbed for a minute but opened as his waders filled and he was swept out into the main body of the river. He was going to be really pissed.

In a pile on the deck, she rubbed the sore spot on her forehead and looked down at the skillet. What was she supposed to do now? The backyard was a river. It was only a matter of time before water filled the house. She couldn't stay here. She picked herself up and went inside.

Out the front door she could see all the low spots in her yard had turned into lakes, and the culvert at the road had clogged and washed out their driveway. Mrs. Ford and her husband at the bottom of the hill had owned this whole side of the mountain once. She'd been very sweet when Bunny and Phil had bought the land. A local who understood the necessity of change. She'd given Bunny some seeds to plant. Bunny hadn't, and she couldn't remember where they were now.

Bunny thought about the Fords' low-lying land. She bet Phil would end up down there. She should go get him before he drowned. She wouldn't go empty handed. She checked her perfectly seasoned skillet for blood, before she put it in the top of the pantry.

She put on her best hiking gear, left Phil a note on the counter just in case, and headed out. She was overwhelmed before she even reached the end of her driveway. Everything was destroyed. She found herself staring like an idiot and reminding herself to breathe. The scale was like nothing she'd ever seen. It felt like a movie about a world war; nothing seemed real; it all felt pretend, theatrical, some kind of illusion, and everything was huge and terrifying. The road was now a river, and there were banks and berms in places that had been flat before. The lush, beautiful green of the North Carolina mountains were now entirely brown. As Bunny walked, picking her way through the trees filled with debris, she kept her on her feet so she wouldn't cry.

Just stepping into Mrs. Ford's yard gave her a bad feeling. When she came in view of the house, she had to rest her hands on her knees and breathe deeply. It was floating. There was water halfway up the front door. Bunny thought she was going to be sick. If Lucille was inside, she wasn't okay. For a split second, Bunny wished Phil was there to tell her what to do.

Bunny put her hand to her forehead. "Christ," she said, and she stood in the muck and watched the house be taken by the river.

❖

The boy looked at Jupiter with wide blue eyes. She knew who he was; he rode her bus. He sat alone at the front with those headphones on, and he got off at the middle school. The other boys weren't nice to him, and he never fought back. He was a long way from his house. There was no way that his mom was okay with him wandering around. Jupiter looked at the glass on the table. He followed her eyes.

"I thought it was apple juice," he said, and then pointed to a bar cart in the corner of the room.

That was a good guess, she had to admit. If you didn't have a dad who drank too much. She walked around the couch and sat on the chair and asked, "why are you here?"

He shrugged. "It's safe. There's no moat though."

Jupiter couldn't help but think of her little brother, who thought the Shipman's was a castle, too. "How'd you get in?"

"Front door," the boy said.

Jupiter smiled. Of course. God, they were stupid. "My friend Canyon is here too, have you seen him?"

The boy shook his head.

Jupiter settled back into the chair. She didn't care where Canyon was. She wished that her mom and little brother were there, though. If her mom was here, she wouldn't have to worry about what to do. That was why the mom always died that the beginning of Disney movies, right? So that the kids would have to make decisions alone. She thought about her own parents, about how the mom in the movies would have to die in order for the kids to be alone, but she guessed that dads could just leave.

"Christ, Juju. It smells like ass in here," Canyon said from the doorway. His arms were full of guns, and bottles of booze.

"What are you going to do with those?" she said, unable to take her eyes off the weapons. Her dad liked guns, but she'd never seen anyone holding so many at once. It was like Canyon's arms were full of firewood, only so, so much worse.

Canyon shook his head like she was an idiot. "This is the whole reason we're here," he said.

The whole house began to shake. The windows rattled, and the glassware on the bar cart clinked against each other. A clamor filled the air.

The boy, Tyler, she finally remembered his name, slid down to the floor at her feet, and wedged himself between the couch and her legs, while he covered his head with his hands.

The thundering turned into a roar, and then to an explosion, as a new cacophony came from the hallway, and Canyon threw himself deeper into the room.

Jupiter thought her head might explode from the pressure and the noise. She buried her face in her lap and covered her head with her arms. She wondered if this was the end. If this was how she was going to die. She hadn't really thought about that before, death, or how it would come, but this felt like it.

When she thought she couldn't take it any longer, and even one more moment would explode her ear drums, it was quieter. A minute later and all that was left was the sound of the wind and the distant rumble of the mudslide moving down the mountain. When she looked up, Canyon was in the doorway shaking his head. "What," she said, untangling her legs from Tyler's arms, and moving towards the door.

"It's gone, the staircase. Most of the hall it's . . ."

She was behind him now, looking for herself. She wouldn't have believed him if she wasn't standing there. This giant indestructible castle had been torn in two by the mountain. Where the other half of the upstairs used to be was a twelve-foot drop and then a river of mud and fallen trees, roots and all. "How will we get out?" she said.

"Jump," he said. "And soon. There might be another one." He was breathing hard. "I dropped a bottle on the stairs. I was going to go back and get it, and then I saw you. If I'd . . ." H e didn't finish. He was pale and trembling. "Come on," he said and grabbed her arm.

Jupiter looked back at Tyler. She could only see the top of his hair. "Him too," she said.

"Whatever," Canyon said. "Just needs to be now."

She went to Tyler. He'd buried his face and was quietly crying. "I'm scared, too," she said, kneeling next to him. "The castle has been breached."

He sighed deeply but didn't look up. She put her hand on his shoulder. He flinched.

"Juju," Canyon said from the doorway. "I can see a way."

"Tyler," she whispered. "Come with me."

"Juju," Canyon repeated, his voice higher and louder.

She was used to this tone from him, usually it was about breaking curfew, or borrowing something that he wouldn't give back, and she usually gave in.

"We can't leave him," she said.

Canyon rolled his eyes.

Jupiter's hands shook. Her mom would have discovered that she was gone at first light, and she would be worried and, lord, what if her mom went out looking for her. She needed to go home. Right now. Canyon could get her home and everything would be okay. But Jupiter couldn't leave this boy. She sat on the floor so she was eye to eye with Tyler.

He looked at her briefly, and then his eyes went back to the floor. "I can't swim," he said. "So, I can't jump."

"Jupiter!" Canyon was hollering now.

"Just go," she shouted back, still looking at Tyler's downcast eyes. When she looked back up at the doorway it was empty. She wasn't surprised. She knew who Canyon was. She was surprised that she was still there, though. She smiled for just a second.

❖

There was no evidence of Phil at Mrs. Ford's so Bunny kept moving, down the mountain, where she thought the river would go, but also toward town. She felt the rumble before she heard it. A tremor beneath her feet. At first, she thought it must be a tree falling; she had witnessed lots of that. Giant trees tumbling in the forest, heavy chunks falling and crashing into the underbrush, while the root balls breached the surface like sea monsters, tentacles snapping. But the sound was too long. And then it was too loud. And then she was turning in circles trying to locate where the avalanche was. Where could she go?

She spotted a ridge and ran. Hoping that a few feet of elevation might save her from whatever was coming. There was a rock outcropping, and she hid beneath it. Perhaps the rocks would take the brunt of the force, she hoped. As she pressed her back to the cold stone, and covered her head, she prayed that if God would just spare her, she'd stop puking. She'd make Phil go to counseling. She'd be a better person. She'd volunteer. She'd actually help with that garden Mrs. Ford told her about. She could even volunteer at the elementary school. She'd start an afternoon art club; it would feel good to share something that she knew. It would feel good to make connections and become a part of the community. She promised the sky and the dirt, as the ground shook, and the air vibrated with the thunder of rocks and trees and destruction. She prayed as her fingernails dug into her palms, as she waited for a wave of brown to crash over her head.

But it didn't. Soon, everything was silent and still.

When it passed, the little valley she'd been standing in only moments before, was now a river of mud and debris. Bunny didn't think she'd ever get used to this. One moment there is no river, and the next, river. She kept waiting for lightning to strike, a volcano to erupt, or for it to start raining locusts. Of course, as soon as she thought, *what's the worst thing that could happen*, men's voices echoed through the silence of the woods. Her heart raced. She hid beneath a falling tree as quietly as she could.

Holding her breath, she tried to guess how many there were based on the crashing sounds, the snapping of branches and footfalls. Men were never careful; they didn't have to be. And here, where everything was already destroyed, what difference did it make? Yet she hadn't been able to bring herself to step on surviving plants, to break twigs unnecessarily. She slowed her breathing. Thought about being completely silent. She couldn't think about what could happen, what had happened to her before, alone with strange men.

She strained to see them when they first came into view, hoping beyond everything that Phil was with them. That would be the best, really. He would be safe, and she would be too, because she wouldn't have to deal with him all alone, and he would protect her from them. There were four of them. In orange. Search and rescue. No Phil.

She was torn. Should she call out? Let them know she was there? They could find Phil and that would be a relief. She came out from behind the tree, but she couldn't make her mouth work. She watched them stride through the forest. Heads up, looking, searching, they hopped over fallen longs and pushed through underbrush. She couldn't find the breath to call out. They were almost past; she was almost out of their sightlines and panic and relief filled her. She couldn't tell her children about this. About how she hadn't done everything she could to save their father. But also, the men were almost gone. She was almost alone and safe, again.

Then one of the men looked to his right and spotted her.

She told them about Phil, about the yellow jacket and river and the waders, and they looked at each other over her head. They told her she was in shock, when she told them that she didn't want to get in their helicopter. She didn't need to be rescued. She was fine. They took her anyway.

❖

After, Jupiter wondered if she'd wanted Canyon to leave. Had she really hoped that he would realize that she needed help with Tyler, and come over, and be kind to the boy, and they'd all have held hands and jumped together. Maybe? But now it was just her and the kid, and it didn't matter.

Jupiter knew that Canyon had felt some sort of panic, but she didn't. When she looked at the hole that used to be the second floor of the Shipman house, she saw a mess, but it wasn't going to get worse. She didn't know what the rush would be. If there was another mudslide, it didn't matter where they were if they were in the unlucky path. She kicked all of the guns Canyon had left on the floor out the hole. She sat next to Tyler on the floor.

"You're on my bus," he said. "You sit at the back."

She nodded. She braced for when he said that she sat with the mean boys, or asked why, but he didn't.

"I like the bus," he said.

"Really?" she said in disbelief. How could he like being the butt of all their jokes. "I hate it." And she did. She hated those mean kids. Their cruel jokes and the pressure to keep up with them. Heaven forbid she didn't laugh at a prank, or she wore the wrong brand of jeans. Forever branded as cold or boring or poor.

"The seat belts in my mom's car are too tight," he said. "And she asks questions the whole way. The bus driver leaves us alone."

Jupiter nodded. Her mom asked a lot of questions, too. It was annoying.

"You can sit with me," he said.

She smiled. "I'd like that," she said, and found that she meant it. Tyler was good company. He didn't make her feel like she had to squeeze herself into some kind of smaller shape. She could breathe.

At first, she thought the vibration in the air was another landslide, but she soon realized what it actually was. "Helicopter," she said, "helicopter!" and rushed to the window. It looked out onto the roof of the porch, but it was too far down.

She ran to the doorway where Canyon had jumped into the water and debris, *ridiculous,* she thought. But then she remembered how Tyler had used the door to get in the house. "Keep it simple," she said aloud to herself as she scanned the room for something to use as a rope. The curtains on the canopy bed were thick and velvet. Perfect.

She yanked down a curtain.

"What's that?" Tyler pointed at a mass of fabric in the middle of the bed.

Jupiter stared at what was obviously the source of the smell: remains of two bodies, entwined. A gun between them. She now had a better Shipman story than anyone.

"Laundry," she said, opening the window and pushing out the screen. She threw the curtain out the window and grabbed Tyler's hand. "You're gonna climb down this," she said. "I'm going to hold you."

His eyes were saucers, and he shook his head.

"I get it," she said. "You don't know yet if you can trust me. I'm really strong. You won't fall. I won't drop you."

Tyler looked at the mass on the bed and shook his head.

"Ty," she whispered. "We can't stay here." She was getting ready to bribe him, like she did with her little brother, but she had nothing good to work with and she was sure that it was going to sound like begging, when he nodded and moved to the window. Was it the bodies? Did he understand what they were? Was it the idea of ending up trapped like them? Or maybe he didn't think she was shitty at everything. Maybe he thought she could do this.

She braced herself, and he climbed down and out onto the roof. She could hear the helicopter but couldn't see it. "Do you see it?" she hollered from the window.

"That way," Tyler said pointing over a line of trees at the disappearing helicopter.

"Shit," she said. "Shit, shit."

◆

As the co-pilot held her, Bunny smacked her hand against the window repeatedly, the diamond in her ring *crack-cracking* against the glass. She was stronger than she looked, a benefit of three years of hard work outside, and he quickly tired of trying to subdue her. She wiggled and thrashed. She was done with making things easy for men. She got her feet in the lap of the pilot and gave him a good heel to the groin, and that did it. She could have screamed for hours, and they wouldn't have listened, but one-well aimed kick and they turned around.

After the helicopter flew off, Bunny could hear the birds again. Her neck hurt from the chokehold, but it felt good to get rid of those overbearing men. She was so tired of being told what to do. Yes, they were helping her look for Phil, but they couldn't just leave that child. Phil had spent the last thirty years telling her he was a man, and unlike her, could take care of himself. She was going to give him the opportunity.

She looked at the girl, "Where are you headed?"

The girl looked back at the mansion, and then met Bunny's eyes while grimacing. "Home. My mom will be worried."

"You want company?" Bunny hoped she wouldn't have to convince her. She didn't want to have a conversation about young girls alone in the woods.

But the girl smiled. "It's not far," she said and started walking.

Moving through the trees, Bunny could smell her own body odor. She thought about going home to shower, about how long it would be before they would be doing anything normal like that again, and if anything could ever be normal again after what they'd lost. *How long would it take to stop discovering things were gone?* She didn't want to see her yard or her house. Didn't want to start cleaning up or figuring out what to do with all her shit. Maybe she wouldn't. Maybe after she walked this girl home, she'd just keep going, find a phone, call her daughter.

It wasn't far, and Bunny found that she was disappointed when the girl led her to a cute craftsman with a red door. The girl pulled her hands through her hair. The house was remarkably unscathed.

"She's just going to be happy you're home," Bunny said.

"I know," the girl said. "But . . ."

Bunny waited.

"I wasn't supposed to leave. I wasn't supposed to be in that house. I don't know where Canyon is. I messed up."

"Did you kill anyone?" Bunny asked.

The girl started laughing. "Of course not."

"To be clear," Bunny said. "Your mom would still want to see you, even if you killed someone. But you survived a hurricane and mudslide. She's gonna forgive you."

The front door opened, and a woman who looked like a thicker version of the girl spilled out and wrapped the girl in her arms.

As the girl wove her arms around the woman, Bunny turned to walk away. *This was good*, she told herself. *She'd helped.*

"Would you like some coffee?" the woman asked. "I got the woodstove going. I have lots, and I'd love some news from out there. The silence is almost the worst part. I hate not knowing. And . . . I have homemade cookies."

"Peanut butter is my favorite," the girl said.

Bunny couldn't remember the last time she had cookies, or real conversation. "I'd love that," she said.

In 2018, there were 14 extreme weather events that resulted in more than $1 billion in damages.

-UN News

Contributors' Biographies

__Editors' Note:__ Where available, online handles have been provided for each of our contributors so you can follow and engage with them on social media. Don't be weird about it.

EDITORS

CURTIS IPPOLITO (RHP Guest Editor; IG: @curtis_sd) is an Anthony Award-winning, and Macavity Award- and Derringer Award-nominated writer. He is the author of the crime novel *Burying the Newspaper Man*. Additionally, his short stories have appeared in numerous prominent publications, as well as being featured in several anthologies. He lives in San Diego and is a member of Sisters in Crime, Mystery Writers of America, and serves as vice-president for the San Diego chapter of Sisters in Crime.

ROGER NOKES (RHP Editor-in-Chief; Threads / IG: @StantonMcCaffery) writes fiction under the pseudonym Stanton McCaffrey. His short stories have been featured in *Tough, Reckon Review, Dark Yonder, Mystery Tribune, Vautrin, Shotgun Honey, Guilty Crime Story Magazine,* and more. He has published two novels: *Into the Ocean;* and ***Neighborhood of Dead Ends***. His short story, "Will I See The Birds When I Am Gone," was featured in *Best American Mystery and Suspense 2024*.

ALBERT TUCHER (Contributing Editor; Facebook: @albert.tucher) is the creator of sex worker Diana Andrews, who has appeared in more than 100 hardboiled stories in venues including *The Best American Mystery Stories 2010*. Her first longer case, the novella *The Same Mistake Twice*, was published in 2013. In 2017, Albert Tucher launched a second series set on the Big Island of Hawaii, in which *Pele's Prerogative* is the latest entry. He is a past president of the Mystery Writers of America NY Chapter, lives in New Jersey, and loves NJ Turnpike jokes.

JAY BUTKOWSKI (Managing Editor; Threads / IG: @jtbutkowski) is a writer of fiction, an eater of tacos and an amateur pizzaiolo who lives in New Jersey. His stories have appeared in online and print publications, including *Shotgun Honey*, *Dark Yonder*, *Tough*, *Yellow Mama*, *All Due Respect*, and *Vautrin*, among others. He is a founding editor at **Rock and a Hard Place Press**, an independent publisher chronicling "bad decisions and desperate people." He's also a father of teenage twins, a doting husband, and a middling pancake chef.

PAUL J. GARTH (Editor; Threads / IG: @PauljGarth) has been published in *Thuglit*, *Tough*, *Needle: A Magazine of Noir*, *Plots with Guns*, *Crime Factory*, ***Rock and a Hard Place Magazine***, and several other anthologies and web magazines. His novella, *The Low White Plain*, part of the "A Grifter's Song" series, was released in June 2022. He writes in Nebraska, where he lives with his family.

MORGAN SULLIVAN (Editor; Bluesky: @thebigleblueski.bsky.social) is a writer of fiction, comedy, and letters to the editor. A recent East Coast transplant, she is enjoying the trees that aren't on fire. Her writing has been featured at *Fireside*

Fiction Magazine, *Shotgun Honey*, and *Tough*, as well as in the *Killing Malmon* and *Murder-A-Go-Go's* anthologies. She has also published an erotic story about a ham sandwich. True story. You can track her down over at govneh.com.

ROB D. SMITH (Editor; Threads / IG: @RobertDominicSmith) is a common man attempting to write uncommon fiction from Louisville, KY. Regarded for darkly humanizing fiction, his story "A Box Full of Soul" was selected for *The Best American Mystery & Suspense 2025*. Rob's Anthony Award-nominated debut thriller *Good-Looking Ugly* is available from Shotgun Honey. His fiction has appeared in *Apex Magazine*, *Reckon Review*, *Thriller Magazine*, *Vautrin*, *Dark Yonder*, *Tough*, and several other crime, horror, and speculative magazines, anthologies, and online publications. Find his work at https://robdsmith.carrd.co/.

ASHLEY-RUTH M. BERNIER's (Acquisition Editor; Threads / IG: @armbernier) work has appeared in *Ellery Queen's Mystery Magazine*, *Black Cat Weekly*, **Stone's Throw**, Smoking Pen Press, *Malice Domestic's Mystery Most Devious* and *Mystery Most Humorous*, *The Best American Mystery and Suspense 2023*, and other esteemed anthologies. Originally from St. Thomas, U.S. Virgin Islands, Ashley-Ruth writes mysteries highlighting the vibrant culture of her home. Her first novel length work is forthcoming from Crooked Lane Books in 2026. She currently lives with her family and teaches first grade in North Carolina.

VICTOR DE ANDA (Acquisition Editor; Bluesky: @victordeanda.bsky.social) is a movie geek and music freak who enjoys writing stories. His fiction has been published in *Dark Waters Vols. 1 & 2*, *Mystery Tribune*, *Shotgun Honey*, *Yellow Mama*, and *Punk Noir Magazine*, with more forthcoming. His story "Bad Man Down" has been included in *The Best American Mystery and Suspense 2025*, edited by Don Winslow and Steph Cha. He can be found living in the suburbs of Philadelphia. Find him online at www.victordeanda.com.

SUSAN JESSEN (Acquisition Editor; Threads / IG: @SuzJay11) enjoys reading, reviewing, and writing fiction of various genres. She received an MFA in Writing Popular Fiction from Seton Hill University. A former Priority Editor at *Flash Fiction Magazine*, she continues to provide editorial feedback during their quarterly contests. Her flash fiction has been published under a pseudonym in anthologies and magazines such as *The Arcanist*, *Lost Balloon*, and *Shotgun Honey*.

CONTRIBUTING WRITERS
(In order of appearance of work)

C.W. BLACKWELL (IG: @cw_blackwell_writer) is an American author from the Central Coast of California. His short stories have appeared with Down and Out Books, *Mystery Magazine*, *Shotgun Honey*, *Tough Magazine*, *Reckon Review*, and **Rock and a Hard Place Press**. He is a two-time Derringer Award winner and five-time nominee. He was included on the Distinguished Author list in the 2024 *Best American Mystery and Suspense* collection. His crime fiction novella *Hard Mountain Clay* was published in January 2023 from Shotgun Honey Books. His debut crime fiction collection ***Whatever Kills the Pain*** was released by **Rock and a Hard Place Press** in July 2025.

MARY THORSON (IG: @mfranzen88) lives and writes in Milwaukee, Wisconsin. She received her BA in Creative Writing from the University of Wisconsin-Milwaukee and her MFA from Pacific University in Oregon. Her stories have appeared in the *Los Angeles Review*, *Reckon Review*, *Cotton Xenomorph*, *Milwaukee Noir*, *Worcester Review*, ***Rock and a Hard Place***, and *Tough*, among others. Her short story, "Book of Ruth," was included in *Best American Mystery & Suspense 2024*, edited by Steph Cha and S.A. Cosby. Her work has been nominated for *Best American Short Stories*, a Derringer, and a Pushcart Prize. She is represented by Lori Galvin at Aevitas Creative Management. Her debut short story collection, ***A Woman's Guide to True Crime***, will be released in early 2026 from **Rock and a Hard Place Press**.

ZAKARIAH JOHNSON (Threads: @pteratorn) plucks banjos and pens thrillers, horror, and mysteries on the banks of the Piscataqua. He's the author of the ecoterrorism murder mystery

Mink: Skinning Time in Wisconsin and the short-story collection *Egg on Her Face*, which includes tales of environmental catastrophes and homicidal trees.

PUJA GUHA (IG: @authorpujaguha) is the author of seven novels and four published short stories. She grew up and has worked all over the world, something she channels into her writing, with settings from New York to Madagascar to Iran. So far, she has traveled to over 60 countries, each of which she hopes to someday include in one of her stories or novels. Her spy thriller series *The Ahriman Legacy* is an Amazon bestseller, and she has been featured on TV and media, including Fox 5, *Reader's Digest*, and the *London Post*.

COLIN BRIGHTWELL (IG: @cbwizzy) is a Kansas City native. His fiction has appeared in *Reckon Review*, *BULL*, *Guilty Crime Story Magazine*, *Dark Yonder*, *Starlite Pulp*, and ***Rock and a Hard Place***. His debut collection, *Nothing Good Ever Happens in a Flyover State*, is available through Cowboy Jamboree Press. He currently teaches middle school English outside Kansas City.

PRISCILLA PATON (IG: @priscillapaton) grew up on a Maine dairy farm and spends time with family in the mountains of northern Maine. She lives in Wisconsin and writes the award-nominated Twin Cities Mystery series, which features feisty Deb Metzger and outdoorsy Erik Jansson. Her recent *When the House Burns*—sex, death, and real estate—follows *Where Privacy Dies* and *Should Grace Fail*. Her fourth, *In Blind Trust*, about the murder of a MedTech executive, will be out in 2026. She participates in environmental and community advocacy programs. You can read more on the web at priscillapaton.com.

CHRISTIAN EMECHETA (IG: @emechetachristian) is a writer, illustrator, and computer scientist. His fiction and poetry have appeared in many online publications and magazines such as *Arts*

Lounge Magazine, *Writefluence Anthology*, 9th Edition of *Chinua Achebe Poetry/Essay Anthology*, *Synchronized Chaos Online Journal*, *The Decolonial Passage*, *Mocking Owl Roost*, and elsewhere. He writes songs when inspired by a tune or lyrics. Christian enjoys reading, watching movies, and getting lost in his imagination. He hopes to travel the world.

Raised on both a farm in north Georgia and the Caribbean island of Trinidad, **RAYMOND J. BRASH** (IG: @raymond.j.brash) currently resides in Denver, Colorado, where he enjoys reading and writing speculative fiction, noir, and anything that crushes multiple genres into a pulpy, edible mash. Raymond has stories published in **Rock and a Hard Place Magazine**, *Shotgun Honey*, and others, and has been nominated for a Best of the Net Award.

EDWARD BARNFIELD (Bluesky: @@edbarnfield.bsky.social) is a writer and researcher living in the Middle East. His stories have appeared in *Triangulation*, *Third Flatiron*, Galley Beggar Press, *The Molotov Cocktail*, Tenebrous Press, *Leicester Writes*, *Strands*, *Cranked Anvil*, and *Shooter Literary*, among others.

KENDALL BRUNSON (IG: @kendallbrunson) is a crime and thriller writer from Florida. Her work has been published in *Kelp Literary Journal*, *100 Word Story*, *Fearsome Critters*, and more. She's written and directed horror shorts that have played at festivals, including Final Girls Berlin Film Fest, The Loft Cinema, and Wasteland Film Festival. She earned her MFA from UC Riverside at Palm Desert and currently lives and works in Jacksonville, Florida.

MICHAEL DOWNING (Twitter / X: @KMWriter01) is a writer originally from New Jersey, now living in a small college town in Georgia. His novel, *Saints of the Asphalt* was released in 2025. His short stories have been featured in various publications and anthologies (some that have even been nominated for Pushcart

Prizes). He is still everything New Jersey: attitude, edginess, and Bruce Springsteen . . . but not Bon Jovi. Learn more at downingfiction.com.

C.E. McKENNA (Bluesky: @ce-mckenna.bsky.social) is a writer, historian, and software engineer from Colorado. She has history theses in the libraries of Reed College and Oklahoma State, and her short stories have found awards and publication with *Writing by Writers, Desperate Literature, The Offing, Cagibi, Lumina, Quarterly West, Northwest Review*, and *Shift*. She is an MFA student at UC Riverside - Palm Desert. Though she's only been to Svalbard once, it made a deep impression.

JIM RULAND (IG: @jimvermin) is an old punk who lives by the sea. He is the author of the novels *Make It Stop* and *Forest of Fortune* and the short story collection *Big Lonesome*. Jim is also the *LA Times*-bestselling author of *Corporate Rock Sucks: The Rise & Fall of SST Records*, which was named a best book of 2022 by *Pitchfork, Rolling Stone* and *Vanity Fair*. Ruland is the co-author of *Do What You Want* with Bad Religion and *My Damage* with Keith Morris. Jim is a frequent contributor to *Razorcake* fanzine and the *LA Times*. He is a veteran of the US Navy and lives in San Diego.

RICHIE NARVAEZ is the author of two novels, *Hipster Death Rattle* and *Holly Hernandez and the Death of Disco*, which received an Agatha Award and an Anthony Award, and two short story collections, *Roachkiller & Other Stories* and *Noiryorican*. You can learn more about his work at www.richienarvaez.com.

MEAGAN LUCAS (IG: @meaganlucasauthor) is the author of the Anthony-nominated collection *Here in the Dark* and the award-winning novel, *Songbirds and Stray Dogs*. Her short work can be found in: *Best American Mystery and Suspense,* **Rock and a Hard Place**, *Dark Yonder,* and *Starlite Pulp,* among others. She is the Editor-in-Chief of *Reckon Review*, teaches in the Great Smokies

Writing Program at UNC-A, and is a JD Candidate at UDayton Law. She lives in the mountains of Western North Carolina.